Gump
& Co.

Books by Winston Groom

Forrest Gump
Gumpisms: The Wit and Wisdom of Forrest Gump
Better Times Than These
As Summers Die
Conversations with the Enemy (with Duncan Spencer)
Only
Gone the Sun
Shrouds of Glory
Gump & Co.

Gump
& Co.

WINSTON GROOM

POCKET BOOKS
New York   London   Toronto   Sydney   Tokyo   Singapore

Gro

This book is a work of fiction. Names, characters, places and incidents are products of the author's imagination or are used fictitiously. Any resemblance to actual events or locales or persons, living or dead, is entirely coincidental.

POCKET BOOKS, a division of Simon & Schuster Inc.
1230 Avenue of the Americas, New York, NY 10020

ISBN: 0-671-52170-5

First Pocket Books hardcover printing September 1995

10 9 8 7 6 5 4 3 2 1

POCKET and colophon are registered trademarks of
Simon & Schuster Inc.

Interior design by Barbara Cohen Aronica

Printed in the U.S.A.

To my lovely wife,
Anne-Clinton Groom,
who has been with Forrest
for lo these lovely years.

THE FOOL'S PRAYER

The royal feast was done; the King
 Sought some new sport to banish care,
And to his jester cried: Sir Fool,
 Kneel now, and make for us a prayer!

The jester doffed his cap and bells,
 And stood the mocking court before;
They could not see the bitter smile
 Behind the painted grin he wore.

He bowed his head, and bent his knee
 Upon the monarch's silken stool;
His pleading voice arose: "O Lord,
 Be merciful to me, a fool!"

. . . .

The room was hushed; in silence rose
 The King, and sought his gardens cool,
And walked apart, and murmured low,
 "Be merciful to me, a fool!"

     —*Edward Rowland Sill, 1868*

Gump
& Co.

Chapter One

Let me say this: Everbody makes mistakes, which is why they put a rubber mat around spitoons. But take my word for it—don't *never* let nobody make a movie of your life's story. Whether they get it right or wrong, it don't matter. Problem is, people be comin up to you all the time, askin questions, pokin TV cameras in your face, wantin your autograph, tellin you what a fine feller you are. Ha! If bullshit came in barrels, I'd get me a job as a barrel-maker an have more money than Misters Donald Trump, Michael Mulligan, an Ivan Bozosky put together. Which is a matter I will go into in a little bit.

But first, let me bring you up to date on my sorry tale. A lot has gone on in my life in the last ten or so years. First, I am ten or so years older, which is not as much fun as some people think. I have got a few gray hairs on my head, an I ain't near as fast as I used to be, which is somethin I found out straightaway when I tried to make me some money playin football again.

It was down in New Orleans, where I had wound up after everthin else happened, an it was just me there. I had got a job sweepin out a strip joint called Wanda's, which didn't close till about three A.M., an so I got my days pretty free. One night I was just settin there in a corner watchin my friend Wanda do her thing on stage when a big fight commenced up front. They was people hollerin, cussin, thowin chairs, tables, beer bottles, an knockin each other in the head, an women screamin, too. I did not think too much of all this, account of it happened about two or three times ever night, except this time, I thought I recognized one of the participants.

It was a big ole feller with a beer bottle in his hand, swingin it in a way that I had not seen since I was up to the University of Alabama way back when. Lo an behole, it was old Snake, the quarterback who one time had thowed the ball out of bounds on fourth down to stop the clock when we was playin them cornshucker bastids from Nebraska in the Orange Bowl twenty years ago. An that, of course, lost us the game an made me have to go to Vietnam an—well, let's don't worry about all that now.

Anyhow, I went over an grapped the beer bottle from Snake, an he was so glad to see me he punched me on top of the head, which was a mistake because it sprained his wrist, an he commenced to holler an cuss, an about that time the police showed up an hauled all of us off to jail. Now, jail is a place I know somethin about, account of I have been there at various times. In the mornin, after everbody else sobered up, the jailer brung us some fried bologna an stale bread an begun astin if we want to call somebody to get us loose. Snake is mad as hell, an he say, "Forrest, ever time I come around your big dumb ass, I wind up in hot water. Here I ain't seen you in years and look what happens. We is thowed in jail!" I just nodded my head, cause Snake is right.

Anyhow somebody come an bail us all out, Snake an

his friends an me, too, an this guy is not very happy, an Snake, he ast me, "What in hell were you doin in that dive anyhow?" When I tole him I was the cleanup man, Snake get a kind of funny look on his face an says, "Hell, Gump, I thought you still had the big srimp company over at Bayou La Batre. What happened? You was a millionaire." An I had to tell him the sad story. The srimp company went bust.

I had left the srimp company an gone on my way after a while, cause I got tired of all the bullshit that comes with runnin a big bidness enterprise. An I put the thing in the hands of my mama an my friends Lieutenant Dan from Vietnam an Mister Tribble, who was the chessmaster that taught me the game. First, Mama died, an that's all I got to say about that. Next, Lieutenant Dan calls me an says he's gonna quit, on account of he's made enough money anyhow. An then one day I got a letter from the Internal Revenue Service, says I ain't paid my bidness taxes an they is fixin to shut me down an take all the boats an buildins an all, an when I went over there to see what was goin on, lo an behole, ain't *nothin* goin on! All the buildins are about empty an weeds is growin up around the place, an they have done pulled out all the phones an turned the electricity off, an the sheriff has nailed up a paper on the front door sayin we are under "foreclosure."

I gone around to see ole Bubba's daddy to find out what had happened. Now, Bubba was my partner an my friend from the army over at Vietnam, which is where he was kilt, but Bubba's daddy had helped me, an so I figgered I would get the real story from him. He is settin on the stoop of his house, lookin sad, when I walked up.

"What is goin on with the srimp bidness?" I ast.

He shook his head. "Forrest," he says, "it is a sad and sorry thing. I'm afraid you have been ruint."

"But why?" I ast.

"Betrayed" is what he answered.

Then he tole me the story. While I was assing around in New Orleans, good ole Lieutenant Dan had took Sue, my friend who was a ape—an orangutang, to be exact—an gone back over to Bayou La Batre to help out with some problems runnin the srimp bidness. The problems was that we was runnin out of srimp to catch. It seems that everbody in the whole world wanted srimp. People in places like Indianapolis who had never even *heard* of srimp a few years before was now demandin that every fast-food restaurant serve them up big platters day an night. We caught srimp fast as we could, but there are just so many srimp to go around an after a few years, we wadn't catchin half what we had when we started, an in fact, the whole srimp industry was in a panic.

Bubba's daddy didn't know exactly what happened next, but whatever it was, things went from bad to worse. First, Lieutenant Dan quit. Bubba's daddy says he saw him drivin off in a big limousine with a lady wearin spike-heeled shoes an a blond Beatle wig, an Dan was wavin two big champagne bottles out the winder. Next, Mister Tribble done quit, too. Just up an left one day, an after that so did everbody else, account of they not gettin paid, an finally, the only one left to answer the phones was ole Sue, an when the phone company pulled out the phones, Sue left, too. Guess he figgered he wadn't bein useful no more.

"I reckon they took all your money, Forrest," Bubba's daddy said.

"Who took it?" I ast him.

"They all did," he said. "Dan, Mr. Tribble, the secretaries and the crews and the office help. They was all luggin stuff out of there. Even ole Sue. Last time I seen him, he was peekin around a corner of the buildin, carryin a computer under his arm."

Well, this was all very bad news. I just couldn't believe it! Dan. An Mister Tribble. An Sue!

"Whatever," says Bubba's daddy. "Forrest, you is wiped out."

"Yeah," I said, "I have been there before."

Anyhow, wadn't nothin to do about it now. Let em have it then. That night I set there on one of our docks. Big ole half moon out over the Mississippi Sound come up an sort of hung over the water. I was thinkin that this wouldn't of happened if Mama had of been here. An also, I was thinkin about Jenny Curran, or whoever she was now— with little Forrest, who is actually my son. An I had promised her my share of the srimp bidness so's little Forrest would have some money to fall back on if he ever needed it. So what am I gonna do? I am ruint. Broke! An that's okay when you are young an don't have no responsibilities. But, hell, here I am more than thirty years old now, an I wanted to do somethin good for little Forrest. An what has happened? I have made a mess of it again. It is the story of my life.

I got up an walked down to the end of the pier. Ole half moon still just hangin right there over the water. All of a sudden I just felt like cryin, an I leaned over on one of the big pilings that holds up the pier. Damn if it didn't bust right off into the water, rotten, an carried me with it. Shit. Here I am again, a fool, standin in the water up to my waist. I wouldn't of minded then if a shark or somethin had swum by an eat me up. But it didn't, so I waded on out an caught the first bus back to New Orleans, just in time to start sweepin up in the strip joint.

A day or so later, ole Snake dropped by Wanda's about closin time. His hand was all bandaged up an in a splint from gettin it sprained on my head, but he had somethin else on his mind.

"Gump," he says, "let me get this straight. After all the shit you have done in life, you are now the cleanup man in a dive like this? Are you crazy? Let me ask you somethin—you still run as fast as you did in college?"

"I dunno, Snake," I said. "I ain't had much practice."

"Well, let me tell you somethin," he says. "I don't know if you know it, but I am the quarterback for the New Orleans Saints. And as you might of heard, we ain't doin so good lately. Like we is oh and eight so far, and everybody's callin us the 'Ain'ts'! We gotta play the goddamn New York Giants next weekend, and the way we are goin, we will then be oh and nine, and I will probably get fired."

"Football?" I ast him. "You still playin football?"

"Well, what else am I gonna play, you idiot—the trombone? Now, listen here, we gotta have some kind of trick against them Giants on Sunday. And I think you might just be it. It won't take much—just one or two plays, that's all you'll have to practice. You do okay, you might make a career for yourself."

"Well, I dunno, Snake. I mean, I ain't played no football since you thowed that pass out of bounds on fourth down to stop the clock an we lost the championship to them cornshuckers from . . ."

"Damnit, Gump, don't remind me of that again—it was twenty years ago! Everybody's forgotten about it by now—except apparently you. For God's sake, here you are moppin up a beer joint at two in the morning and you're turning down the opportunity of a lifetime? What are you, some kind of nut?"

I was about to answer yes when Snake interrupted me an begun scribblin on a bar napkin.

"Look, here's the address of the practice field. Be there tomorrow at one sharp. Show them this note, and tell them to bring you to me."

After he left I stuck the napkin in my pocket an went back to cleanin up the place, an that night when I went home I laid up in bed till dawn, thinkin about what Snake had said. Maybe he was right. Anyhow, might not hurt to try. I remembered those times back at the University of Alabama all them years ago, an Coach Bryant an Curtis an Bubba an the guys. An when I did, I got kind of misty-eyed, account of they were some of the best times of my life, when that crowd was roarin an yellin, an we almost always won all our games. Anyhow, I got dressed an gone out an got some breakfast, an by one o'clock I had arrived on my bicycle at the New Orleans Saints's practice field.

"Who you say you are again?" the guard asts when I shown him Snake's napkin. He is lookin me up an down pretty suspiciously.

"Forrest Gump. I used to play ball with Snake."

"Yeah, I'll bet," he says. "That's what they all say."

"I did, though."

"Well, wait a minute, then." He looked at me kind of disgusted like an went off through a door. Few minutes later he comes back, shakin his head.

"All right, Mr. Gump. Follow me." An he takes me back to the locker room.

*　*　*

Now, I have seen some big fellers in my time. I remember them University of Nebraska players, an *they* was big. But all these fellers, they is not big—they is *huge!* In case I ain't tole you yet, I am six-six an weigh about two hundrit forty—but these guys—they look about seven feet an three or four hundrit pounds apiece! One feller, dressed kind of official, comes up an says to me, "You lookin for somebody here, old-timer?"

"Yeah," I says. "Snake."

"Well, he ain't here today. Coach made him go to the doctor on account of he sprained his hand hittin some idiot on the head in a bar."

"I know," I says.

"Well, anything else I can do for you?"

"I dunno," I tole him. "Snake says for me to come by here an see if y'all want me to play ball for you."

"Play ball? For us?" He got kind of a funny little squint in his eye.

"Uh huh. See Snake an I was on the same team back at Alabama. He tole me last night to . . ."

"Wait a minute," the feller says. "Your name ain't Forrest Gump, by any chance, is it?"

"Yup, sure is."

"Yeah, yeah," he says. "I heard about you, Gump. Snake says you run like a bat out of hell."

"Dunno about that anymore. I ain't run in a while."

"Well, I tell you what, Gump, Snake asked me to give you a tryout. Why don't you come in here and let's get you suited up—By the way, my name's Coach Hurley. I coach wide receivers."

He took me back to the uniform room, an they found some clothes an shit for me. Lord it was different from back at the University. All them clothes have changed now. They got twice as many pads an pieces of rubber an stuff, so's

when you get all suited up, you look like a Mars-man or
somethin, an when you stand up, you feel like you gonna
tump over. When I finally get dressed, everbody else is
already out on the field doin they exercises an shit. Coach
Hurley motion me over to his group, which is runnin pass
patterns, an say for me to get in line. I remembered this part
from my playin days—just run out about ten yards an turn
around an they thow you the ball. When my turn comes, I
run out an turn around an the ball hits me square in the face,
an it surprised me so much I tripped an fell on the ground.
Coach Hurley shake his head, an I ran on back to the end of
the line. Four or five times later, I ain't caught a ball yet an
all the other guys be kind of avoidin me. Like I needed a
bath or somethin.

After a while, Coach begun hollerin an shoutin, an
everbody gone on into the scrimmage. They was divided up
into two teams an after a few plays, Coach Hurley motion
me over to him.

"All right, Gump," he says. "I don't know why I am
doin this, but you go on in there at wide receiver and see if
you can catch a ball, so Snake, whenever he gets here, is not
going to be a laughingstock—or, for that matter, me either."

I run into the huddle an tell them I am there. The
quarterback looks at me like I'm nuts, but says "Okay,
eight-oh-three corner post—on two—Gump, you hit it
straight for about twenty yards, look out once then look
back in." An everbody breaks an gets into their position. I
don't even know where my position is, so I go on out to
where I think it is, an the quarterback, he sees me an
motions me in closer. He counts an the ball is snapped, an I
run out what I figger is twenty yards, do a little jig, an then
look back, an sure enough the ball be headed right for me.
Fore I know it, it is there, right in my hands, an I grapped it
an begun to run hard as I could. Damn if I ain't gone twenty

more yards when two big ole guys slam into me an knock me on the ground.

Then all hell broke loose.

"What in hell was *that!*" one of the guys shouts.

"Hey—that ain't right. What the hell's he doin!" another one says.

Two or three more come up an begun hollerin an cussin an wavin their arms at Coach Hurley. I got up an run on back to the huddle.

"What's wrong with them guys?" I ast the quarterback.

"Hell, Gump, them guys are so dumb they don't know what to do when they see somethin they ain't seen before. They were expectin you to do what I said—go out twenty, jig, and then corner post. You did half of that—and even that was backwards. It ain't in the playbook. Lucky I spotted you. But that was a nice catch, anyway."

Well, rest of the afternoon I caught five or six more passes, an everybody ceptin the defense was happy. Ole Snake had come back from the doctor by then an was standin on the sidelines, grinnin an jumpin up and down.

"Forrest," he says, when the scrimmage is finally over, "we is going to have us a *time* next Sunday afternoon against them New York Giants! It is a lucky thing that I went to your strip joint that night!"

But I am wondering if this is so.

Anyhow, I practiced the whole rest of that week, an by Sunday, I was feelin pretty good about mysef. Snake had got his hand out of the splint an was first-string quarterback again an was playin his heart out during the first two quarters, so's when we went into the locker room we was only behind 22 to 0.

"Okay, Gump," Coach Hurley said. "Now we gonna show em somethin. I think we have lulled them New York Giants into a false sense of security now. They gonna be lookin for a easy ride. You will not give it to them." Then he an some other coaches say a bunch of other bullshit an we gone on back out to the stadium.

First play, somebody on our side fumbles the kickoff an we are back on our own one yard line. Just like Coach Hurley say, we have lulled them Giants into a false sense of security. Coach Hurley pat me on the butt an I went into the game. The crowd all of a sudden got sort of quiet, an then a kind of low mumbling begun—I guess because they ain't had time to put my name into the program.

Snake, he look at me with eyes flashin an say, "Okay, Forrest, now's the time. Just do it." He called the play, an I went out toward the sidelines. On the snap, I hauled ass downfield an turn around, an the ball ain't there. Snake is being chased around in the backfield by five or six Giants men, back an forth, back an forth in our own end zone—he must of gained a hundred yards, but it was the wrong way.

"Sorry about that," he says, when we get back into the huddle. He reached down in his britches an pulled out a little plastic flask an took a long slug from it.

"What is that?" I ast.

"A hundrit percent pure orange juice, you fool," Snake says. "You don't think I'd be runnin around out drinkin whisky at my age, do you?"

Well, they say some things never change, but they also say wonders never cease, an I am glad ole Snake is doin the right thing.

Well, Snake calls the same play to me, an I run out again. By now the crowd is booin us an throwin paper cups an programs an half-eaten hotdogs onto the field. This time I turn aroun an got hit in the face by a big half-rotten tomato that somebody in the stands had brought along to indicate their displeasure, I guess. As you can imagine, it thowed me off just a little, an I put my hands up toward my face, an lo an behole, Snake's pass catches me right there—so hard it knocked me down, but we is at least out of the hole.

Now it is first an ten on our twenty, an Snake call the same play again. I am tryin to wipe the tomato off my face when Snake says, "You sort of got to watch out for them folks thowin things from the stands. They don't mean nothin by it. It's just their way down here."

I am wishin they would find another "way."

Anyhow, out I go, an this time before I line up I hear all this real vulgar cussin an name callin directed toward me, an I look across the line an I'll be damned if there ain't ole Curtis, the linebacker from my Alabama days, wearin the uniform of a New York Giant!

Now, Curtis had been my ole roommate at the University for a while, at least till he thowed the outboard motor out of the athletic dorm winder onto a police car, which got him into some trouble. An later I gave him a job at the srimp company at Bayou La Batre. Long as I had known him, Curtis did not say nothin without startin it with about ten sentences of profanity, an so it was sometimes hard to figger out just what he wanted—especially when you only have about five seconds before the play starts, which was now the case. I gave him a little wave, an this seemed to surprise him so, he looked over at somebody else on his team, an that's when our play went off. I was past Curtis like a shot, even though he tried to trip me with his feet, an headed downfield, an Snake's ball was right there. I didn't even lose a step—went right on into the end zone. Touchdown!

Everbody was jumpin all over me an huggin an all that, an when I was walkin off Curtis come up an say to me,

"Nice catch, asshole," which was about as high a compliment as Curtis ever gave. Bout that time, somebody thowed a tomato an hit *him* with it, square in the face. It was the first time I ever saw Curtis speechless, an I felt sort of sorry for him. "Hey," I says, "they don't mean nothin by that, Curtis. It's just their way down here in New Orleans. Why, they even thow stuff at people off their Mardi Gras floats." But Curtis wadn't havin none of that, an so he took out toward the stands yellin an cussin an givin everbody the finger. Good ole Curtis.

Well, it was a interestin afternoon. By fourth quarter we was ahead 28 to 22, an I iced the game by makin a forty-yard catch that was thowed by the second-string quarterback who had come in for Snake, who was on the sidelines gettin his leg stitched up after a Giant bit a chunk out of it. All during the last part of the game the fans be chantin, "Gump! Gump! Gump!" an when it was over, about a hundrit photographers an newspaper reporters come up an mobbed me on the field, wantin to know who I was.

After that, my life done definitely changed. For that first game against the Giants, the Saints people gave me a check for ten thousan dollars. Next week, we done played the Chicago Bears, an I caught three more touchdown passes. The Saints people figgered out a way to pay me, they says, on "an incentive basis," which was that they would give me one thousan dollars for ever pass I catch, an a ten-thousan-dollar bonus for each touchdown I score. Well, after four more games I got nearly sixty thousan dollars in the bank an we is now 6 an 8 an movin up in the conference standins. The week before the next game, which is against the Detroit Lions, I sent Jenny Curran a check for thirty thousan dollars for little Forrest. After we whup the Detroit Lions an then the Redskins, Colts, Patriots, 49ers, an Jets, in that order, I done sent her another thirty thousan dollars, an I am figgerin that by the playoffs I will be on easy street for sure.

But it was not that way at all.

We done won the conference championship for our division an next have got to play the Dallas Cowboys on their home turf. Everthin is lookin up pretty good. Our men are all very confident an be slappin each other on they asses with towels in the locker room. Ole Snake, he even stopped drinkin, and was in the prime of health.

One day one of the fellers come up to me an says, "Look here, Gump, you need to get yourself an agent."

"A what?" I ast.

"Agent, you dummy. Somebody to represent you and get you all the money you ever wanted. You ain't gettin paid enough around here. None of us are. But at least we got agents to deal with them bastids up at the organization. Why, you ought to be makin three times as much as you are now."

So I took his advice an got me an agent. Mister Butterfield was his name.

First thing Mister Butterfield does is go an start an argument with the people at the Saints organization. Pretty soon I get called in an everbody is mad at me.

"Gump," they says, "you has already signed a contract for one thousand dollars a pass and ten thousand dollars a touchdown for this season. Now you want to go back on it. What the hell is this!"

"I dunno," I said. "I just got this agent to . . ."

"Butterfield! Agent my ass! That man is a crook. Don't you know that?"

When I said I didn't, they tole me that Mister Butterfield had threatened to hold me out of the playoff game if they didn't give me triple what they were now.

"Let me tell you this, Gump," the owner says, "if you miss just *one* game because of this ridiculous attempt at highway robbery, I will not only kick you off the team personally, but I will see to it you don't never get another job playing football anyplace—at least for money. You understand that?"

I said I did an went on out to practice.

That week I finally quit my job sweepin up at Wanda's strip joint. The hours was kind of gettin to me. Wanda said she understood, an anyway, she said she was gonna fire me anyhow account of it wadn't "dignified" for me to be playin football for the Saints an be her janitor at the same time. Besides, she said, "Them people ain't comin in here to look at *me* anymore, they is comin to look at *you*, you big oaf!"

Well, the day before we was fixin to leave for the Dallas game, I gone to the post office an there is a letter there from Mobile, Alabama. It is from Jenny's mama. Now, I always get kind of excited when I hear from Jenny or anybody even connected with her, but this time, I dunno, somethin felt kind of funny. Inside the envelope was another letter, not even opened. It was the one I had sent Jenny with the last check for thirty thousan dollars. I begun to read what Mrs. Curran was tryin to tell me, but even before I finished, I wished I was dead.

"Dear Forrest," she said. "I don't know how to tell you this. But Jenny got very sick about a month ago, and her husband, Donald, did, too. He died last week. And the next day, Jenny did, too."

There was a bunch of other stuff she said, also, but I don't remember much of it. I kept lookin at them first lines, an my hands started tremblin an my heart begun to beat so hard I thought I was gonna faint. It was not true! It couldn't be. Not Jenny. I mean, I had knowed her all these years, ever since we was in grade school, an I had loved her too—only person besides my mama I'd ever really loved. An I just stood there while big ole tears run down onto the letter an blot out the ink except for the last few lines, which said, "I have little Forrest here with me, and he can stay as long as I can care for him, but I'm not too well myself, Forrest, and if you can find the time between your football games to come and see us, I think we'd better have a talk."

Well, I ain't sure exactly what I done next, but somehow I got back home an thowed some stuff in a bag an caught the bus to Mobile that afternoon. It was the longest bus drive of my life, I think. I just kept goin back over all them years with Jenny an me. How she always helped me out of trouble in school—even after I accidentally tore off her dress in the movie theater—an in college when she sang with the folk music band an I screwed up by haulin the banjo player out of the car while they was makin out, an then up in Boston when she was singin with The Cracked Eggs an I went to Harvard University an got in the Shakespeare play—an even after that, when she was up in Indianapolis workin for the retread tire company an I became a rassler an she had to tell me what a fool I was makin of mysef. . . . It just can't be true, I kept thinkin, over an over again, but thinkin don't make it so. I knew that deep down. I knew it was true.

When I got to Mrs. Curran's house, it was nearly nine o'clock at night.

"Oh, Forrest," she says, an thowed her arms around me an begun to cry, an I couldn't help it an begun cryin, too. In a little while, we went inside an she made me some milk an cookies an tried to tell me about it.

"Nobody knows exactly what it was," she said. "They both got sick about the same time. It was very fast and they just kind of slipped away. She wasn't in any pain or anything. In fact, she was more beautiful than ever. Just laid in the bed, like I remember her as a little girl. Her very own bed. Her hair all long and pretty, and her face was just like it always was, like an angel. And then, that morning, she . . ."

Mrs. Curran had to stop for a while. She wadn't cryin anymore. She just looked out the winder at the streetlight.

"And when I went in to see her, she was gone. Lying there with her head on the pillow, almost like she was sleeping. Little Forrest was playing out on the porch, and, well, I wasn't sure what to do, but I told him to come in an kiss his mama. And he did. He didn't know. I didn't let him stay that long. We buried her the next day. Out to the Magnolia Cemetery in the family plot, alongside her daddy and her granny. Under a sugar maple tree. Little Forrest, I don't know how much he understands about it all. He don't know about his daddy. He died up in Savannah, with his folks. He knows his mama's gone, but I don't think he really understands about it."

"Can I see it?"

"What?" Mrs. Curran ast.

"Where she was. Where she was when . . ."

"Oh, yes, Forrest. It's right in here. Little Forrest is sleeping in there now. I've only got two . . ."

"I don't want to wake him up," I says.

"Why don't you," says Mrs. Curran. "It'll make him feel better, maybe."

An so I gone into Jenny's bedroom. There was little Forrest asleep in her bed, didn't know nothin really about what was happenin to him. Had a teddy bear he was huggin an a big blond curl across his forehead. Mrs. Curran started to wake him up, but I ast her not to. I could almost see Jenny there, peaceful an asleep. Almost.

"Maybe he ought to just rest tonight," I says. "They'll be time in the mornin for him to see me."

"All right, Forrest," she says. Then she turned away. I touched his face an he turned over an give a little sigh.

"Oh, Forrest," Mrs. Curran says, "I don't believe all this. So quick. And they all seemed so happy. Things sure do turn out bad sometime, don't they?"

"Yes'm," I says. "They shore do." We went on out of the room.

"Well, Forrest, I know you're tired. We've got a sofa here in the living room. I can make you a bed."

"You know, Mrs. Curran, maybe I could sleep on that swing out on the porch. I always liked that swing, you know. Jenny an I used to sit on it an . . ."

"Of course, Forrest. I'll get you a pillow and some blankets."

So that's what I did. An all that night the wind blew, an sometime afore dawn, it begun to rain. It wadn't cold or nothin. Just a regular ole fall night for around here where I grew up. An I don't think I slept much neither. I was thinkin about Jenny an little Forrest an about my life, which, come to think of it, hadn't been much. I have done a lot of things, but I ain't done many of them very well. Also, I'm always gettin into trouble just about the time things start goin good. Which, I suppose, is the penalty you pay for bein a idiot.

Chapter Two

Well, the next mornin Mrs. Curran come out on the porch with a cup of coffee an a doughnut. The rain had let up a little bit, but the sky was a dark pearly gray an there was thunder growlin off someplace like God was mad.

"I guess you'll want to go out to the cemetery," Mrs. Curran said.

"Yeah, I guess so," I tole her. I didn't really know if I wanted to or not. I mean, somethin was tellin me I oughta, but it was the last place I really wanted to go.

"I've got little Forrest ready," she says. "He ain't been there since . . . Well, I think it would be a good thing for him to go along. Just to kind of get used to it."

I looked behind her an there he was, standin behind the screen door, lookin sort of sad an puzzled.

"Who are you?" he ast.

"Why, I'm Forrest. You remember when I met you a while back? Up at Savannah."

"You're the one with the funny monkey?"

19

"Yeah. Sue. But he's not a monkey. He's a purebread orangutang."

"Where is he now? He here?"

"Nope. Not this time," I says. "He got bidness someplace else, I reckon."

"We're gonna go see my mama now," the little boy says, an I like to choked up right then.

"Yeah, I know," I says.

Mrs. Curran, she put us in the car an we drove out to the cemetery. Whole time, I got these horrible butterflies in my stomach. Little Forrest, he just lookin out the winder with big ole sad eyes, an I am wonderin what in hell is gonna happen to us all.

It was a really pretty cemetery, as them things go. Big ole magnolia an oak trees, an we wound around an wound around till we got to a big tree an Mrs. Curran stopped the car. It was a Sunday mornin, an someplace church bells were chimin away. When we got out, little Forrest come up beside me an looked up, an so I took him by the hand an we walked to Jenny's grave. The ground was still wet from the rain, an a lot of leaves had blown down, pretty red an gold ones, shaped just like stars.

"Is that where Mama is?" little Forrest ast.

"Yes it is, darlin," Mrs. Curran says.

"Can I see her?"

"No, but she's there," says Jenny's mama. He was a brave little boy, he was, an didn't cry or nothin, like I would of if I'd been him. An after a few minutes he found hissef a stick to play with an walked off a ways by hissef.

"I just can't believe it," Mrs. Curran said.

"I can't neither," I says. "It ain't right."

"I'll go back to the car now, Forrest. You probably want to be alone for a while."

I just stood there, kind of numb, twistin my hands.

Everbody I really cared for seemed to have died or somethin. Bubba an Mama, an now poor Jenny. It had begun to drizzle a little bit now, an Mrs. Curran went an got little Forrest an put him in the car. I started to walk away mysef when I heard a voice say, "Forrest, it's okay."

I turned aroun, but ain't nobody there.

"I said it's okay, Forrest," the voice says again. It was . . . It couldn't be . . . It was Jenny!

Cept there still ain't nobody there.

"Jenny!" I says.

"Yes, Forrest. I just wanted you to know everything's gonna be all right."

I must be goin crazy, I figgered! But then alls of a sudden I kind of seen her, just in my mind, I guess, but there she was, as beautiful as always.

"You're gonna have to take little Forrest now," she says, "an raise him up to be strong and smart and good. I know you can do it, Forrest. You've got a very big heart."

"But how?" I ast. "I'm a idiot."

"No you're not!" Jenny says. "You might not be the smartest feller in town, but you've got more sense than most people. You've got a long life ahead of you, Forrest, so make the best you can of it. I've told you that for years."

"I know, but . . ."

"Anytime you really get stumped, I'll be there for you. Do you understand that?"

"No."

"Well, I will. So go on back and get busy and try to figure out what you're gonna do next."

"But, Jenny, I just can't believe it's you."

"Well, it's me all right. Go on, now, Forrest," she says. "Sometimes you act like you ain't got sense enough to get in out of the rain."

So I gone on back to the car, soakin wet.

"Was you talkin to somebody out there?" Mrs. Curran ast.

"Sort of," I said. "I guess I was talkin to mysef."

That afternoon, me an little Forrest sat in Jenny's mama's livin room an watched the New Orleans Saints play the Dallas Cowboys—or whatever it was they did with them. The Cowboys done scored four touchdowns the first quarter, an we ain't scored none. I had tried to call the stadium to explain where I was, but ain't nobody answered the phone in the locker room. I guess by the time I got around to callin, they had all done gone out on the field.

Second quarter it was worse, an by half-time the score was forty-two to nothin, an the sportscasters were all talkin about how I wadn't there an nobody knew where I was. I finally got through to the locker room, an all of a sudden Coach Hurley got on the phone.

"Gump, you idiot!" he hollered. "Where in hell are you!"

I tole him Jenny had died, but he didn't seem to understand.

"Who in hell is Jenny?" he screamed.

It wadn't too easy to explain all this, so I just tole him she was a friend of mine. Then the owner got on the phone.

"Gump, I tole you that if you don't show up for a game, I'm gonna fire your ass myself! And that's what I'm doin. Your ass is fired!"

"But see," I tole him, "it was Jenny. I just found out yesterday . . ."

"Don't hand me that bullshit, Gump! I know all about you and your so-called agent, Mr. Butterbutt, or whatever his name is. This is just another cheap trick to get more money. An you ain't gonna do it. Don't *never* come around my football team again. You hear—never!"

"Did you explain it to them?" Mrs. Curran ast, when she came back into the room.

"Yeah," I said. "Sort of."

An so that ended my professional football playin days. Now I had to find some kind of job to help support little Forrest. Jenny had put most of the money I'd sent her into a bank account, an with the other thirty thousan dollars Jenny's mama had sent back to me, there was enough to earn a little interest. But it weren't gonna be enough for everthin, so I knew I had to find me some work.

Next mornin, I looked through the papers at the job ads. Wadn't much goin on. Mostly they wanted secretaries an used car salesmen an such, an I figgered I needed somethin, well, more dignified.

Then I spotted a ad in the column marked "Other."

"Promotional Representative," it says. "No experience necessary! Huge profits for hard workers!" An it give an address for a local motel. "Interviews at 10 A.M. sharp." "Must be able to deal with people" was the final line.

"Mrs. Curran," I says, "what is a 'promotional representative'?"

"I'm not sure, Forrest. I think it's . . . Well, you know the guy who dresses up like that big peanut outside the peanut store downtown and hands out little samples of nuts to folks? I think it's something like that."

"Oh," I says. Frankly, I was expectin somethin a little higher up on the ladder. But I am thinkin about them "huge profits" the ad talked about. An besides, if it *was* bein a peanut man or somethin, at least people wouldn't know it was me inside the costume.

As it turned out, it was not the peanut man. It was somethin very very different.

"Knowledge!" says the feller. "Everthin in the world depends on *knowledge!*"

They was about eight or ten of us done answered the ad for "Promotional Representative." We had arrived at this dinky little motel an was sent into a room that had a bunch of foldin chairs set up an a phone settin on the floor. After about twenty minutes, the door suddenly bust open an in comes this tall, thin, suntanned guy wearin a white suit an white buck shoes. He don't say his name or nothin, just comes marchin into the room an gets in front of us an begun to give us a lecture. His hair is slicked back an greasy, an he has a little pencil mustache.

"Knowledge!" he shouts again. "And here it is!"

He unfolded a big color-poster-size sheet of paper an begun pointin out the various forms of knowledge, which are printed on it. They is pictures of dinosaurs an ships an farm crops an big cities. They is even pictures of outer space an rocket ships, of TVs an radios an cars, an I don't know what-all else.

"This is the opportunity of a lifetime!" he hollers. "To bring all this knowledge into people's homes!"

"Wait a minute," somebody ast. "Does this have anything to do with selling encyclopedias?"

"Certainly not," the man answers, sort of hurt like.

"Well, it looks like it does to me," the feller says. "If it's not selling encyclopedias, what the hell is it?"

"We do not *sell* encyclopedias!" the man replies. "We *place* encyclopedias in people's homes."

"Then it *is* about selling encyclopedias!" the first man shouts.

"With an attitude like that, I don't think you should be here," said the feller. "Leave us now, so the others can be informed."

"Damn right I'll leave," says the first man, walkin out. "I got roped into sellin encyclopedias one time before, an it's a total bunch of bullshit."

"Nevertheless!" hollers the feller in the white suit, "you will be sorry when all these other guys are rich and famous." An he slammed the door so hard the room shook an I was afraid the doorknob might of hit the first man in the asshole.

It took us about a week to go through our "trainin" period. This consisted of havin to learn a long speech, word for word, about how good the encyclopedias we was sellin was. *Book of Worldwide Information* was what they was called. Our instructor was the feller in the white suit, who was also the regional sales manager for the encyclopedia company. Mister Trusswell was his name, but he told us to just call him Slim.

Like Slim said, we was not goin out there to *sell* encyclopedias. We was gonna *place* them in people's homes. Actually, the deal was this: We gave the people the encyclo-pedias for free, provided that they would sign a contract agreeing to buy a new two-hundrit-and-fifty-dollar annual yearbook ever year for the rest of their lives. In this way the people got their free set of encyclopedias an the company got about ten thousan dollars for sellin the yearbooks, which cost about five dollars apiece to print. I would get fifteen percent of ever contract I made. An Slim got five percent of that. Now, how could anybody lose on a deal like this?

It was on a Monday when we was given our first

assignments. We was tole to wear a coat an tie an be sure to get shaved an clean under our fingernails. An there was to be no drinkin on the job, either. We reported to the motel, an there was a big ole flatbed truck waitin for us. Slim herded us on board like cattle, an away we went.

"Now, listen up," Slim says. "Each of you is gonna get dropped off in a neighborhood. What I want you to look for is children's toys—swings, sandboxes, tricycles—that kind of shit. We want to sell these things to young parents! That way, they got longer to have to pay for the annual yearbook! You don't see no children or children's toys outside, don't waste your time!"

So that's what we did. Everbody, me included, got dropped off in some neighborhood. They wadn't very nice neighborhoods, either, but Slim says that's okay, cause people in nice neighborhoods is probly too smart to fall for the kind of scam we is tryin to pull. Anyhow, first house I see with a set of children's swings, I go up an knock on the door. A woman answers an opens the screen door. Immediately I stick my foot in it, like I have been tole to do.

"M'am," I says, "you got a minute?"

"Do I *look* like I got a minute?" she answers. Her hair is up in curlers an she is wearin a nightgown, an they is all sorts of racket comin from the little kids in the backgroun.

"I want to talk to you about the future of your children," I says, which is part of the rehearsed speech.

"What is your interest in my children?" she asts, sort of suspiciously.

"They are badly in need of knowledge," I answers.

"What are you, one of those religious nuts?" she says.

"No, m'am, I am here to make a free gift to your home of the world's best encyclopedias."

"Encyclopedias! Ha," she says. "Do I look like I can afford to buy encyclopedias?"

I could see her point, but anyhow, I went on with the speech: "M'am, as I have said, I'm not astin you to *buy* encyclopedias. I am gonna *place* them in your home."

"What do you mean—*loan* them to me?"

"Not exactly," I says. "If I could just come in for a minute . . ."

So she let me in an set me down in the livin room. Slim had done tole us if we got this far, we was almost home free! I opened my kit an begun explainin everthin to her, just like Slim had said to do. The speech was about fifteen minutes long, an she just looked an listened. Three little kids about the age of little Forrest come in an begun crawlin all over her. When I am through, she bust into tears.

"Oh, Mr. Gump," she says. "I wish I could afford them encyclopedias. But I just can't." An then she begun to tell me her sad tale. Her husband done run off with a younger woman an left her without a cent. She lost her job as a diner cook cause she fell asleep from overwork fryin eggs an ruint the griddle. The power company done shut down her electricity, an the phone company is about to do the same. She also got to have a operation but can't afford it, an the kids is hungry half the time. That night the landlord is comin around to collect the fifty-dollar rent an she ain't got it, so she's about to be thowed out of her house. An there is a bunch of other stuff, too, but you get the gist of it.

Anyhow, I done loaned her the fifty bucks an got out of there. Man, she was pitiful.

All that day I done knocked on doors. Most people wouldn't even let me in. About half of them says they have already been taken by other encyclopedia salesmen, an they was the unhappiest ones of all. Four or five slammed the door in my face, an somebody sicced a big ole ugly dog on me. By late that afternoon, when Slim's truck pulled up to haul us off, I was exhausted an discouraged.

"Now, don't none of you worry about this first day," Slim says. "First day's always the hardest. Just think, if any of you had sold just one of them contracts, you would be a thousand dollars richer. It don't take but one, an I guarantee you there is plenty of suckers out there." Then he turns to me.

"Gump," he says, "I been watchin you. You got *energy* boy! An charm, too. You just need a little practice with an expert! An I am the man to show you. Tomorrow mornin, you are comin along with me!"

That night when I got back to Mrs. Curran's, I didn't even feel like eatin no supper. Here I was, a great "Promotional Representative," fifty bucks poorer an got nothin to show for it but thinner shoe soles an a hole in my pants where the dog got me.

Little Forrest was playin on the livin room floor, an ast me where I been.

"Sellin encyclopedias," I said.

"What kind of encyclopedias?"

An so I showed him. I did just what I was tole to do. I gave my whole speech, openin out the folder with all the pictures an layin down the samples of the encyclopedias an yearbooks. When I was finished, he looked at one of the books an says, "This is a bunch of shit."

"What is that?" I said. "Who taught you to talk that way?"

"Sometimes my mama would say that," he replied.

"Well, it ain't no proper way for a seven-year-ole boy to be talkin," I says. "Besides, why you call my books that?"

"Because it's true," he said. "Look at all this stuff. Half of it's wrong." He points to a part of the encyclopedia that's open. "Look at this," he says, pointin to a drawin that said "1956 Buick." "That's a fifty-*five* Buick," he says. "The fifty-six didn't have fins like that. And look at this, too," he said. "That's an F-eighty-five fighter plane—not an F-one-hundred!" Little Forrest gone on to point out a bunch of other stuff, too, he said wasn't right.

"Any dummy would know all this is wrong," he says.

Well, *almost* any dummy, I figgered. I didn't know if he was right or not, but I intended to ask Slim about it next mornin.

"You got to catch em at just the right time," Slim says. "Right after the husband has gone off to work an before they take their kids to school. If you see a yard with toys for little kids who ain't old enough to go to school, save it for later in the day."

We had got off the truck in a neighborhood an was walkin down the street, an Slim was teachin me the tricks of the trade.

"Next best time," he says, "is right after the soap operas is over an before they got to go pick up the kids again, or the husband gets home from work."

"Look," I said, "I need to ast you somethin. Somebody done tole me a lot of the things in the encyclopedia ain't right."

"Yeah, who tole you that?"

"I'd rather not say. Question is, is it true?"

"How the hell would I know?" Slim says. "I don't read that crap. I'm just here to get people to buy it."

"But what about the folks who do?" I says. "I mean, it don't seem fair to be gettin them to pay all that money for stuff that ain't so."

"Who cares?" Slim answers. "Ain't any of them people know the difference—an besides, you don't think they actually use this shit, do you? They get it to put on a shelf, and it probly don't ever get opened up."

Anyhow, Slim pretty soon spotted the house he was gonna make a sale at. It needed some paint an all, but outside there was an old tire hangin from a tree branch by a rope an some small bikes on the porch.

"This is it," Slim said. "I can feel it in my bones. Two kids, just about school age. I bet Mama's in there right now opening her checkbook for me."

Slim knocked on the door, an pretty soon a lady appeared, sort of sad-eyed an tired lookin. Slim went right into his pitch. As he kept on talkin, he just sort of worked his way inside the house, an the next thing the lady knew, the two of us was settin in her livin room.

"But I really don't need any more encyclopedias," she says. "Look I've already bought the *Encyclopedia Britannica* and the *Encyclopedia Americana*. We'll be payin on those the next ten years."

"Exactly!" Slim says. "And you won't be using them until then, either! You see, them encyclopedias are for older kids—late high-school and college students. But you gotta have somethin *now*, while your kids are still young— somethin they can get interested in! And here it is!"

Slim begun handin the lady all his samples, pointin out how many pictures an all were there an how the writin was simplified an much more understandable than them other encyclopedias the lady already had bought. Time he was through, Slim had got the lady to serve us some lemonade, an when we left, Slim walked away with a contract in his hand.

"Now, Gump! See how easy it is! Lookee here, I just made myself a thousand dollars for twenty minutes' work— just like takin candy from a baby!"

In fact, he was correct. Cept I didn't feel exactly right about it. I mean, what was that poor lady gonna do with all them encyclopedia sets? But Slim said she was just the kind of "client" he liked. "They believe all the bullshit you can lay on em," he said. "Most of em are grateful just to have somebody to talk to."

Anyway, he says for me to go on now an start pushin the encyclopedias on my own, an he expects me to have a sale or two by the end of the day—now that he has showed me how to do it.

So that's what I did. But by late that afternoon, I had knocked on two-dozen doors an hadn't even once got ast inside. Four or five times the people wouldn't even open the door—they spoke through the mail slot an tole me to go away. One lady was hoein some crabgrass out of her driveway an when she found out why I was there, she ran me off with the hoe.

I was walkin on back to the truck pickup point when I looked down a street that was different from the ones I had been workin on. This was a nice street, with real pretty houses an gardens an expensive cars in the driveways. An at the very end of the street, up on a little hill, was the biggest house of them all—a mansion, I guess you could call it. I figgered, what the hell. I know Slim has tole us these kinds of folks don't buy encyclopedias, but I got to try *somethin*, an so I gone on up to the mansion an rang the doorbell. It was the first doorbell I seen all day. First, nothin happened, an I figgered ain't nobody home. I rang two or three more times, an was about to go on my way, when suddenly the door opened. It was a lady standin there, wearin a red silk gown, an carryin a cigarette holder in her hand. She was older than me, but she was still very beautiful, with long wavy brown hair an a lot of makeup. When she saw me, she looked me over two or three times, an then gave a big ole smile. Afore I had a chance to say anythin at all, she opened the door an invited me in.

Mrs. Hopewell was her name, but she says for me to call her Alice.

Mrs. Hopewell—Alice—took me into a great big room with high ceilins an a lot of fancy furniture an ast me if I wanted somethin to drink. I nodded, an she says, "What'll it be then, bourbon, gin, scotch?" But I remembered what Slim had tole us about drinkin on the job, so I tole her a CokeCola would be just fine. When she come back with the CokeCola, I went into my spiel. About halfway through, Mrs. Hopewell says, "Thank you, Forrest. I have heard enough. I'll buy them."

"What?" I ast. I ain't believin my luck.

"The encyclopedias," she says. "I'll take a set."

She ast me how much to write the check for, an I explained about how she ain't really buyin them, just makin a contract to buy the annual yearbook for the rest of her life, but she waved me off. "Just show me where to sign," she said, an that's what I did.

Meantime, I took a swig of the CokeCola. *Uggh!* It tasted horrible! For a moment I thought she done poured me somethin else besides CokeCola, but in fact she hadn't, account of she done left the can right there on the side table.

"And now, Forrest, I am gonna go slip into somethin more comfortable," Mrs. Hopewell says.

I am thinkin she looks comfortable enough already, but of course, this is none of my bidness.

"Yes'm," I says.

"Just call me Alice," she says, and disappears out of the room with her skirts sashayin behind her.

I set there lookin at the CokeCola an gettin thirstier an thirstier. I really wish I had a RC or somethin. Anyhow, I figger she is gonna be a few minutes, so I gone on back to where the kitchen was. I have never seen such a kitchen as this! I mean, it is bigger than the whole house Jenny growed up in, with tiles an wood an stainless stuff an lights that come out of the ceiling! I looked in the icebox to see if there was another CokeCola, thinkin maybe that one had just gone bad. To my surprise there was about fifty cans of it in there, an so I popped open another one an took a great big swig. *Arrrrragh!* I had to spit it out. It tasted like shit!

Well, actually it didn't taste exactly like shit, whatever shit tastes like. It tasted more like a combination of turpentine an bacon grease, with a little sugar an fizzy-water thowed in. I am thinkin somebody done played a trick on Mrs. Hopewell.

Just about this time, Mrs. Hopewell come through the door. "Ah, Forrest, I see you have found the CokeCola. I didn't know you were that thirsty, you poor boy. Here, let me put that in a glass for you." She had put on a little pink nighty that showed everthin she had, which was considerable, an was wearin little fluffy pink slippers, an I am thinkin that she must be gettin ready for bed.

But now I was really on the spot. She got a fresh glass that sparkled like a rainbow an poured the CokeCola over some ice. I could hear it cracklin in the glass an was wonderin how I was gonna drink it when Mrs. Hopewell says she will be right back, that she is goin to "freshen up."

I was about to thow the CokeCola out again, when a idea come to me. Maybe I could make it better. I was rememberin the time back at the University when I wanted a limeade so bad I could just taste it, but there wadn't no limes, an my mama had sent me some peaches an I made a *peach-ade* by squeezin the peaches through a sock. Bad as it was, I am thinkin that I can salvage somethin out of this CokeCola, account of my tongue is dry as my toe an I might even be dyin of thirst. I could of just got me some water, but by now, I have definitely got CokeCola on my mind.

They was a big ole pantry, an inside it was hundrits of little jars an bottles of all sorts of sizes an shapes. One says cumin, an another says Tabasco, an another says tarragon vinegar. They was jars an bottles an little boxes of other stuff, too. I found some olive oil I figgered might cut the bacon grease taste some, an then a jar of chocolate sauce that might take off some of the turpentine flavor. I mixed up about twenty or thirty different things in a bowl that was settin out on the counter, an when I was finished, I mushed them all together with my fingers an then dipped out a couple of spoonfuls an thowed it into the CokeCola glass. For a moment, the stuff begun to boil an hiss like it was gonna blow up, but the more I stirred it in with the ice, the better it looked, an after a few minutes, it begun to look like CokeCola again.

At this point I was startin to feel like one of them desert gold prospectors that was bakin to death under the sun, an so I lifted the glass an drunk it down. This time, it gone on down pretty good, an while it wadn't exactly CokeCola, it didn't taste like shit, neither. It was so good, in fact, that I poured mysef another glass.

Just then, Mrs. Hopewell returned to the kitchen.

"Ah, Forrest," she says, "how is that CokeCola?"

"It is pretty good," I tole her. "Matter of fact, I'm gonna have some more. You want some?"

"Ah, thank you, but thank you, no, Forrest."

"Why not?" I ast. "Ain't you thirsty?"

"Why, as a matter of fact I am," she says. "But I'd prefer, well, a little libation of a different sort." She went over an poured hersef a glass about half full of gin an then put some orange juice in it.

"You see," she says, "I am always amazed that anybody can drink that crap. My husband, in fact, is the feller that invented it. Somethin they want to call 'New Coke.'"

"Yeah?" I say. "Well, it don't exactly taste like the ole one."

"You're tellin me, buster! I never had anything so wretched in my life. Kinda tastes like—hell, I dunno— *turpentine* or something."

"Yeah," I says. "I know."

"Some stupid deal his bosses up at the Coke company in Atlanta have dreamed up. 'New Coke' my ass," she says. "They always screwing with something just so's they can figger a new angle to sell it with. Ask me, it's gonna be a bunch of bullshit."

"That so?" I ast.

"Damn right. Matter of fact, you're the first person ever got a whole glass of it down without gagging. You know, my husband's the vice president of CokeCola—in charge of research and development. Some research—some development, if you ask me!"

"Well, it ain't half bad if you put some other stuff in it," I says. "Just fix it up a little."

"No? Well, that's not my problem. Look," she says, "I didn't get you in here to talk about my husband's hare-brained schemes. I bought your goddamn encyclopedias, or whatever they are, now I want a favor. I had a masseuse coming over this afternoon and he didn't show. You know how to give a back rub?"

"Huh?"

"A back rub—you know, I lie down and you give me a rub. You're so big on books about world knowledge, you gotta know how to rub somebody's back, right? I mean, even an idiot can figure out how to do that."

"Yeah, well . . ."

"Listen, buster," she says, "bring the goddamn CokeCola and come with me."

She took me around to a room that had mirrors on all the walls an a big old raised bed in the middle of it. Music was playin through speakers in the ceilin, an they was a big ole Chinese gong settin there by the bed.

Mrs. Hopewell got up on the bed an thowed off her little slippers an nighty an put a big towel over her bottom half, an she was laid down on her stomach. I tried not to look at her while this was goin on, but account of the whole room was mirrors, this was not very easy to do.

"Okay," she says, "start rubbing."

I got sort of aside of her an begun to rub her shoulders. She begun to make little *oh-ah* sounds. The more I rubbed, the louder they got. "Lower. Lower!" Mrs. Hopewell says. I gone on an rubbed lower, an the more I did, the *lower* I got! It was beginnin to get awkward for sure. In fact, I was now at the top of the towel. Finally she begun to pant an then she reaches over an hits the Chinese gong! It made the room shake an the mirrors seem like they gonna fall off the walls.

"Take me, Forrest," she moans.

"Where you want to go?" I ast.

"Just take me!" she screams. "Now!"

At this point I suddenly begun to think about Jenny an about a bunch of other things, an Mrs. Hopewell was grappin at me an writhin an pantin on the bed, an this shit seemed about to get out of hand when, without no warnin, the door to the mirror room bust open an they is a little man standin there wearin a suit an tie an steel-rimmed glasses, kinda look like a Nazi German.

"Alice," he shouts, "I think I have got it figured out! If

we put some steel-wool shavings into the formula, it will make it quit tasting like turpentine!"

"Jesus God, Alfred!" Mrs. Hopewell hollers. "What are you doing home this time of day!" She done bolted upright an was tryin to pull the towel up around hersef to look decent.

"My researchers," the feller says, "have found the solution!"

"Solution! Solution to what?" Mrs. Hopewell asts.

"The 'New Coke,'" he says. The feller strides into the room, actin like I'm not even there. "I think we got a way to get people to drink it."

"Oh, for godssake, Alfred. Who would want to drink that crap anyhow?" Mrs. Hopewell looks like she's about to burst into tears. She ain't got but that one towel, an she is tryin to cover hersef up, bottom an top, with it. Ain't workin too good, an so she is grappin for her nighty, which is on the floor, but ever time she graps for it, the towel falls off. I am tryin to look away again, but the mirrors won't give me no other view.

About this time, Alfred, I guess was his name, noticed me.

"Are you the masseuse?" he ast.

"Sort of," I says.

"That your CokeCola?"

"Yup."

"You're drinking it?"

"Uh huh."

"No shit?"

I nodded. I didn't exactly know what to say, account of it is his new invention.

"And it don't taste awful?" His eyes got big as biscuits.

"Not now," I says. "I fixed it."

"Fixed it? How?"

"I put some stuff in it from the kitchen."

"Let me see that," he says. He took the glass an helt it up to the light an examined it, sort of like a person will examine somethin nasty in a laboratory jar. Then he drunk a little sip of it an got a kind of squinty look in his eyes. He look at me, then at Mrs. Hopewell, then he slugged down a big ole swallow.

"My God!" he says. "This shit ain't half bad!"

He drunk some more an get a real amazed look on his face, like he was seein a vision or somethin.

"You *fixed* this!" he shouts. "How in hell did you *fix* it?"

"I done put a few things from that pantry in it," I says.

"*You!* The *masseuse?*"

"He's not exactly a masseuse," Mrs. Hopewell says.

"He's not? Then what is he?"

"I'm a encyclopedia salesman," I says.

"Encyclopedias—Huh?" Alfred says. "Then what are you doing here? With my wife?"

"It is kind of a long story," I tole him.

"Well, it doesn't matter," he says. "We'll get to that later. What I want to know now is what in hell did you do to this CokeCola? Tell me! My God, tell me!"

"I dunno, exactly," I says. "It was like, well, it didn't taste so good at first, an I thought it could have stood some doctorin up, you know?"

"Didn't taste good! Why, you moron, it tasted like shit! Don't you think I know that? And you have made it at least drinkable! Do you have any idea what something like this is worth? Millions! Billions! C'mon now, try to remember. What was it, er—What's your name, anyhow?"

"Gump," I says. "Forrest Gump."

"Yes, Gump—well, c'mon now, Gump—let's go real slow through exactly what you did to this stuff. Show me what you put in it."

So that's what I did, except I couldn't remember everthin. I got out some of the little bottles an jars an stuff an tried to do it again, but I never could seem to get it quite right again. We tried an tried again, maybe fifty times, until it was way past midnight, but each time ole Alfred spit the stuff out in the sink an says it ain't like the first batch. Meantime, Mrs. Hopewell is about on her twentieth gin an orange juice.

"You fools," she says once. "There ain't no way to make that crap any good. Why don't we all go lay down in the bed an see what happens?"

"Shut up, Alice," Alfred says. "Don't you see this is the opportunity of a lifetime!"

"Opportunity of a lifetime is what I just suggested," says Mrs. Hopewell, an she goes back out in the mirror room an starts beatin on the gong. Finally, Alfred leans up against the icebox an puts his head in his hands.

"Gump," he says, "this is incredible. You have snatched me from the jaws of defeat, only to throw me back again. But I'm not finished yet. I am gonna call the police to seal this kitchen off. And tomorrow, we are gonna get an entire staff down here to pack up every conceivable thing you might have put in this stuff and ship it all back to Atlanta."

"Atlanta?" I ast.

"You bet your sweet ass, Gump. And the most prized item of all is going to be yourself!"

"Me?" I ast.

"Goddamn right, Gump. Your big ass is coming along to our lab in Atlanta to put this thing together right. Just think of it, Gump. Today Atlanta! Tomorrow the *world!*"

Mrs. Hopewell's face is smilin from the winder as I leave, an upon considerin all this, I have a feelin that trouble lies ahead.

Chapter Three

Anyhow, I gone on back to Mrs. Curran's that night an phoned up Slim at his motel to say I ain't gonna be placin no more encyclopedias in people's homes.

"Well, Gump, so this is how you repay me for all my kindness!" he says. "Stabbed in the back! I should of known better." An he concludes with a bunch of other shit that ain't any nicer, after which, he hung up in my face. At least I got that over with.

Little Forrest is of course long asleep in the bedroom time I get through with all that, an Mrs. Curran ast me what is goin on? I tole her I am quittin the encyclopedia bidness to go up to Atlanta an help Alfred make his new CokeCola, an that I figger I got to do this, account of it is a lot of money involved an we need to fix up little Forrest with some backup income. She agrees with me, cept she say she thinks I oughta have a conversation with little Forrest fore I go, an explain to him about exactly who I am, since his mama an daddy are dead now. I ast her don't she think *she'd* be better off explainin all that, but she say no.

"There comes a time, Forrest, when I believe a person has got to take the responsibility on himself, and that time is now. Might not be easy, but you gotta do it. And you gotta do it right, because it is gonna make a lastin impression on him."

In this, I know Mrs. Curran is correct, but it is not somethin I look forward to.

Next mornin I get up bright an early, an Mrs. Curran made me some cereal an helped me get my bag packed. Alfred says he is gonna pick me up at nine A.M. sharp, an so I have got to deal with little Forrest right about now. When he gets finished eatin his breakfast, I call him out on the porch.

"I have got to be gone for a while," I says, "an there is some things you better know before I go."

"What is that?" he ast.

"Well, for one thing, I don't know how long I'm gonna be gone, an I want you to be real nice to Mrs. Curran while I'm away."

"She's my grandma; I'm always nice to her," little Forrest says.

"An I want you to do real good in school, an don't get into no kind trouble, okay?"

A kind of frown come over his face, an he look at me sort of funny.

"Say, you ain't my daddy. Why you tellin me all this?"

"I guess that's what I want to talk to you about," I says. "You see, I *am* your daddy."

"No you're not!" he hollers. "My daddy's sick back home. He's comin to get me just as soon as he gets well."

"That's somethin else I got to tell you," I says. "Your daddy ain't gonna get well, Forrest. He's with your mama now, you see?"

"He is *not!*" Forrest says. "Grandma says he's comin to get me pretty soon! Any day now."

"Well, your grandma's wrong," I says. "You see, he

done took sick like your mama, an he didn't get well, an so I am gonna have to take care of you now."

"You!—That's not so! My daddy is comin!"

"Forrest," I says. "You got to listen to me, now. I didn't want to have to tell you this, but I got to. You see, I'm your real daddy. Your mama tole me that a long time ago. But you was livin with them, an I was just—well, like a bum or somethin, an it was better that you stayed with them. But see, they gone now, an ain't nobody but me to take care of you."

"You're a liar!" he says, an begun to beat on me with his little fists, an then he begun to cry. I knew he was gonna, an it was the first time I seen him do it, but I figger it is good for him now—although I still don't think he understands. I would rather be doin anythin but this.

"Forrest is tellin you the truth, son." Mrs. Curran had been standin in the doorway durin all this. She come out on the porch an pick the little boy up an set him in her lap.

"I didn't want to have to tell you this myself," she says, "so I got Forrest to do it for me. I should have tole you, but I just couldn't."

"It's not so. It's not so!" he shouts, an begun to kick an cry. "You're liars. You're both liars!"

About this time a big ole black limousine pull up in front of the house an Alfred get out an motion for me to come on an get inside. I can see Mrs. Hopewell's face grinnin out the backseat winder.

An so I took my bag an went on down the sidewalk to the car, an behind me, all I could hear was little Forrest screamin, "Liar, liar, liar!" If this is what Mrs. Curran meant when she says tellin little Forrest the truth will make a "lastin impression," I sure do hope she is wrong.

* * *

Anyhow, we went on up to Atlanta, an the whole time Mrs. Hopewell is puttin her hands on my leg an stuff like that, an ole Alfred, he is pourin over papers an books an talkin to hissef a lot. When we arrive at the CokeCola headquarters buildin, they is a big ole mob of people there to welcome us, an when I come in everbody be pumpin my hand an clappin me on the back.

They led me down a long hall to a door marked Experimental Research Lab, Top Secret, Keep Out! When we gone inside, I like to fainted! They has set up a whole kitchen exactly like Mrs. Hopewell's, right down to the half-empty glasses where I had drunk the CokeCola.

"Everthing is right here, Gump, just like you left it back at Mobile," Alfred says. "Now, what we want you to do is just what you did when you fixed that CokeCola. Trace every step you took, and think real hard, because the fate of this whole company might be riding on it!"

To me, it seems a sort of unfair burden to shoulder. After all, I ain't done anythin but try to fix me somethin to drink. Anyhow, they put me in a big ole white smock, like Dr. Kildare or somethin, an I begun the experiment. First I take a can of the "new CokeCola" an put it in a glass with some ice cubes. I tasted it, just like I done at Mrs. Hopewell's, an it still taste like shit or whatever.

So I gone into the pantry, where all the stuff is on the shelves. Truth is, I can't remember exactly what I put in the CokeCola that might of improved it. But I went on anyhow an started mixin the shit up. All the time, four or five fellers be follerin me around, takin notes whenever I do somethin.

First I took a pinch of cloves an a dab of cream of tartar. Next I put in some root beer extract an meat tenderizer an popcorn cheese seasoning an added some blackstrap molasses an crab boil. After that I done opened a can of chili con carne an skimmed the little orange fat that floats around the top an put that in, too. An then I added a little bakin soda, for good measure.

Finally, I stirred the whole thing up with my finger, just like I done at Mrs. Hopewell's, an I took a big ole swig of it. Everbody be holdin their breaths an watchin me with they eyes all bugged out. I swished the stuff around in my mouth for a second, then said the only thing that come to mind, which was *"Ugggh!"*

"What's wrong?" one of the fellers ast.

"Can't you see he don't like it?" says another.

"Say, let me taste that," Alfred says.

He takes a drink an spits it out on the floor. "Christ! This shit is worse than the stuff *we* made!"

"Mr. Hopewell," one of the fellers says, "you spit that out on the floor. Gump spit his in the sink. We're losin control of the experiment."

"Yeah, well, all right," Alfred says, an he got down on the floor an wiped up the Coke with his handkerchief. "But that don't seem too important to me, *where* he spit it. Main thing is, Gump, we gotta get back to work."

So that's what we did. All that day an most of the night. I got so confused at one point I accidentally poured half a saltcellar in the CokeCola instead of garlic powder, which I thought might take some of the edge off the turpentine taste. When I drank it down, it made me half crazy for a while, like they say happens to people in lifeboats that drink seawater. Finally Alfred says, "Okay, I guess that's enough for today. But we gotta get back at this bright an early tomorrow mornin. Right, Gump?"

"I reckon so," I says, but I am figgerin we might be up against a hopeless cause.

* * *

All that next day an the next weeks an the next months that gone by, I done tried to fix the CokeCola. Didn't work. I put in cayenne pepper an Spanish saffron an vanilla extract. I used cumin an food colorin an allspice an even MSG. The fellers follerin me aroun had gone through about five hundrit notebooks by now, an everbody was gettin on everbody else's nerves. Meantime, at night I would go back to the big ole hotel suite where we was all stayin, an sure enough, there would be Mrs. Hopewell, loungin aroun in next to nothin. Couple of times she ast for a back rub an I give it to her, but when she ast for a front rub, that's where I drawed the line.

I am beginnin to believe this whole thing is a bunch of crap. They feed me an give me a place to stay, but I ain't seen no money yet, an that's why I am here, on account of I gotta take care of little Forrest. One night lyin in bed, I am wonderin what I'm gonna do, an start thinkin about Jenny an some of the good ole times, an all of a sudden, I see her face in front of me, just like I did at the cemetery that day.

"Well, you big bozo," she says. "Can't you figger this one out for yourself?"

"What you mean?" I ast.

"You ain't never gonna be able to make that stuff taste right. Whatever you did the first time was just a fluke or something."

"Well, what I'm gonna do, then?" I says.

"Quit! Leave! Go find yourself a real job, before you spend the rest of your life trying to do what's impossible!"

"Well, how?" I ast. "I mean, these people are countin on me. They says I am their only hope to save the CokeCola Company from rack an ruin."

"Screw em, Forrest. They don't care anything about you. They're just trying to save their jobs, and using you as a fool."

"Yeah, well, thanks," I says. "I guess you're right. You usually were."

An then she is gone, an I am alone again.

Next mornin I am up at the crack of dawn when Alfred come an got me. When we got in to the experiment kitchen, I gone through the motions of makin the CokeCola good again. Bout halfway through the day, I done mixed up a batch of some shit, but this time, when I drunk it down, instead of sayin "Uggh!" an spittin it out, I done grinned an says "Ahhhh!" an drunk down some more.

"What's that?" one of the fellers shouts. "He *likes* it?"

"I reckon I got it," I says.

"Praise the Lord!" hollers Alfred, an slaps himself in the forehead.

"Gimme that," says one of the other fellers. He takes a sip an sort of rolls it around in his mouth.

"Say, that ain't half bad!" he says.

"Let me taste it," Alfred says. He takes a swallow an gets a really funny look on his face, like he is goin through an unusual experience.

"*Ahhhh!*" Alfred says. "It is wonderful!"

"Let me have some, too," another feller asts.

"No, no, damnit!" Alfred says. "We gotta save this shit for chemical analysis. What's in this glass is worth billions! Do you hear me, billions!" He rushes out an calls in two armed guards an says for them to take the CokeCola glass to the vault an to guard it with their lives.

"Gump, you have done it!" Alfred shouts, an begun poundin hissef on the knee with his fist an get so red in the face he looks like a beet. Them other fellers is holdin hands an jumpin up an down, an hollerin, too. Pretty soon the door to the experimental kitchen bust open, an there is a tall, gray-haired man standin there, lookin very distinguished in a dark blue suit.

"What is all this?" he ast.

"Sir, we have performed a miracle!" Alfred cries. "Gump, this is the chairman of the board and chief executive officer of CokeCola—go shake his hand."

"What is the miracle?" the feller ast.

"Gump here has made the New Coke taste good!" says Alfred.

"Yeah? How you do that?" he ast.

"I dunno," I says. "Just lucky I guess."

Anyhow, a few days later, the CokeCola Company has arranged for a big preview tastin party to be held at their headquarters at Atlanta, an have invited about five thousan people consistin of press, politicians, socialites, stockholders, an other elite folks—even includin about five hundrit grade-school kids from around the city. Outside, big spotlights crisscross in the sky, an them what wadn't invited were standin behind ropes wavin at them what was. Most everbody wearin tuxedos an ball gowns, an they is all millin aroun an makin small talk when suddenly a curtin on the stage is pulled back, an me an Alfred an Mrs. Hopewell an the president of CokeCola are standin there.

"Ladies and gentlemen," says the president, "I have a momentous announcement to make." Everbody get real quiet an be lookin straight at us.

"The CokeCola Company is proud to announce a new product that is gonna revitalize our bidness. As you know, CokeCola has been around for more than seventy years, an we have not once changed our original formula, because we figgered everbody liked CokeCola. But that is not the way of the nineteen-eighties. Everbody got to change sometime.

WINSTON GROOM • 48

General Motors changes about every three or four years. So does politicians. People change clothes once or twice a year . . ."

At this last remark, there is some low mumblin from the audience.

"What I meant was," the president goes on, "that clothes designers change their product with great regularity —and just look at the money they make!"

He lets this sink in for a moment an then proceeds: "And so we here at CokeCola have decided to throw away our time-honored formula for CokeCola and try somethin different. 'New Coke' is what it is called, and we have to thank for this a brilliant young scientist, Forrest Gump, who has invented this amazing product! Now, right at your tables, our staff is passing out bottles and cans of New Coke for your enjoyment, but first, I think a few words from its inventor are appropriate. Ladies and gentlemen, I give you Forrest Gump!"

He leads me to the speaker's stand, an I am dumbfounded. I am so scared, what I am thinking is, I got to pee, but I ain't gonna say it this time. Nope. So I just says, "I hope it is good," an stepped back away from the microphone.

"Wonderful," the president shouts when the applause dies down. "And now, let the tasting begin!"

All over the auditorium you can hear the sounds of cans poppin an bottles bein opened, an then you can see the people drinkin the new CokeCola. At first there is some *ooohs* and *ahhs,* an a few people be lookin at each other an noddin their heads. But then there come a cry from one of the little kids they has invited, says, "*Ugggh!* This shit is awful!" an spits it out. Then the other kids start doin the same thing, an in no time, seemed like everbody be spittin the New Coke on the floor an gaggin an cussin. Some people even spit it on other people, an this began to cause a disturbance out in the audience, an all of a sudden seems like a fight or somethin break out. Pretty soon, the people be thowin the cans an bottles of New Coke at us an at each other, too, an you can see all sorts of fists flyin an kickin an gougin, an tables turned over an all. Some of the ladies' dresses be ripped off, an they gone screamin out into the night. Cameras be flashin an the TV people is tryin to capture it all on film. Me an the president an Alfred an Mrs. Hopewell are just standin on the stage, dodgin the bottles an cans, an we are sort of dumbstruck. Somebody shouts, "Call the police!" But I am lookin out at the crowd, an the police seem to be in the middle of everthin themselfs.

After a little bit, the whole thing spills out onto the street, an we hear a lot of sirens an so on. The president an me an Alfred an Mrs. Hopewell try to make our way out, but we get caught up in the thing, too, an it ain't long fore Mrs. Hopewell's dress is ripped off. We is covered with Coke an shit, an also with stuff from cupcakes an Moon Pies, which the CokeCola Company has thoughtfully handed out with the New Coke. Somebody shouts that the mayor of Atlanta has declared "a state of emergency," on account of there is a riot, an afore it is all over, they has busted out all the winders on Peachtree Street an looted most of the stores, an a few people is now settin fire to the buildins.

We is all standin under the awnin outside the CokeCola headquarters when somebody recognize me, shouts, "There he is!" an before I know it, about a thousan people commenced chasin me, includin the president of CokeCola an Alfred an even Mrs. Hopewell, who is only wearin her underpants! This ain't somethin I got to think about long! I start runnin fast as I can, across the Interstate an up hills an side roads, rocks an bottles landin all around me. Shit, seems like I been here before. Anyhow, I outrunned the mob, cause that is my specialty, but let me say this: It was scary!

Pretty soon, I found mysef on a ole two-lane highway leadin I knew not where, but along come a pair of head-lights an I stuck out my thumb. The headlights stopped, an lo an behole, it was a pickup truck. I ast the driver where he was headed, an he say, "North, to West Virginia," but that if I want a ride, I gotta ride in the back, account of he's got a passenger in the front. I look over at the passenger, an damn if it weren't a great big ole sow pig, must of weighed four hundrit pounds, settin there gruntin an pantin.

"This is a registered Poland China swine," the feller say. "Name's Gurtrude. Gonna make me rich one day, so she gotta ride in the cab. But you can bunk out in the back, there. Them other hogs is just common swine. Might root you around a little, but they don't mean no harm."

Anyhow, I got on the truck an away we went. They was about a dozen of them pigs in there with me, oinkin an squeelin an gruntin an all, but after a while they settled down an give me some livin space. Pretty soon it begun to rain. What I am thinkin is, I have had my ups an downs.

About sunup that next mornin the pickup done pull up at a truck stop, an the driver gets out an comes around to the back.

"Say," he says, "you sleep okay?"

"Pretty good," I answer. At this point I am lyin under a hog that is twice as big as me, but at least it kept me warm.

"Let's go in an get a cup of coffee an somethin to eat," he says. "By the way, my name's McGivver."

Outside the restaurant is a newspaper box with a copy of *The Atlanta Constitution,* headline says: **MORON WOULD-BE INVENTOR CAUSES RIOT IN CITY.**

The story reads somethin like this:

THE ATLANTA CONSTITUTION

A sometime Alabama encyclopedia salesman who professed knowledge of a new formula for the CokeCola Company caused one of the most violent riots in Atlanta's history yesterday when his scam was uncovered before several thousand of this city's most prominent citizens.

The incident broke out at about 7 P.M. when Forrest Gump, an itinerant tinkerer and peddler of phony reference books, was introduced by the president of the CokeCola Company as having conceived a new brand of the nation's favorite soft drink.

Witnesses said that when the new concoction was served to the audience for the first time, it induced a violent reaction in all present, which included the mayor and his wife, as well as various council members and their spouses and corporate chairpeople of all descriptions.

Police called to the scene described the melee as "uncontrollable" and told of horrible depredations inflicted on Atlanta's most fashionable citizens, including the ripping off of women's gowns and dresses and fighting and throwing objects of all descriptions.

At some point, the affair spilled out into the streets and turned into a riot, causing extensive damage in the chic downtown area. One source prominent in Atlanta's high society who wished to be unnamed said: "It was the wust thing I ever seen since Lester Maddox begun handin out them axe handles at his restaurant back in sixty-four."

Little is known of the perpetrator, Mr. Gump, who witnesses said fled the scene shortly after the brouhaha started. Sources said that Gump, thought to be in his early forties, was once a football player at the University of Alabama.

An assistant football coach at Georgia Tech who wished to remain anonymous recalled that "Yeah, I remember that Gump feller. Wadn't too smart, but the sombitch sure could run."

Police have put out an all-points bulletin for Gump, and the CokeCola Company, headquartered here, has offered a $1 million reward for his capture, dead or alive. . . .

Anyhow, I kind of hid the newspaper an we went on into the restaurant an set down, an Mister McGivver begun tellin me about his farmin operation in West Virginia.

"It ain't too big right now," he says, "but someday, I'm gonna be the greatest hog raiser in the world."

"Yeah?" I says. "That's nice."

"Nice—shit on nice, Gump. It's a dirty, low-down, smelly business, but there's money in it. 'Bring home the bacon' and all that crap. You just gotta be flexible. The hogs don't take a whole lot of work, but there are other problems to contend with."

"Such as what?" I ast.

"Well, for one thing, the people in Coalville, the little town where my farm is, they all the time complainin about the smell. Now, I admit that hogs smell, but the hell with that, Gump. Business is business. I got a thousand hogs and all they do is eat and shit all day. Of course it's gonna smell. I got used to it, why can't they?"

Anyhow, he goes on for a while about the hog bidness, an then he ast me about mysef.

"Say," he says, "was you involved in that disturbance in Atlanta last night? It looked like some kind of riot was goin on."

"Well, not exactly," I says, which I guess was sort of a lie, but I just didn't want to get into all that right now.

"Where you headed?" Mister McGivver ast.

"I dunno," I said. "I gotta go someplace an get me a job."

"What line of work are you in, Gump?" he says.

"Oh," I says, "I guess you could say I done a lot of things. Right now I just gotta get back on my feet."

"Well, why don't you come work for me awhile? There's a lot to do around the farm."

So that's what I did.

Chapter Four

Next year or two, I learned more about hog farmin than anybody got a need or even a right to know.

They was all sorts of hogs Mr. McGivver kept: big ole Poland Chinas an registered Hampshires, Mangalitzas, Durocs, Berkshires, Tamworths, an Cheshires. He even had a few merino sheep, which was sort of funny lookin, but Mister McGivver said he had em cause they was "nicer to look at."

My job, I figgered out pretty soon, was to do just about everthin. I slopped the hogs in the mornin an afternoon. Then I'd go around with a shovel an try an get up as much of the pig shit as possible, which Mister McGivver would sell to crop farmers for manure. I fixed fences an tried to keep the barn cleaned. Every month or so I'd load up the truck with whatever pigs Mister McGivver wanted to sell, an take them to market up at Wheeling or wherever.

One time I'm comin back from a trip to a pig auction, when a great idea come over me. I am drivin on the outskirts of this big ole army base, when it occur to me that they is wastin a lot of food that might be useful. I mean, when I was in the army a long time ago, I spent a lot of time on KP, account of I was always in hot water. An one of the things I remembered was that there was a lot of food an stuff that just got thowed out in the garbage from the mess halls, an it suddenly occurs to me that maybe we can use this food to slop the hogs. This is on account of hog food is expensive, an Mister McGivver say this is the main reason he cannot expand the pig farmin as fast as he wants. An so I stopped by the headquarters an ast to see whoever was in charge. They shown me into a little office, an lo an behole, there is this big ole black feller settin behind a desk, an when he turned around, it was Sergeant Kranz, from my ole company back in Vietnam. He took one look at me an liked to jumped out of his skin!

"Great godamighty! Is that *you*, Gump? What in hell are you doin here?"

When I tole him, he bust out laughin till he liked to split his pants.

"Pig farmer! Why, hell, Gump, with your record— Congressional Medal of Honor an all—you ought to be a general by now—or at least a sergeant major, like me! Mess hall leftovers for pigs, why—well, why not? Hell, Gump, you go see the mess hall first sergeant. Tell him I said to give you all the garbage you want." We talked about some of the ole times back in the war—about Bubba an Lieutenant Dan an some of the other fellers. I tole him about the Ping-Pong stuff in China an gettin involved with the NASA people an startin up the srimp bidness an playin football for the New Orleans Saints. He say that all sounds pretty peculiar, but what the hell, to each his own. For him, he says, he is a "thirty-year" man in the army, after which he is gonna retire an open a saloon that won't allow any civilians in, whatsoever, includin presidents of the United States. Finally Sergeant Kranz clapped me on the back an sent me on my way, an when I got back to the farm with a load of garbage for the hogs, Mister McGivver was beside hissef.

"Goddamn, Gump," he shouts. "This is the most brilliant idea I've ever heard of! Why didn't I think of it myself! With all this slop from the army, we can double—hell, quadruple our operation in a matter of months!"

Mister McGivver was so happy he done give me a fifty-cents-an-hour raise an let me have Sundays off. I used the time to go down to the town an sort of ass around. Coalville wadn't much of a place. A few thousan people maybe, an a lot of them was out of work account of the coal seam that caused the town to be there in the first place had done played out. The mine entrance was just a big ole hole in the side of the hill overlookin the town now, an a lot of the guys set around the courthouse square an played checkers. There was a diner there called Etta's, where some of the ole miners gone to drink coffee, an sometimes I'd set there an drink coffee alongside em an hear them tell their stories about when the mine was runnin. Tell the truth, it was kind of depressin, but it was better than hangin around the hog farm all the time.

Meanwhile, it became my job to arrange for the mess hall slop to be brought to our hog farm. First thing we had to do was to separate the pig food from the other shit, like napkins an paper bags an boxes an cans an all. Sergeant Kranz done figgered out a way to do this, however. He made all the KPs in the various barracks divide the garbage into separate cans, marked Edible Trash an Inedible Trash. This worked good enough till visitors' day at the army base came around an some of the mamas an daddies of the soldiers complained to the general about what their sons might be gettin to eat around there. After that, we figgered out a new code for the cans, but it worked just as well. In a few months our operation was workin so good Mister McGivver had to buy us two new trucks just to haul the garbage to our farm, an within a year, we had seven thousan an eighty-one hogs to our name.

One day I done got a letter from Mrs. Curran. She says it is gonna be summertime pretty soon, an she thinks it might be a good idea for little Forrest to spend some time with me. She don't put it exactly in the letter, but I get the impression little Forrest is not doin too good. It is like "boys will be boys," but also she adds that his school grades ain't high as they used to be an "it might be helpful if he could spend some time with his daddy." Well, I wrote her back, sayin to send him on up on the train when school let out, an a few weeks later, he arrived at the station in Coalville.

When I first see him, I can hardly believe it! He has grown about a foot an a half an is a fine-lookin boy, with sandy brown hair an good clear blue eyes like his mama had. But when he sees me, he ain't smilin.

"How's it goin?" I ast.

"What is this place?" he says, lookin around an sniffin like he has arrived at the city dump.

"It is where I live now," I tole him.

"Yeah?" he says.

I get the impression little Forrest has developed an attitude.

"They used to mine coal here," I say, "afore it run out."

"Grandma says you are a farmer—that so?"

"Sort of. You wanna go on up to the farm?"

"Might as well," he says. "I don't see no reason to stay here."

So I took him up to Mister McGivver's farm. Half a mile fore we arrive, little Forrest be holdin his nose an fannin the air. "What is that smell?" he ast.

"It is the hogs," I say. "What we raise on the farm is hogs."

"Shit! You expect me to stay here all summer with a bunch of stinkin hogs!"

"Look," I say, "I know I ain't been that good a daddy to you, but I am tryin to get us both by, an this is the only work I got right now. An I got to tell you, you ain't sposed to be using words like 'shit' around here. You is too young for that."

He didn't say nothin for the rest of the drive, an when we got to Mister McGivver's house, he gone on inside to his room an shut the door. Didn't come out till suppertime, an when he did he mostly just sat at the table an played with his food. After he gone to bed, Mister McGivver lit up his pipe an say, "The boy don't seem to be very happy, does he?"

"I reckon not," I says, "but I think he'll come around in a day or so. After all, he ain't seen me in a pretty long time."

"Well, Gump, I think it might be a good thing for him to pull his weight around here, you know. Might make him grow up a little bit."

"Yeah," I says, "maybe so." I gone on to bed mysef an was feelin pretty low. I closed my eyes an tried to think about Jenny, hopin she'd turn up to help me, but she didn't. This time, I am on my own.

Next mornin I got little Forrest to help me slop the pigs, an the whole time he acted disgusted. All that day an the next, he didn't say nothin to me cept when he had to, an then it wadn't but a word or two. Finally I had a idea.

"You got a dog or anythin at home?" I ast.

"Nope."

"Well, you want a pet?"

"Nope."

"You know, I bet you do, if I showed you one."

"Yeah? What sort of pet?"

"Foller me," I says.

I took him to a little stall in the barn, an there is a big ole Duroc sow, nursin half-a-dozen piglets. They is about eight weeks ole, an I had my eye on one of them in particular for a while. I figger it be the pick-of-the-litter, so to speak. It has good clear eyes an comes when you call it, an it is white with little black spots, an its ears perk up when you talk to it.

"I call this one Wanda," I says, pickin it up an handin it to little Forrest. He don't look too happy takin it, but he does, an Wanda begun rootin an lickin him like a puppy will.

"How come you call her Wanda?" he says finally.

"Oh, I dunno. I sort of named her after a ole friend of mine."

Well, after that, little Forrest seemed happier. Not so much with me, but Wanda become his constant companion. She was ready to be weaned anyhow, an Mister McGivver says it is okay with him, if it makes the boy happy.

One day it is time to truck some hogs up to Wheeling for the auction. Little Forrest helped me load them in the truck, an we set off early in the morning. Took half a day to get there, an then we got to come back for another load.

"How come you always drivin all those hogs up to Wheeling in this old truck?" he ast, which is probly the longest words he has had for me so far.

"Cause we gotta get em there, I guess. Mister McGivver's been doin it for years."

"Well, don't you know there's a railroad runs right through Coalville? Goes up to Wheeling, cause it said so when I rode in here on it. Why don't you just put the hogs on the railroad an let them take em up?"

"I dunno," I says. "Why?"

"Because you'd save time, for cryin out loud!" He looks very exasperated at me.

"What's time to a hog?" I ast.

Little Forrest just shakes his head an looks out the winder. I guess he is now figgered out that he has got a pea brain for a daddy.

"Well," I says, "maybe that is a good idea. I'll talk to Mister McGivver about it in the mornin."

But little Forrest ain't impressed. He just settin there with Wanda in his lap. Lookin kinda scared an alone.

"Fantastic!" shouts Mister McGivver. "Trains to carry the hogs to auction! It'll save us thousands! Why in hell didn't I think of that!"

He is so excited he's about to bust, an he picks up little Forrest an give him a big ole hug. "You're a genius, my boy! Why, we're all gonna be rich!"

Anyhow, Mister McGivver give us both a raise an let us have Sunday *an* Saturday off, an so on weekends I'd take little Forrest down to Coalville to Etta's diner an we'd get to talk to the ole miners an other folks that come around. They bein real nice to little Forrest, an he is all the time astin them questions about stuff. It weren't a bad way to spend the summer, actually, an as the weeks gone by I felt that little Forrest an me is gettin somewhat closer.

Meantime, Mister McGivver is tryin to solve a very messy problem, namely, what we gonna do with all the pig shit that is pilin up as our operation expands? By now, we has got more than ten thousan hogs, an that number is expandin ever day. By the end of the year, Mister McGivver say we ought to have upwards of twenty-five thousan hogs an, at about two pounds of pig shit per hog per day . . . well, you can see where this is leadin to.

Anyways, Mister McGivver is sellin the hog shit for manure at a pretty fast clip, but at this point he is about run out of folks to buy it, an besides, the folks in town are complainin louder an louder about the smell we are creatin.

"We could try to burn it," I says.

"Hell, Gump, they already bitchin about the odor as it is. How you think they'd react to a bonfire of fifty thousand pounds of pig shit ever day?"

Over the next few days we kicked around a few more ideas, but ain't none of them gonna work, an then one night at the supper table when the conversation turned to pig shit again, little Forrest piped up.

"I been thinkin," he says, "suppose we use it to generate power?"

"Do what?" ast Mister McGivver.

"Look here," Little Forrest says, "we got that big ole coal seam runnin right underneath our property. . . ."

"What makes you think that?" says Mister McGivver.

"Cause one of the miners tole me so. He says the coal mine goes for nearly two miles from where the entrance is in town right across this land where the hogs are, and stops just before it gets to the swamp."

"Is that so?"

"It's what he tole me," little Forrest says. "Now, looka here . . ." He pulls out a composition book he has brought an lays it out on the table. When he opens it up, damned if it don't contain some of weirdest drawins I have ever seen, but it look like little Forrest might have saved our asses again.

"My God!" Mister McGivver hollers after he has looked at the drawins. "This is wonderful! First rate! You deserve a Nobel Prize, young man!"

What little Forrest has come up with is this: First we plug up the entrance to the coal mine back in town. Next, we drill holes down to the shaft under our property an bulldoze the pig shit into it ever day. After a while, the pig shit will begin to ferment an give off methane gas. Once that happens, we have a vent for the gas that runs through some kind of machinery an stuff that little Forrest has figgered out, an in the end winds up in a big ole generator that will produce enough power not only to run our farm, but it will run the power for the whole *town* of Coalville!

"Just think of it," Mister McGivver shouts, "a whole *city* run on pig shit! And furthermore, it's so simple an idiot can run it!" I am not so sure about this last statement.

Well, that was just the beginnin. It took the rest of the summer to get the operation goin. Mister McGivver had to talk to the city fathers, but they come up with a government grant to let us start the deal. Pretty soon we got all sorts of engineers an drillers an EPA people an equipment drivers an construction workers millin around on the farm, an people are installin the machinery in a big ole blockhouse they built. Little Forrest is named "honorary chief engineer." He is so proud, he is about to bust!

I gone on about my duties sloppin hogs an cleanin barns an pens an so on, but one day Mister McGivver comes an says for me to get the bulldozer, because it is time to start shovelin the pig shit into the mine shaft. I worked at that bidness for a week or so, an when I am done, they put a big mechanical seal over the holes they has drilled an little

Forrest say now all we got to do is set an wait. That afternoon as the sun begins to go down, I watched him disappear over a little hill that leads down to the swamp, ole Wanda trottin along beside him. She's gettin big now, an so is he, an I ain't never been prouder of anythin in my life.

A week or two later, when it is almost the end of summer, little Forrest come an say it is finally time to start up the pig-shit-power operation. He took Mister McGivver an me into the blockhouse just before dark, where there is a big heap of machinery with a bunch of pipes an dials an gauges, an he begun to explain to us how the thing works.

"First," he says, "the methane gas is released from the mine shaft through this pipe, an a flame ignites it here." He points to what look like a big ole hot water heater. "Then," he says, "the condenser gets the steam compressed an it turns this generator, which makes electricity that moves out through these wires, and that's where the power comes from." He stands back, grinnin from ear to ear.

"This is wonderful!" cries Mister McGivver. "Edison, Fulton, Whitney, Einstein—none of them have done better!"

Little Forrest suddenly begun turnin valves an handles an thowin switches, an pretty soon the needles on the pressure gauges begun to climb an the meters on the wall begun to turn around. All of a sudden, lights flickerd on in the blockhouse an we is all jumpin for joy. Mister McGivver rushes outside an begun to holler—all the lights in the house an barns be on, bright as day, an in the distance we can see lights comin on in Coalville, too.

"Eureeka!" shouts Mister McGivver. "We have turned a sow's ear into a silk purse, an we are now eatin high on the hog!"

Anyhow, next day little Forrest got me back into the blockhouse an begun showin me how the operation ran. He explained all the valves an gauges an meters, an after a while, they didn't seem so hard to understand. I just had to check it all once a day an make sure that one or two of the gauges was not registerin more than they should be, an that this or that valve was turned on or off. I guess Mister McGivver was right, even a idiot like me could run this thing.

"There is somethin else I been thinkin about," little Forrest says at supper that night.

"What is that, my brilliant lad?" says Mister McGivver.

"Well, I been thinking. You said you were having to slow down the breeding a little bit cause there are just so many hogs you can sell in Wheeling and the other places around here."

"That is correct."

"So what I'm thinking is, why not ship the hogs overseas? South America, Europe—even China?"

"Ah, well, my boy," says Mister McGivver, "that is another fine idea. The problem is, it costs so much to ship hogs that it becomes uneconomical. I mean, time you get em to some foreign port, the shipping costs eat up your profit."

"That's what I been thinkin about," he says, an he pulls out the little composition book, an damned if they ain't another whole section of sketches he's drawn.

"Fantastic! Unbelievable! Terrific!" Mister McGivver cries, leaping up. "Why, you should be in the Congress or something!"

Little Forrest has been at it again. He has done sketched a model of a hog transport ship. I did not understand all of it exactly, but the gist of it is this: Inside the ship the hogs is kept in layers from top to bottom. The floorin is nothin but heavy mesh steel, an so when the hogs on the top layer shit, it drops on the second layer an the second on the third an so on, until finally all the hog shit winds up in the bottom of the boat, where there is a machine like we have made here that runs the entire ship.

"So the energy costs are virtually nil!" Mister McGivver roars. "Why, think of the possibilities! Shipping hogs for less than half the normal cost! This is simply amazing! Whole fleets of ships powered by shit! And it doesn't have to stop there, either! Think of it—trains, planes, airplanes! All of it! Even washers and dryers and television sets! Screw atomic energy. This may usher in a whole new era!" He is so excited he is now wavin his hands, an for a minute I worry he is gonna have a fit or somethin.

"I'm gonna turn this over to somebody first thing in the mornin," Mister McGivver says. "But first, I want to make an announcement. Gump, you have been so helpful around here that I want to show my gratitude by cutting you in on one third of our profits. Now, how about that?"

Well, I was kind of surprised, but it sounded pretty good, an I tole him so.

"Thanks," I said.

Finally the time come for little Forrest to go back to school. I was not lookin forward to it, but it had to be. The leafs was just beginnin to turn on the sycamore trees when I carried him to the train station in the truck. Wanda was ridin in the back, account of she was too big now for the cab.

"I want to ask you somethin," little Forrest says.

"What is that?"

"It's about Wanda. I mean, you ain't gonna . . ."

"Oh, no—no, I ain't gonna do anythin like that. I think we'll keep her on here as a brood hog, you know? She'll be fine."

"You promise?"

"Yeah."

"Well, thanks."

"I want you to be good when you get home, hear? An do what your grandma tells you, okay?"

"Yeah."

He just set there lookin out the winder, an I got the feelin there was somethin wrong.

"You ain't unhappy about anythin, is you?"

"Well, I was sort of wondering, why can't I just stay here and help run the hog farm?"

"Cause you too young, an you gotta go back to school. We'll see about that later, you know? But it ain't time right now, okay. Maybe you can come back for Christmas or somethin, huh?"

"Yeah, that'd be good."

We got to the station an little Forrest gone around to the back of the pickup truck an got Wanda down. We set on the depot platform, an he was huggin her around the neck an kind of talkin to her, an I felt real sorry for him. But I knowed I was doin the right thing. Anyhow, the train come along an he hugged Wanda one last time an got on board. Him an me, we just shook hands, an I watched him through the winder as the train pulled out. He give me an Wanda a little wave, an then we gone on back to the farm.

Well, let me say this: The days that follered was crazy, an Mister McGivver, he was busy as a one-legged man at an ass-kickin contest! First, he done expanded the hog breedin operation tenfold. He is even *buyin* hogs from all over, an so in the months that come, we has got upward of fifty or sixty thousan hogs—they is so many of them, we lost count. But it don't matter, cause the more hogs we got, the more methane gas we produce, an by now we is not only lightin up Coalville, but two other little towns down the road. People from the federal government up at Washington says they is gonna use us as a model example an even want to give us an award ceremony.

Next, Mister McGivver has gone to work on the project of buildin the pig-shit fleet, an almost within no time, he has got three huge ships under construction over on the Atlantic Ocean at Norfolk, Virginia. This is where he spends so much of his time now, he has left most of the hog farmin bidness to me. Also, we has had to employ about a hundrit workers from the town, which was a great relief to them, as most was out-of-work miners.

Furthermore, Mister McGivver has expanded the hog-slop garbage collection to ever military base within three hundrit miles, an we is got fleets of trucks pickin up the garbage, an what we don't use ourselfs, we sell to other farmers.

"We are becoming a great national enterprise," Mister McGivver says, "but we are leveraged up to the hilt."

I ast him what that meant, an he says, "Debt, Gump, debt! We have had to borrow millions to build those ships and buy more land for the hog farm and trucks for the garbage operation. Sometimes at night I worry about goin broke, but we are in too deep now to quit. We are gonna have to expand the methane gas operation to meet expenses, and I'm afraid we're gonna have to raise our prices."

I ast him what I could do to help.

"Just keep shoveling shit fast as you can," he says.

So that's what I did.

By the end of that fall, I figgered that we has got somewhere between eight hundrit thousan an one million pounds of pig shit down in the mine, an the operation is runnin full steam night an day. We had to double the size of the plant just to keep it goin.

Little Forrest is due to arrive for Christmas, but about two weeks before that they has scheduled the ceremony to honor us for our contributions to society. The whole town of Coalville is decked out in Christmas decorations an little colored lights an stuff—all run by our plant. Mister McGivver cannot come home for the celebration on account of he is too busy tryin to get the ship fleet built, but he tells me to accept the award in his absence.

The day of the ceremony, I put on my suit an tie an drove into town. There is people there from all over—not only Coalville, but the little towns nearby an also a bunch of buses with folks representin civic an environmental organizations. From Wheeling, the governor an the attorney general has come down, an from Washington, they has come a United States senator of West Virginia. Sergeant Kranz has also come over from the army post, an the mayor of Coalville is already makin a speech when I arrive.

"Never in our wildest dreams," he says, "did we ever believe that our deliverance was at hand—saved, as it were, by a herd of swine, an the ingenuity of Mr. McGivver and Mr. Gump!"

The ceremony was takin place in the town square below the little hill where the mine entrance was, an the platform was decked out with red, white, an blue buntin an little American flags. When they seen me comin, the high school band interrupted the mayor's speech an begun playin "God Bless America," an the five or six thousan people in the crowd begun to holler an clap an cheer as I walked up the platform steps.

Everbody there shook my hand—the mayor, governor, attorney general, an the senator, as well as they wives—

even Sergeant Kranz, who was wearin his dress uniform. The mayor concludes his talk by sayin what a fine feller I am, an thankin me for "revitalizin the town of Coalville by creatin this marvelous invention." He then says everbody should stand for the playin of "The Star-Spangled Banner."

Just before the band begun to play, there was a slight sort of tremor in the ground, but nobody much seemed to notice it but me. Durin the first verse, the rumblin in the ground begun again, an this time some folks started lookin around kinda nervous like. When they got to the high part of the song, there was a third rumble, a lot louder than the first, an it caused the ground to shake, an a pane fell out of a winder of a store across the street. It was about now it dawned on me that somethin bad was fixin to happen.

I had been so nervous that mornin when I was tryin to get into my suit an my tie an all that I had forgot to release the main pressure gauge at the power plant. Little Forrest had always tole me this was the most important thing to do ever day, account of somethin serious might go wrong. By now, most folks are still singin, but some is sort of mumblin to each other an turnin they heads to see what is happenin. Sergeant Kranz lean over to me an ast, "Gump, what in hell is goin on?"

I was fixin to tell him, when he found out for hissef.

I looked up at the hill where the plugged-up mine entrance was, an suddenly they was this humongous explosion! A big flash of light an flames, an then *KA–BLOOIE!* the whole thing done blowed up!

Next instant, everthin got completely dark, an I thought we had all been kilt! But soon I heard a kind of low moanin around me, an when I wiped my eyes an looked around, it was a sight to see. Everbody on the speakin platform was still standin there, kinda in shock or somethin, an they was all covered in pig shit, head to toe.

"Oh, my God!" shouts the governor's wife. "Oh, my God!"

I looked around some more, an damned if the whole town ain't covered in pig shit, includin, of course, the five or six thousan people in the crowd out in front. The buildins, cars, buses, ground, streets, trees—everthin, about three or four inches deep! The guy playin the tuba in the band was the strangest sight of all. He was so surprised, I guess, that when the explosion happened, he was blowin a long note an didn't quit—just kept on tryin to blow his note with the tuba full of pig shit, an it looked sort of like a soufflé about to get done.

I turned around again, an there was Sergeant Kranz, starin me right in the face, eyes all bugged out, teeth bared—somehow he'd even managed to keep his army hat on.

"Gump!" he hollers. "You fuckin idiot! What is the meaning of this?"

Before I could answer, he reach out to grap me by the throat, an I figgered what is comin next, so I leaped over the railin an run away as fast as I can. Sergeant Kranz an everbody else, them what was able, anyway, begun to chase me, too. It seemed like a familiar situation.

I was tryin to get home to the farm, but I realized they ain't no place to hide there, probly—at least not from a mob that has just been hit with a million pounds of Poland China pig shit, an blamin it on me. But I runned just as fast as I could, which is considerable, an by the time I got to the house, I has outdistanced them somewhat. I was gonna try an pack my bag, but suddenly, here they come up the road, hollerin an yellin, an so I run out the back door an go into the barn an get Wanda, who look at me kinda funny but follows me anyhow. I runned past the pens an across the pasture, an damn if all the hogs don't start chasin us, too—even the ones in the pens, what broke through an joined the mob.

Only thing I can think of is maybe to get into the swamp, so that's what I did. I hid there till sundown, while there was a lot of cussin an shoutin all around me. Wanda, she had enough sense to keep quiet, but when night come, it is cold an wet an there is flashlights shinin through the swamp, an ever so often I can pick out a person carryin a pitchfork or hoe, just like in the Frankenstein movie. They even got helicopters overhead, shinin their lights, an loud-speakers demandin that I come out an surrender.

To hell with that! I say, an then along comes my salvation. I hear a train in the distance on the far side of the swamp an figger this is my only chance to make a break for it! Wanda an me, we slogged out onto higher ground an by some miracle managed to jump on board a boxcar. Inside, there is a little dim candle burnin, an I make out a feller settin there in a heap of straw.

"Who in hell is you?" he ast.

"Gump's my name," I says.

"Yeah, who's that with you?"

"Her name's Wanda."

"You got a girl with you?"

"Sort of," I says.

"What you mean, sort of—you got some kind of transvestite there?"

"Nope. She's a polled Duroc hog, might win some prizes one day."

"Hog?" he says. "Greatgodamighty! I ain't had nothin to eat in a week."

I can see this might be a long trip.

Chapter Five

After a little bit on the train, the feller's candle burnt out, an after he coughs for a while, it seem like he has dozed off. An so we rode on in the dark with the wheels clackin an the boxcar swayin an rockin, an finally Wanda done put her head in my lap an gone to sleep. Me, though, I stayed up for a while, wonderin how in hell I am always gettin myself into these kinds of fixes. Everthin I touch, it seems, turns directly to shit. Literally.

Next mornin there is a faint little light comin in through the doors of the boxcar, an the feller in the corner begins to stir an starts coughin again.

"Hey," he says, "why don't you open the doors a little an get us some fresh air?"

I gone over an opened the door about a foot or so. We is passin by houses an some dingy ole buildins, an everthin is gray an cold, cept for a few little Christmas decorations on people's doors.

"Where we headed?" I ast.

"Near as I can figger, Washington, D.C.," the feller say.

"Hell, I been there," I says.

"That a fact."

"Yup, long time ago. I went to see the President."

"What of?"

"The United States."

"What, was there a parade or somethin?"

"Nah, it wadn't no parade. I went to his house."

"Yeah, I bet that pig of yours flew over it, too."

"Huh? Wanda don't fly."

"I know," he says.

I turned aroun to look at him, an there is somethin terribly familiar about the feller's eyes, though his face is covered with a black beard an he is wearin a ole hobo-lookin hat.

"Say," I ast, "what's your name, anyhow?"

"What's it to ya?"

"Well, you look sort of like somebody I knowed once, that's all."

"Yeah? Who?"

"A feller from the army. Way back in Vietnam."

"What'd you say your name was again?"

"Gump."

"Yeah? I knew a Gump one time. What's your first name?"

"Forrest."

"Oh, shit!" the feller says, an he thows his arms up over his face. "I might of known it!"

"Well, who in hell *are* you?" I ast.

"Goodgodamighty, Forrest, don't you recognize me?"

I crawled across the straw an got up real close to his face.

"Why, you're . . ."

"No, I reckon you don't. I wouldn't expect you to—I've kinda gone down recently," he says in between coughs.

"Lieutenant Dan!" I shouted, an grapped him by the

shoulders. But when I looked into his eyes, they is a awful sort of milky white, like he can't see or somethin.

"Lieutenant Dan—what has happened to you?" I says. "Your eyes . . ."

"I'm mostly about half blind now, Forrest."

"But how?"

"Well, it's a lot of things," he says. An when I get a better look, it is really terrible. He is thin as a rail an dressed in rags. The little stumps where his legs was are pitiful lookin, an his teeth are bad.

"I suppose it's all that stuff from Vietnam catchin up with me," he says. "You know, it wasn't just my legs that was shot—it was all up in my chest an stomach, too. I reckon after a while it caught up with me. Say—what's that smell? Is that you? You smell like shit!"

"Yeah, I know," I says. "An it is a long story."

Well, Lieutenant Dan begun to cough again so hard I laid him down an gone over to my side of the boxcar, thinkin it might be my smell that was makin him do it. I just couldn't believe it! He looked like a ghost, an I am wonderin how he wound up in such sorry shape, especially after all the money he got from our srimpin bidness, but I figger there is time to ast about that later. In a little bit, he stop coughin an dozed off again, an I am settin there with Wanda, wonderin what is gonna happen to us all.

About a hour to two later, the train slowed down. Lieutenant Dan starts coughin again, so I reckon he is awake.

"All right, now, Forrest," he says, "we gotta get off of here before the train comes to a full stop, else they will call the police on us and put us in jail."

I looked out the crack in the doors, an we is comin into a big ole railroad yard with a bunch of rusty freight cars an junk an ole cabooses, an a lot of trash an garbage blowin in the cold wind.

"This is the Union Station," Dan says. "They have remodeled it just for us."

Just then, the train come to a stop an then begun to back up slowly.

"Okay, Forrest, now's our chance," Dan says. "Open that door and let's get out of here."

I thowed open the doors an jumped out. Ole Wanda is standin there with her snout pokin out of the boxcar, an I runned up beside her an grapped her by the ear an pulled her down. She let out a big "oink" when she hit the ground. Next, I runned up to where Dan was settin, right behin her in the boxcar door, an grapped him by the shoulders an set him down easy as I could. He was carryin his artificial legs with him, but they was pretty scuffed up an dirty.

"Let's crawl under that freight over there before the engine comes by an they see us," Dan says. So that's what we did. Finally we has arrived in our nation's capitol.

It is freezin cold an the wind is whippin up around us, an there are little snowflakes in the air.

"Forrest, I hate to tell you this, but I think you gotta get cleaned up before we go out an take in the sights," Dan says. "I saw a pretty big mud puddle back there, if you know what I mean."

So, while Dan strapped on his artificial legs, I gone over to the mud puddle an took off my clothes an got in an tried to rinse off as much pig shit as I could. Wadn't easy, cause it had mostly dried by now, specially in my hair, but somehow I did it, an after that, I washed my clothes an put em back on. It was not the most pleasant experience of my career. When I was finished Wanda took a turn hersef, figgerin, I spose, she was not gonna be outdone.

"Let's walk on up to the station," Dan says. "Least it's warm in there and you can dry out."

"What about Wanda?" I ast.

"I been thinkin about that," he says. "Here's what we do."

While I am takin my bath, Dan has found a ole piece of rope, an when Wanda got through with hers, he ties it around her neck for a leash. He has also picked up a long stick, an when he takes Wanda's leash in his hand an walks behin her with the stick, tappin it on the ground, damn if he don't look like a blind man on the street! Well, sort of, anyhow.

"We'll see how this works," he says. "You let me do the talking."

So we gone on into the Union Station, which is filled with all sorts of fancy-lookin people, most of who is lookin right at us.

I looked down on a empty bench an there is a copy of *The Washington Post*, all messed up, but somebody done turned to a page inside that says: IDIOT CAUSES NOXIOUS BLAST IN WEST VIRGINIA. I just couldn't help but read it:

The Washington Post

Longtime Senator Robert Byrd of West Virginia said he has "seen some shit in his lifetime," but nothing to compare with the humiliating experience he underwent in the small mining village of Coalville yesterday.

Byrd, a staunch supporter of businesses small and large in his native state, was standing on a speakers' platform with a dozen other luminaries, including representatives of the U.S. Army and the federal EPA, when a terrible methane gas explosion tore through the town, covering everything and everyone in sight with an unsightly patina of swine manure.

The explosion apparently was set off when a certified idiot, later identified as Forrest Gump, of no fixed address, failed to properly attend a cutoff valve in a plant that received federal funds to convert pig manure into energy.

Police Chief Harley Smathers described the scene this way: "Well, I cain't hardly describe it at all. I mean, they was all them important people standin there up on the stage. And after it happened, ain't none of them said nothin for a moment or two, I reckon they was just too startled or something. Then the ladies, they begun to holler and cuss, and the men, they begun to sort of flinch around an mutter—look like the Swamp Thing character on TV. After a while, they must of figgered who the culprit was—this Gump feller, I guess—an organized a posse of sorts to run him down.

"We chased after him for a while till he took into Mud Bottom Swamp. Apparently he had a accomplice with him, big ole fat feller disguised as a pig or somethin. We lost him there after dark. Legend around here is, don't go into Mud Bottom Swamp at night. No matter who's in there."

"You got any money?" Dan ast.

"Bout ten or fifteen dollars," I says. "How bout you?"

"Twenty-eight cents."

"Well, maybe we can get some breakfast," I says.

"Hell," Dan says. "I sure wish we had enough to go to the oyster bar. Man, what I wouldn't give for a dozen oysters on the half shell right now. Served up over crushed ice, with one of them little crystal bowls for sauce on the side—lemons and Tabasco and some Worcestershire an horseradish."

"Well," I says, "I reckon we could do that." Matter of fact, I know I ain't got much cash on me, but what the hell. I remember ole Lieutenant Dan in Vietnam, always talkin about how much he liked raw oysters. I figger, bad off as he is now, why not?

Ole Dan, he is so excited he is about to bust, an his legs begun to clatter as we go down the hallways.

"Assateague or Chincoteague oysters," he says, "don't matter which. Even good ole Chesapeake Bay oysters'll do! Hell, mysef, I prefer the Pacific Coast variety—Puget Sound salties, or some of the Oregon State breeds. Or, then, down from the Gulf Coast, where you come from—Bon Secour or Heron Bay oysters, or over at Apalachicola, Florida, they used to have some delicious mollusks!"

Dan was kinda gettin beside hissef, an I think his mouth was waterin as we walked across a great big marble-floored hall toward where the signs say Restaurant an Oyster Bar. But just afore we go inside it, a policeman come up an order us to halt.

"What you clowns think you're doin?" he ast.

"Gettin our breakfast," says Dan.

"That so?" says the policeman. "An what's that hog doin here?"

"That is a licensed seein-eye hog," Dan says. "Can't you see I'm blind?"

The cop be lookin at Dan pretty hard in the face, an finally he say, "Well, you look kinda blind, but we can't let no hog inside the Union Station. It's against the rules."

"I tole you, this is a seein-eye hog. It's perfectly legal," Dan says.

"Yeah, well, I heard of seein-eye dogs. But ain't no such thing as a seein-eye *hog*," say the cop.

"Yeah," say Dan. "Well, I am livin proof that there

is—ain't that right, Wanda?" He reach down an patted Wanda on the head, an she give out a single loud grunt.

"So you say," the policeman answers, "but I ain't never heard of any such thing. Besides, I think you better show me your driver's licenses. You fellers look kinda suspicious."

"Driver's licenses!" Dan shouts. "What kind of people would give a driver's license to a blind man?"

The cop, he thinks a minute, an pointin his thumb at me, says, "Yeah, maybe you're right—but what about him?"

"*Him!*" Dan shouts. "Why he's a certified idiot. You want *him* drivin around in your city?"

"Yeah, well, how come he's all wet?"

"On account of he fell down in a big mud puddle outside the station here. What kind of people are you, allowin such mud puddles? Why, I think you oughta be sued or somethin."

The cop be scratchin his head now, an I guess tryin to figger out how to deal with this situation without makin hissef look like a fool.

"Well, all this may be so," he says, "but if he's a idiot, what's he doin here? Looks like maybe we oughta lock him up or somethin."

"It's his *hog*," Dan answers. "He is the best seein-eye hog trainer in the world. He might not be smart, but it's one thing he *can* do. Hogs are smarter than dogs—most of em even smarter than people. But they need a good trainer."

At this, Wanda give out another big grunt an then peed right on the nice marble floor.

"All right—that's it!" the cop holler. "I don't care what you say! You bozos are outta here!"

He grapped Dan an me by the collars an start draggin us to the doors. In the confusion, Dan done dropped

Wanda's leash, an by the time the cop turn aroun to see where she was, he suddenly got a real funny look on his face. Wanda is back about twenty yards behin, lookin at the cop with them squinty little yeller eyes of hers, an she is pawin the marble an gruntin an snortin to beat the band. Then, without no further warnin, she done charged across the floor straight at us, but Dan an me, we knew who she's aimin at, an so does the cop.

"Oh, my Lord! Oh, my Lord!" he shouts an takes off runnin fast as he can. I let Wanda chase after him for a moment or two an then called her back. Last we see of that cop, he is headed for the Washington Monument. Dan picks up the end of Wanda's leash again, an we walked on out the door of the Union Station an onto the street, with Dan tappin the ground with his stick.

"Sometimes a man gotta stand up for his rights," he says.

I ast Dan what we gonna do next, an he say we need to go on down to Lafayette Park, across from the White House, account of it is the prettiest piece of public property in the town, an is also the main place in the city where they let folks like us camp out an do our thing.

"All we gotta do is get us a sign," Dan says. "Then we become legitimate protesters, an ain't nothin nobody can do to us. We can live there long as we want."

"What kinda sign?"

"Don't matter, long as it is against whatever the President stands for."

"What is that?" I ast.

"We'll think of something."

So that's what we did. I found a big ole piece of

cardboard, an we spent twenty-five cents on a red crayon, an Dan tole me what to write on the sign.

"Vietnam Veterans Against the War," he say.

"But the war's over."

"Not for us it ain't."

"Yeah, but it's been ten years . . ."

"Screw it, Forrest, we'll tell em we been here all that time."

Anyhow, we gone on down to Lafayette Park across from the White House. They was all sorts of protesters there, an bums an beggars, too. They all gots signs, an some are hollerin across the street an a lot have got little tents or cardboard boxes to live in. They is a fountain in the middle, where they get their water from, an two or three times a day everbody get together an pool their money an send out for some cheap sambwiches an soup.

Dan an me, we set up our operation on a corner of the park, an somebody tole us where a appliance store was so that we can get a couple of refrigerator cartons that afternoon, which will be our homes. One of the fellers say it is a lot better now that wintertime has come, account of when it is halfway warm, the Park Service turns on the sprinkler system deliberately in the middle of the night, to drive us away. Lafayette Park is kinda different than the last time I was here—or at least the President's house was. Now they has got a big iron fence around it an concrete posts ever few feet, an a bunch of armed guards pacin back an forth. It is like the President don't want nobody to come see him.

Anyhow, Dan an me commenced to beggin from the passersby, but ain't too many people interested. End of the day, we has made about three bucks. I am beginnin to get worried about Dan, account of all his coughin an how thin he is an all, an I remembered how back when we come home from Vietnam he had gone on up to the Walter Reed Hospital an they fixed him up.

"I don't want no more of that place, Forrest. They done fixed me up once, an look where it got me."

"But, Dan," I says, "ain't no reason for you to be sufferin. You still a young man."

"Young, hell! I'm a walkin corpse—Can't you see that, you idiot?"

I tried, but there wadn't no talkin him out of it—He just wadn't goin to the Walter Reed Hospital. That night we was in our boxes, an things was pretty dark an quiet in the Lafayette Park. We was gonna get a crate for Wanda, too, but I decided she could sleep with Dan, account of she might help keep him warm.

"Forrest," Dan says after a while, "I know you think I must of stolen the money from the srimp bidness, don't you?"

"I dunno, Dan. I mean, that's what some other people say."

"Well, I didn't. Wadn't none there to steal when I left."

"What about drivin off in the big car with the girl?" I ast. I just had to ast it.

"That wasn't nothin. That was the last money I had in the bank. I just figured what the hell, ya know. If I'm gonna be broke, I might as well go out in style."

"Then what happened, Dan? I mean, we had a lot of money in that bidness. Where'd it go?"

"Tribble," he says.

"Mister Tribble!"

"Yeah, that sombitch run off with it. I mean, he must have, cause he was the only one who could have. He had all the accounts an all, an after your mama died, he was runnin the whole show. One day he says to everybody that there ain't enough money to meet the payroll this week, but to stick around an there will be, an the next week, that sombitch is gone!"

"I can't believe it. Why, Mister Tribble was honest as the day is long!"

"Yeah—a chessman. I reckon you might believe so. But I think he's a crook. You know, Forrest, you got some good sides to you, but your main problem is, you trust everybody. You don't think there are people out there who are gonna screw you any chance they get. They take one look at you, an they say 'sucker.' An your big dumb ass don't know the difference. You treat everybody like they are your friend. It ain't that way in the world, Forrest. A lot of people ain't your friend. They are just lookin at you the way a banker looks at somebody comes in for a loan—How I'm gonna fleece this rube? That's the way it is, Forrest. That's the way it is."

Then Dan, he commenced to start coughin again, an finally he gone on to sleep. I got my head out of the icebox crate, an the sky have cleared an it is cold an still, an the stars are all shinin, an I am just about asleep when they is like a warm mist come above me an all of a sudden, there is Jenny, sort of smilin an lookin at me!

"Well, you sure did it this time, didn't you?"

"Yup, I reckon I did."

"You had it right in your hand, didn't you? And then you get so excited about the ceremony that you forget to release the pressure valve—and look what happens."

"I know."

"And what about little Forrest? How's he gonna take this?"

"I dunno."

"Well, I can imagine," Jenny says, "that he's gonna be real disappointed. After all, all that stuff was his idea in the first place."

"Yup."

"So don't you think you ought to tell him? After all, he

was gonna come up there and spend Christmas with you, right?"

"It's what I was gonna do tomorrow. It ain't like I have had much time."

"Yeah, well, I think you better get it done."

I could tell she was sort of mad, an I wadn't feelin too good about things mysef.

"I guess I done made a fool of mysef again, huh?"

"Well, let me say this, you was a sight, runnin across those fields covered in pig shit, bein chased by that mob an all them hogs, too."

"Yup, I spose I was, but you know, I kinda figgered you might of been able to help me out there a little—You know what I mean?"

"Forrest," she says, "it wadn't my turn to watch after you."

An then the mist sort of dissolved an I was lookin at the sky again, an a big ole silver cloud sailed across the stars, an the last thing I remember was Wanda done give out a big ole grunt from Dan's icebox carton.

Next mornin, I got up early an found a pay phone an called Mrs. Curran's number. Little Forrest had already gone off to school, but I tole her what had happened. She seemed kinda confused by it all, an so I said I would call again that night.

When I get back to Lafayette Park, I seen Lieutenant Dan in some kinda argument with a man in a marine's uniform. I couldn't hear what they was sayin, but I figgered it was a argument because Dan was givin the man the finger an the man was givin the finger back. When I get up to our boxes, Dan sees me an says to the feller, "and if you don't like it, my friend Forrest, here, will whip you ass!"

The marine turn around an look at me, up an down, an all of a sudden he gets a sort of shit-eatin smile on his face, an I can see he has got picket teeth in front an he is a officer an is carryin a briefcase.

"I am Colonel Oliver North," he says to me, "and who are you, gonna whip my ass?"

"My name is Forrest Gump, an I don't know nothin about this ass-whippin bidness, but if Lieutenant Dan say to do it, that's good enough for me."

Colonel North sort of size me up, an then gets a look on his face kinda like a lightbulb went off inside his head. He is all spit-an-polish from shoes to hat, an on his uniform he is wearin about a dozen rows of ribbons.

"Gump? Say, you ain't the Gump won a Congressional Medal of Honor over at Vietnam?"

"That's him," says Dan. An Wanda, who is still inside her box, give out a big ole grunt.

"What the hell was that?" Colonel North asts.

"That's Wanda," I say.

"You fellers got a girl in that carton?" says the colonel.

"Wanda's a pig," I say.

"Yeah, I don't doubt it, hangin out with a couple of slackers like you. How come you against the war?"

"Cause it's easier to be against somethin that don't exist, you dummy," Dan answers.

Colonel North scratches his chin for a second, then nods. "Yeah, I can see your point about that, I guess. Say, listen, Gump, what's a guy like you who has won the Congressional Medal of Honor doin here actin like a hobo, anyway?"

I started to tell him about the pig farm an all, but I figgered it might sound strange, so I just said, "I got in a bidness venture that went sour."

"Why, you oughta have stayed in the army," the

colonel says. "I mean, here you are a big war hero. You gotta have *some* sense."

An then the colonel, he gets this *real* odd look in his eyes, an squints off in the distance for a minute, toward the White House, an when he turns back, he says, "Look here, Gump, I might be able to use a guy like you. There is something I'm involved with in which your talents could be very useful. You got time to come over across the street an hear me out?"

I looked at Dan, but he just nodded, an so the colonel an me, that's what we did.

Chapter Six

First thing Colonel North says to me when we out of earshot of Dan is "Your clothes are awful; we gotta get you cleaned up." An so he took me over to some army fort an tole them to fit me with a brand-new private's uniform, an then he took me to where I could get a bath an to a barbershop for a haircut an a shave. When we was through, I was spic-an-span an feelin like I was back in the army or somethin—which was weird.

"Well, Gump, that is an improvement if I do say so," the colonel says. "Now, look here, I want your ass spit-an-polish from now on in. If it's necessary, I want you to even spit-shine your asshole—you got that?"

"Right, Colonel," I say.

"And now," he says, "I am gonna confer on you the title of 'special assistant for covert operations.' But you ain't to tell anybody anything about any of this—no matter what. Right?"

"Right, Colonel," I says.

"Listen, Gump," says Colonel North when we get inside the White House, "we are going to see the President of the United States, so I want you to be on your best behavior—you got that straight?"

"I already seen him," I says.

"When? On TV or something?"

"Right here—about eight or ten years ago."

"Yeah, well, they got a new president now. You ain't met this one yet—An he don't hear too good, either, so you got to speak up if he says something to you. An for that matter," Colonel North adds, "he don't *listen* too well, either."

We gone on into the little round room where the President was, an sure enough, it was not neither of the ole presidents I had met, but a new one this time. He was a older, kindly gentleman with little rosy cheeks an look like he might of been a cowboy at some point, or maybe a movie actor.

"Well, Mr. Gump, I am proud to make your acquaintance," the President says. "Colonel North, here, tells me you won the Congressional Medal of Honor."

"Yessir," I says.

"And what did you do to get it?"

"I runned."

"Beg your pardon?" says the President.

"He said he ran, sir," Colonel North interrupted, "but he didn't tell you he ran carryin five or six of his wounded buddies out of the line of fire."

"Well, Colonel, there you go again," say the President, "putting words in people's mouths."

"Sorry, sir," says the colonel. "I was just trying to clarify matters. Put them in a proper perspective."

"You leave that to me," the President say. "That is my

job, not yours—By the way, Colonel North, have we met
before?"

Anyway, we finally got on down to bidness. In a corner
of the room is a TV set, an the President, he has been
watchin *Concentration*.

"Why don't you turn that shit off, Colonel," the
President says. "It confuses me."

"Right, sir," says the colonel. "Personally, I prefer *The
Price Is Right*, myself."

"Last time I was here," I says, tryin to get in the
conversation, "the President, he sometimes watched *To Tell
the Truth*. But that was a long time ago."

"I ain't too fond of that one," Colonel North says.

"Listen," says the President, "we ain't got time to screw
around talkin about TV shows. Just what you got on your
mind, Ollie?"

"That sombitch the Ayatolja of Iran," he says. "We is
fixin to make a fool of him an get back our hostages, too,
and while we are at it, we gonna do in them communist
jackoffs in Central America, as well. It is the scheme of a
lifetime, Mr. President!"

"Yeah? How you gonna do all that, Ollie?"

"Well," say the colonel, "all it takes is a little tact and
diplomacy—Now, here is my plan . . ."

For the next few hours the colonel he explainin his
scheme to the President. Once or twice the President dozed
off, an the colonel had to stop an wake him up by ticklin his
nose with a feather he kept in his uniform pocket for that
purpose. I did not foller much of Colonel North's stuff,
account of everthin seemed to depend on everthin else an
they was a bunch of names thowed out that was just about
unpronounceable. When he was finished, I didn't under-

stand any more about what we is sposed to do than when he started, but I figgered the President did.

"Yeah, Ollie, that all sounds pretty good to me, whatever it was, but let me ask you this: What is the Ayatolja of Iran got to do with it?" the President says.

"Huh?" say the colonel. "Why, the Ayatolja *is* the plan! Don't you see—arms for hostages! An then we use the money they pay us to finance the gorillas fighting in Nicaragua! It couldn't be neater, Mr. President!"

Me, I was wonderin why the gorillas in Nicaragua was fightin, an it reminded me of ole Sue.

Poor ole Sue.

"Well," says the President, "it all sounds kinda fishy to me—but if you say so, Ollie—But just remember—no arms for hostages, *per se*—you know what I mean?"

"It will make you a great national hero, sir," the colonel says.

"One other thing I don't understand," says the President, "is what is Mr. Gump's role in all this?"

"Well, Mr. President," the colonel answers, "I believe that the two greatest enemies of all Americans are ignorance and apathy, and Private Gump is living proof that these can be overcome. He will be a great asset to us."

The President looked kinda puzzled an turned to me. "What'd he say? Somethin about ignorance and apathy, wadn't it?"

"I don't know, an I don't give a shit," I says.

At this, the President scratch his head an get up an turns on the TV set again.

"Whatever you want to do, Ollie," he says, "but now I got to watch *Let's Make a Deal*."

"Yes, that's a fine show, Mr. President."

"The one I really liked was *Queen For a Day*, but it don't come on no more," the President says, lookin kinda sad.

"You just leave it to me and Private Gump, here, Mr. President. I assure you, we will reflect great credit on you and this office."

But the President, he seem like he ain't really listenin. He is watchin *Let's Make a Deal.*

Anyhow, after all that I gone on back to Lafayette Park with Colonel North an am wonderin what to do about Lieutenant Dan an Wanda, account of I can't leave em there alone. The colonel, he has figgered out a plan for Dan, say he is gonna have him committed to Walter Reed Hospital for "observation," an ain't no time goes by but what a big ambulance pulls up an hauls Lieutenant Dan off.

Wanda, Colonel North says, is gonna have a temporary home at the "National Zoo."

"She will be 'exhibit B,'" he says, "in case we get arrested."

"Arrested for what?" I ast.

"Well, Gump, you never know," the colonel says.

Meantime, I tole the colonel I gotta go see little Forrest afore we go flyin off all over the world, an he says I can use "Air Force One" to do it, account of the President, he says, "that sombitch ain't goin nowhere today anyhow."

Comin into Mobile on Air Force One is not like arrivin on a regular plane. They have got a brass band to welcome me an a limousine to drive me around, an when I get to Mrs. Curran's house, they is a lot of people hangin around in the yard. Mrs. Curran come out to greet me, but I can see little Forrest standin behind the screen door, kinda like he don't want to see me. When I gone inside, I found out this was true.

"I told you, you had to check the pressure valve at least twice a day, din't I?" was the first thing he said.

"Yup," I says. "An you shore was right."

"Yeah, I know, cause you ruined everything. We could of been millionaires. And now we're broke, I suppose."

"That's about the size of it, son."

"Don't call me son. Never. I ain't your son."

"I just meant it like . . ."

"I don't care what you meant. It was the easiest thing in the world to just check that valve. And now look what's happened."

"Little Forrest, I am sorry about it, but I can't do nothin to fix it now. What's over is over, an I gotta get on with other stuff."

"Like what—goin into the army or something? How come you wearing that uniform?"

"Well, I reckon I sort of am. I mean, I was in the army once afore, you know."

"So you told me."

"An I gotta do one more thing for Colonel North. Cause he ast me to, an, well, I just gotta do it."

"Yeah, I spose you do—cause you screwed up everything else."

He turned around an I seen him ball up his fist an put it up like he was wipin his eye. It was a very painful thing to see, feelin to mysef like he was ashamed of me. I reckon he had a right to be, though, on account of·I have messed up good this time.

"What about Wanda?" he ast. "I spose you have sold her to the butchers."

"That ain't so. She is at the National Zoo in Washington, D.C."

"So she's just gonna be there for everybody to make fun of, huh?"

"Nah, it ain't like that. The colonel is gonna get her special treatment."

"Huh," he says. "I bet."

Anyhow, that was the way it went. To say the least, little Forrest was not pleased to see me, an I was feelin pretty low when I left. The one thing that give me a little encouragement was just before I walked out the door.

"By the way, what was it like when the shit pit blew out?" he ast.

"Well," I says, "it was a sight."

"Yeah," he says. "I bet." An I thought I might have seen a little smile on his face just then, but I ain't sure.

An so we gone on over to Iran.

It was a big city with a lot of bulblike things on top of the buildins, look like upside-down turnips, an them fellers was all dressed in black robes an wearin hats look like a overturn basket on they heads an tryin to look fierce an everthin.

Fiercest lookin of them all was the Ayatolja.

He be glarin an scowlin, an is not exactly the most pleasant-lookin feller I would want to meet.

Colonel North whispers to me, "Just remember, Gump, 'tact and diplomacy.' It's all that matters!" Then he done stick out his hand an try to shake it with the Ayatolja, but the Ayatolja, he just set with his arms crossed an scowl at the colonel an don't say nothin.

Colonel North look at me an say, "This sombitch is weird, man. I mean, everbody I ever met was willin to shake hands—you know what I'm sayin?"

Standin behin the Ayatolja was two guys in baggy-lookin diapers, have big swords in they belts, an one of em say, "Don't you never call the Ayatolja a 'sombitch.' He might figger out what it means an then we gotta chop off your heads."

In this, I figger he is correct.

Anyhow, I am tryin to break the ice, so to speak, so I ast the Ayatolja how come he is always so fierce an mad-lookin an scowlin all the time?

"It is because," he say, "that for thirty years I have been tryin to become president of the World Council of Churches, an them heathen assholes won't even let me in! Who is more religious than the Ayatolja, anyhow?"

"Why you let that worry you?" I ast, an he says back, "On account of I am a dignified feller, an don't take no shit off nobody, an who is these turds that will not let me in the World Council of Churches? I am the Ayatolja of Iran, after all. I am a big cheese, you dummy."

"Now, wait a minute," say Colonel North. "My man Forrest, here, might not be the brightest feller around, but you oughtn't be callin him names."

"The Ayatolja does whatever he wants—You don't like it, kiss my ass."

"Yeah, well, I am a marine colonel and I don't kiss asses."

At this, the Ayatolja commenced slappin his thighs an bust out laughin.

"Very good, Colonel, very good. I think we can do some bidness here."

Anyhow, Colonel North done start explainin his deal to the Ayatolja.

"Look here," he says, "some of your fellers over in Lebanon done took a bunch of our people for hostages, and it is causin considerable embarrassment to the President of our United States."

"Oh, yeah," the Ayatolja says. "So why don't you just go over there and get em out?"

"It ain't that easy," the colonel says.

The Ayatolja begun to chuckle. "Really. Tell me about it. I know somethin about hostage takin mysef, you know. Look what happened when that other numbnuts president of yours came over here an tried to screw with our hostage-takin enterprise. What was his name . . . ?"

"It don't matter, he ain't there anymore," say the colonel.

"Yeah, I know all about that, too!" The Ayatolja begun to laugh again, an slap his thighs.

"Well, that may be true," the colonel says, "but look here, we gotta get down to bidness. Time is money, you know?"

"What is time to the Ayatolja?" he say, holdin his palms up in the air, an just about then, one of them fellers with the baggy underpants an the swords beat twice on a huge gong, sort of like the one Mrs. Hopewell, from the CokeCola scheme, had in her rubdown room.

"Ah, speakin of time," announces the Ayatolja, "we are about ready for lunch. You boys had anythin to eat yet?"

"No, sir," I piped up, an Colonel North, he gave me a dirty look.

"Well, then," the Ayatolja shouts, "let the feast begin!"

At this, about a hundrit A-rabs come runnin into the room carryin trays an platters of all kinds of shit, an it is the most mysterious-lookin food I have ever seen. They is big heaps of what appear to be salami wrapped in cabbage an hams an olives an fruits an maybe cottage cheese or somethin—an I don't know what-all else. They laid it all down in front of us on a big Persian rug an stood back with they arms folded across they chests.

"Well, Mr. Gump, and what would you like to eat?" says the Ayatolja.

"Maybe a ham sambwich," I answered.

"Father of God!" screams the Ayatolja. "Don't say them kinds of things in here! We people ain't ate no nasty ham in three thousand years!" He begun wavin his hands an scowlin again.

Colonel North be givin me the real evil eye now, an from the corner of my own eye, I seen them fellers in the baggy diapers have begun drawin they swords. I figger I have said somethin wrong, so I says, "Well, how about a few of them olives or somethin."

A feller begun collectin a plate of olives for me, an I am thinkin that this is okay, too, account of I reckon I ate enough ham back at the pig farm to last me a lifetime.

Anyhow, when the food was served to Colonel North, he begun eatin it with his fingers an oohin an ahin about how good it was, an I picked up a olive or two an put em in my mouth. The Ayatolja took out a fork an started eatin his lunch with it, an kinda raised his eyebrows at the colonel an me. When we was finished, the A-rabs took the plates away, an the colonel tried to get down to bidness again.

"Listen," he says, "we got enough missiles we can lay our hands on to blow up half of Christendom. Now, you want some of these, you gotta promise to make them crackpots over in Lebanon let our fellers go free. Is that a deal?"

"The Ayatolja don't make deals with the Great Satan," he says.

"That so?" the colonel answers. "Well, why don't you make your own missiles then?"

"We ain't got time to," say the Ayatolja. "We are too busy with our prayers."

"Oh, yeah." The colonel snickers. "Then why don't you pray yourself up some missiles, then?"

The scowl on the Ayatolja's face become darker an darker, an I could see that the colonel's tact an diplomacy was fixin to get us into a lot of hot water. An so I tried to lighten the tension with a little joke.

"Scuse me, Mr. Ayatolja," I says. "Have you heard the one about the drunk caught drivin down a one-way street?"

"Nope."

"Well, the policeman says to him, 'Say, din't you see them arrows?' An the drunk says, 'Arrows? I din't even see the Indians!' "

"For Chrissakes, Gump . . ." the colonel hisses, but just then the Ayatolja busts out in a big laugh an begun slappin his thighs an stampin his feet.

"Why, Mr. Gump, you do have a sense of humor, don't you? Why don't you an me take a little walk in my garden?"

So that's what we did. I looked back over my shoulder as we was goin out the door, an Colonel North was just standin there with his jaw hangin down past his chin.

"Look here, Mr. Gump," the Ayatolja says when we get outside, "I don't like this Colonel North of yours. His diplomacy is too slick, and my impression is that he is tryin to put a fast one over on me."

"Oh, I don't know about that," I says. "He seems to me like a truthful feller."

"Well, be that as it may, I ain't got all day to listen to his bullshit. It's about time for me to go pray again. So tell me, what do *you* think of all this arms for hostages stuff?"

"I don't know much about it. I mean, if it's a fair trade, I guess it's okay. The President seemed to think it was. But, like I say, it ain't exactly in my sphere of influence."

"Just what *is* your sphere of influence, Mr. Gump?"

"Well, I was a pig farmer, before all this."

"Father of God," the Ayatolja mutters, claspin his hands an rollin his eyes up toward heaven. "Allah has sent me a swine merchant."

"But basically," I added, "I guess I am a military man."

"Ah, that is a little better I suppose. So, from that standpoint, how do you think these missiles will help the poor ole Ayatolja in his war against the infidels in Iraq?"

"Damn if I know."

"Ah—that's the kind of answer the Ayatolja likes to hear. Not this slick car salesman crap of your Colonel North. You go back and tell your people we got a deal. Arms for hostages."

"You gonna get our hostages out, then?"

"I can't promise it, of course. Those fellers in Lebanon are a bunch of maniacs. All the Ayatolja can do is try—You just make sure them missiles get here on the double."

So that's how it was. Colonel North, when he got through chewin me out for hornin in on his diplomacy, he was happy as a pig in sunshine, so to speak.

"Great God, Gump," he says on the flight home, "this is the deal of a lifetime! We have finally tricked that old moron into givin us back our hostages for some old beat-up missiles that an army of Norwegians wouldn't know what to do with. What a lovely *coup!*"

All the way till we landed, the colonel be pattin hissef on the back for his brilliance. Me, I figger I might have found some kind of career in this bidness, so's I can send some money home for little Forrest. As it turned out, that was not the way it worked.

* * *

We ain't back in Washington but a while when all hell breaks loose.

But meantime, I tried to get my affairs straight. First, I gone on up to Walter Reed Hospital, and, sure enough, just like Colonel North said, there is ole Lieutenant Dan, lyin up in a hospital bed. And he was lookin one hell of a lot better than when I seen him last.

"Where've you been, you big asshole?" Dan ast.

"I have been on a top secret mission," I says.

"Yeah? Where to?"

"To Iran."

"What for?"

"To see the Ayatolja."

"What'd you go to see that sombitch for?"

"We was there to make a deal for arms for hostages."

"That so?"

"Yup."

"What kind of arms?"

"Bunch of ole rusty missiles."

"What kind of hostages?"

"Them over in Lebanon."

"Deal go through?"

"Sort of."

"What you mean, sort of?"

"Well, we give the Ayatolja his missiles."

"You get back the hostages?"

"Not yet."

"Yeah, an you never will, you dumb cluck! Not only have you just revealed to me, a civilian, all this top secret bullshit—which is a firin-squad offense—but it sounds like you have been had again! Forrest, you are a shit-for-brains for sure."

Well, after exchangin our pleasantries, I took ole Dan in

his wheelchair down to the cafeteria to get some ice cream. Since they don't serve oysters on the half shell at the hospital, ice cream has become Dan's favorite food. He says that aside from raw oysters, ice cream is sort of easy on his teeth. Anyhow, it kind of made me remember when I was a little kid settin out on Mama's back porch, churnin away on Saturday afternoons, makin our own ice cream, an Mama would always let me lick the paddles when the ice cream was good an soft an cold.

"What you reckon is gonna happen to us, Dan?"

"What the hell kind of question is that?"

"I dunno. It just sort of come to me."

"Hell it did—You been thinking again—which is not exactly your specialty."

"Yeah, sort of, I guess. I mean, seems like everthin I touch turns to shit. I can't keep no job more than a while, an even when it's goin okay, I screw up. An I am always missin my mama an Jenny an Bubba an everbody. An now there is little Forrest to look after. Listen, I know I am not the smartest feller around, but people half the time be treatin me like some kinda freak. Seems like the only way I'm gettin anyplace is when I dream at night. I mean, when's this shit gonna stop?"

"Probly it won't," Dan says. "That's just the way it is sometimes. Folks like us, we is just screw-ups, an there's no getting around it. Me, I ain't worried what's gonna happen, cause I know. I ain't long for this earth, myself, an far as I'm concerned, good riddance."

"Don't say that kind of stuff, Dan. You're about the only friend I got left."

"I'll say the truth if I want to. I probly done a lot of wrong shit in my life, but one thing you can't say is that I don't tell the truth."

"Yeah, but that's not how it is. Nobody can know how long they gonna live."

"Forrest," he say, "you got the mind of a mole."

Anyway, this will sort of give you an idea of Dan's frame of mind. Me, I was feelin pretty low mysef. I had begun to realize that Colonel North an me has been bamboozled by the Ayatolja, who has now got his missiles, an we ain't seen no hostages returned. Colonel North done been busy arrangin for the money we got for the missiles to be sent down to Central America to the gorillas, an he is not feelin nearly as bad about things as me.

"Gump," he says one mornin, "I gotta go up to Congress in a day or so to testify to some committee about my activities. Now, they may call you, too, or they may not, but in any case, you don't know nothin about any deals for arms for hostages, do you?"

"I know somethin about the arms, but I ain't seen no hostages yet."

"That's not what I meant, you big ox! Don't you realize what we have done is illegal! We could all go to jail! So you better keep your big mouth shut and do what I tell you, you hear?"

"Yes, sir," I says.

Anyhow, I had other shit to worry about, namely, that Colonel North had got me billeted at the marine barracks, an it was not goin too pleasant there. Marines is different from army folks. They is always goin aroun hollerin at everbody an chewin ass an makin you keep everthin clean as a whistle. The one thing it seemed they liked least was havin an army private in their barracks, an frankly, they made my life so miserable that I finally moved out. I didn't have nowhere to go, so I gone on back to Lafayette Park to see if I could find my crate. Turned out, somebody was usin it, so I went an found me another one. An after I got things fixed up, I got the bus out to the National Zoo to see if I could find ole Wanda.

Sure enough, she was there, right next to the seals an the tiger.

They had her in a little cage with some straw an shavins on the floor, an she was lookin pretty unhappy. Sign on the cage says *Swinus Americanus.*

When she seen me, she recognized me immediately, an I reached out over the fence an give her a pat on the snout. She give out a big ole grunt, an I felt so sorry for her I didn't know what to do. If I could of, I'd of busted in that cage an turned her loose. Anyhow, I went on up to the concession stand an bought some popcorn an a Twinkie, an took it back to Wanda's cage. I almost bought her a hotdog, but thought better of it. I gave her the Twinkie an was feedin her the popcorn, when a voice behin me says:

"An just what do you think you're doin?"

I turn aroun an it is a big ole zoo guard standin there.

"I am givin Wanda some food."

"Oh, yeah? Well, don't you see that sign right there, says Do Not Feed the Animals?"

"I bet it wadn't the animals put that sign there," I says.

"Oh, a smartass, huh?" he say, an grapped me by the collar. "Let's see how funny you are in the lockup."

Well, frankly, I have had enough of this shit. I mean, I am feelin so low I almost got to look up to look down, an everthin is goin wrong, an all I done was try to feed little Forrest's pig, an this bozo is givin me a hard time, an well, that was it!

I grapped him back an lifted him up in the air. Then I spun him aroun a few times, like I remember from my rasslin days with The Professor and The Turd, an then I let him loose. He sailed in the air over a fence, kinda like a Frisbee, an landed right in the middle of the seal pool with a big splash. All the seals done jumped in the water an come rushin up to him an whoppin him with they flippers, an he is hollerin an shoutin an shakin his fist. I walked on out of the zoo an caught the bus back downtown. Sometimes a man has got to do what he has got to do.

Sombitch is lucky I didn't thow his ass in the tiger pit.

Chapter Seven

Well, it wadn't long before the shit hit the fan.

It seems that the bidness we had been doin with the Ayatolja was not exactly viewed in a good light by the folks on Capitol Hill, who thought that tradin arms for hostages was not such a hot idea, especially when the money we got was turned over to help the gorillas in Nicaragua. An what them congressmen had in mind was that the President, hissef, was behind the scheme, an they was out to prove it.

Colonel North done so good testifyin before the Congress the first time that they invited him back again, an this time they had a bunch of slick Philadelphia lawyers tryin to trip him up. But the colonel, now, he is pretty slick hissef, an when he is usin his tact an diplomacy, he is pretty hard to trip up.

"Colonel," asts one of the lawyers, "what would you do if the President of the United States told you to commit a crime?"

"Well, sir," says the colonel, "I am a marine. And

marines obey the orders of their commanders-in-chief. So even if the President told me to commit a crime, what I would do is, I would salute smartly an charge up the hill."

"Hill? What hill? Capitol Hill?"

"No, you jackass—any hill! It's a figure of speech. We are the marines! We charge up hills for a living."

"Oh, yeah, then how come they call you 'jarheads'?"

"I kill you, you sombitch—I rip your head off, an spit down your neck!"

"Please, Colonel, don't let us be vulgar. Violence will get you nowhere. Now, Colonel, what you are tellin me is that this was *not* the President's idea?"

"That's what I am tellin you, you asshole."

"So whose idea was it then? Was it yours?"

"Of course not, you jerk." (The colonel's tact an diplomacy is now gettin into full swing.)

"Then whose was it?"

"Well, it was a lot of people's. It just sort of evolved."

"Evolved? But there must of been a 'Prime Mover,' Colonel. Things of this magnitude just do not simply 'evolve.'"

"Well, sir, in fact there probably was a person who thought it through the most thoroughly."

"So this person, he would be the 'Prime Mover' of all these illegal schemes, is that correct?"

"I suppose you could say that."

"And this person, was it Admiral Poindexter, the security adviser to the President of the United States?"

"That pipe-smokin butthole? Of course not. He ain't got the sense to pour piss out of a boot, let alone be a Prime Mover."

"Then, can you tell us, sir, who was it?"

"Why, yessir, I can. It was Private Forrest Gump."

"Who?"

"Gump, sir, PFC Forrest Gump, who has been a special assistant to the President for covert activities. It was all his idea."

At this, all the lawyers an senators got into a huddle an begun to whisper an wave they hands an nod they heads.

So that's how I got dragged into the mess.

Next thing I knowed, two goons in trenchcoats come up to my crate in Lafayette Park in the middle of the night an start bangin on the top. When I crawled out to see what was goin on, one of em shoved a paper in my hand, say I got to appear in the mornin before the Special Senate Committee to Investigate the Iran-Contra Scandal.

"An, I suggest you get that uniform pressed before you get there," one of the goons says, "because your big ass is in a heap of trouble."

Well, I didn't know what to do next. It was too late to wake up Colonel North, who I figgered would have it all thought out with his tact an diplomacy, so I wandered aroun the city for a while an finally wound up at the Lincoln Memorial. The lights was shinin down on the big ole feller, all done up in his marble statue an lookin kinda sad, an a mist was blowin in off the Potomac River, an it had begun to drizzle a little rain. I was feelin pretty sorry for mysef, when lo an behole, out of the mist I seen Jenny sort of walkin toward me!

Right off the bat, she says, "Well, looks like you have done it again, Forrest."

"I reckon," I says.

"Didn't you get in enough trouble the last time you went into the army?"

"Yup."

"So what is it? You think you had to do this for little Forrest?"

"Yup."

She brushed her hair back an tossed her head, just like she used to do, an I just stood there, twistin my hands.

"Feelin kinda sorry for yourself, huh?"

"Uh huh."

"Don't want to go up there to the Congress and tell the truth, do you?"

"Nope."

"Well, you better, cause this is a serious bidness, sellin arms for hostages—At least those bozos think so."

"So I'm tole."

"So what you gonna do?"

"I dunno."

"My advice is, I'd come clean with the whole thing. And don't be coverin up for anybody. Okay?"

"Yeah, I guess," I said, an then another big ole cloud of white mist come waftin in from the river, an Jenny, she just sort of vanished into it, an for a moment I wanted so bad to go runnin after her, maybe to catch her somehow, an bring her back—but even I am not so stupid as that. So I just turned aroun an started back for my crate. Anyhow, I am left on my own again. An as it turned out, it was the last time I did not take Jenny's advice about tellin the truth.

"Now, tell us, Private Gump, just when was it you first got the idea to swap arms for hostages?"

I be settin at a big ole table facin all the senators an lawyers an other muckity-mucks in the congressional hearin room, an the TV cameras be rollin an lights shinin in my face. A little young-lookin, blond-haired lawyer guy be astin the questions.

"Who says I did?" I ast.

"I am asking the questions here, Private Gump. You just answer em."

"Well, I don't know how I can answer that," I says. "I mean, you don't even ast me *whether* I did—You just ast me *when* . . . ?"

"That's right, Private Gump, when was it, then?"

I looked over at Colonel North, uniform all full of medals, an he be glarin at me an slowly noddin his head, like I am sposed to answer somethin.

"Well, it was when I first met the President, I reckon."

"Yes, and did you not tell the President that you had conceived a scheme to swap arms for hostages?"

"No, sir."

"What did you tell the President then?"

"I tole him the last time I met a president, he wanted to watch *To Tell the Truth*, on the TV."

"Issat so! An what did the President say?"

"He says he would rather watch *Let's Make a Deal*."

"Private Gump! I remind you that you are under oath here!"

"Well, actually, he was watchin *Concentration*, but he said it confuses him."

"Private Gump! You are evading my question—and you are under oath. Are you tryin to make the United States Senate look ridiculous? We can hold you in contempt!"

"I reckon you already do," I says.

"Sombitch! You are covering up for all of them—the President, Colonel North, here, Poindexter, and I don't know who-all else! We are gonna get to the bottom of this if it takes all year!"

"Yessir."

"So, now, Gump, Colonel North has told us you conceived the whole nefarious plan to swap arms for hostages to the Ayatolja and then divert the money to the Contras in Central America. Isn't that so?"

"I don't know nothin about any Contras—I thought the money was goin to some gorillas."

"Ah—an admission! So you *did* know about this horrible scheme!"

"I understood the gorillas need the money, yessir. That's what I was tole."

"Ha! I think you are lying, Private Gump. I suggest that it was *you* who devised the entire operation—and with the President's complicity! Are you trying to play dumb?"

"It ain't exactly playin, sir."

"Mr. Chairman!" the lawyer says. "It is obvious that Private Gump, here, the 'special assistant for covert operations to the President of the United States,' is a fraud and a faker, and that he is deliberately tryin to make the United States Congress look like fools! He ought to be held in contempt!"

The chairman, he sort of drawed hissef up an look down at me like I was a bug.

"Yes, it does appear that way. Uh, Private Gump, do you understand the penalty for makin the United States Congress look like fools?"

"No, sir."

"Well, we can thow your ass in jail—not to put too fine a point on it."

"Oh, yeah," I says, tryin to imitate Colonel North's tact an diplomacy strategy, "start thowin then."

So here I am again, thowed in jail.

Headline in *The Washington Post* next day says: **MORON DETAINED IN CONTEMPT OF CONGRESS CASE.**

The Washington Post

An Alabama man, who sources close to the Post identified as a "certified idiot," has been charged with contempt of Congress in the Iran-Contra scandal, which this paper has covered from top to bottom.

Forrest Gump, of no fixed address, was sentenced to an indefinite prison term yesterday after he began ridiculing members of the Select Senate Committee appointed to investigate charges that key members of the Reagan administration conspired to swindle the Ayatolja Koumani of Iran out of cash in an arms-for-hostages scam.

Gump, who apparently has been involved in numerous shady activities involving the U.S. Government, including its space program, was described by sources as "a member of the lunatic fringe of American intelligence operations. He's one of those guys who comes an goes in the night," the source said.

A senator on the committee, who asked not to be identified, told the Post that Gump "will rot in that jail until he repents for trying to make fools of the U.S. Congress. Only the U.S. Congress itselves, and not some shitheaver from Alabama, is permitted to do that," said the senator, to quote his own words.

Anyhow, they give me some clothes with black an white prison stripes on em, an stick me in a cell I got to share with a forger, a child molester, a dynamite bomber, an some nut called Hinckley who is always talkin about the actress Jodie Foster. The forger is the nicest one of the bunch.

Anyhow, after reviewin my employment qualifications, they set me to work makin license plates, an life settled down to a dull routine. It was about Christmastime—

Christmas Eve, to be exact, an it was snowin—when a guard come up to the cell an say I got a visitor.

I ast him who it was, but he just says, "Listen, Gump, you is lucky to have *any* kind of visitor, considerin the crime you have committed. People that go around makin a fool of the U.S. Congress are lucky they don't get thowed in 'the hole'—so get your big ass out here."

I gone on down to the visitors room with him. Outside, a group of carolers from the Salvation Army is singin "Away in a Manger," an I can hear a Santa Claus ringin his bell for donations. When I set down in front of the wire booth, I am absolutely floored to see settin across from me little Forrest.

"Well, merry Christmas, I guess" is all he says.

I don't know what else to say, so I says, "Thanks."

We just set lookin at each other for a minute. Actually, little Forrest is mostly starin down at the counter, ashamed, I guess, to see his daddy in the pokey.

"Well, how'd you come to get here?" I ast.

"Grandma sent me. You was in all the papers and on TV, too. She said she thought it might cheer you up if I came."

"Yeah, well it does. I really appreciate it."

"It wadn't my idea," he said, a comment which I thought was unnecessary.

"Look, I know I've screwed up, an right now I ain't exactly somebody you can be proud of. But I been tryin."

"Tryin to do what?"

"Tryin not to screw up."

He just kep starin at the counter, an after a minute or so, he says, "I went out to the zoo to see Wanda today."

"She okay?"

"Took me two hours to find her. Seemed like she was

cold. I tried to put my jacket in there for her, but some big ole zoo guard come up an start hollerin at me."

"He didn't mess with you, did he?"

"Nah, I tole him it was my pig, an he says somethin like, 'Yeah, that's what some other crackpot tole me, too,' an then he just walked off."

"So how's school?"

"It's okay, I guess. The other kids been givin me a hard time on account of you bein thowed in the slammer."

"Well, don't let that bother you, now. It ain't your fault."

"I don't know about that . . . If I'd just kept remindin you to check those valves and gauges at the pig farm, maybe none of this would have happened."

"You can't look back," I says. "Whatever is, is what is meant to be, I reckon." That was about the only face I had left to put on it.

"What you doin for Christmas?"

"Oh, they probably got a big ole party for us here," I lied, "probably have a Santa Claus an presents an a big turkey an everthin. You know how prisons are, they like to see the inmates enjoyin themsefs. What you gonna do?"

"Catch the bus back home, I guess. I reckon I seen all the sights. After I got back from the zoo, I walked by the White House an up to Capitol Hill an then down to the Lincoln Memorial."

"Yeah, how was that?"

"It was kinda funny, you know. It had started snowin, an was all misty, an . . . an . . ."

He begun shakin his head, an I could tell by his voice he was startin to choke up.

"An what . . ."

"I just miss my mama, that's all . . ."

"Your mama, was she . . . You didn't see her, did you?"

"Not exactly."

"But sort of?"

"Yeah, sort of. Just for a minute. But it was only a dream. I know that! I ain't stupid enough to really believe it."

"She say anythin to you?"

"Yeah, she says I gotta look out for you. That you all I got, besides Grandma, an that you need my help now."

"She said that?"

"Look, it was just a dream, like I said. Dreams ain't real."

"You never know," I says. "When's your bus?"

"About an hour. I guess I better be goin."

"Well, you have a good trip home, okay. I'm sorry you had to see me like this, but maybe it won't be too long afore I get out."

"Yeah, they gonna turn you loose?"

"Could be. There is a feller comes here for charity work with the inmates. A preacher. He says he is tryin to 'rehabilitate' us. He says he thinks he can get me out in a few months on a 'federal work-release program' or somethin. Says he's got a big ole religious theme park down in Carolina an needs fellers like me to help him run it."

"Yeah, what's his name?"

"The Reverend Jim Bakker."

So that's how I come to go to work for the Reverend Jim Bakker.

He had a place in Carolina he had named Holy Land, an it was the biggest theme park I had ever heard of. The reverend had a wife called Tammy Faye, looked like a Kewpie doll with eyelashes long as a dragonfly's wings an a lot of rouge on her cheeks. They was also a younger woman hangin aroun, name of Jessica Hahn, that Reverend Bakker described as his "secretary."

"Look, Gump," Reverend Bakker says, "if that ignoramus Walt Disney can do it, so can I. This is the grandest scheme of the grand. We will attract Bible thumpers from all over the goddamn world! Fifty thousand a day—maybe more! Every scene in the Bible—every parable—will have its place here! And at twenty dollars a head, we'll make billions!"

In this, the Reverend Bakker was correct.

He had more than fifty rides an attractions, an was plannin for more. People got to walk through some woods where they was a guy dressed up like Moses, an when they got close he stepped on a button that set off a gas valve that shot a fire twenty feet in the air—"Moses and the Burnin Bush"! An as soon as the gas fire bust out, the visitors all jump back an begun hollerin an ooohin an ahhhin, like to scared them to death!

There was a stream, too, where a little baby Moses was floatin aroun in a plastic boat wrapped in a towel—"Moses in the Bulrushes"!

Then there was "The Red Sea Parting," where Reverend Bakker has figgered out a way for a whole lake to be sucked up on both sides on command, an the people get to walk across on the bottom, just like the Israelites—an furthermore, when they got to the other side, the reverend has a bunch of goons from the prison-release program dressed up like Pharaoh's Army start chasin after em, but when the goons tried to get across the sea, the pumps thowed all the water back in the lake an Pharaoh's Army got drownded.

He had it all.

They was "Jacob in His Coat of Many Colors" an the

entire "Story of Job," which was about as much sufferin as I
have ever seen a man go through on a daily basis. After the
first bunch had walked through "The Red Sea Parting," a
second group got to come to the lake to watch Jesus turn
loafs of bread into fishes. The reverend, he had figgered out
a way to save money by lettin the fishes eat the bread till
they got fat enough, an then he served them up to the
visitors at the fish-fry pavilion for fifteen dollars a plate!

They have got "Daniel in the Lion's Den" an "Jonah in
the Belly of the Whale," too. On Mondays, when Holy Land
is closed, the reverend rents out the lion an his tamer to a
local bar for fifty bucks a night, where they bet people that
nobody can beat the lion in a rasslin match. The whale is a
big ole mechanical whale, an it was all workin pretty good
till the reverend discovered that Jonah was hidin a bunch of
whisky behin the whale's tonsils. Ever time the whale
gobbled him up he'd run back an slug down a drink. End of
the day come, Jonah is pretty drunk, an the finale arrived
when Jonah commenced to give the crowd the finger just
before the whale's jaws clamped shut. Reverend had to put
a stop to that, account of some of the mamas complained
that their kids was givin the finger back.

But the most spectacular ride of all was "Jesus Ascend-
ing into Heaven," which was run on somethin the reverend
called a skyhook. In fact, it was like one a them bungee-
jumpin things in reverse, where the guy in the Jesus suit gets
hooked up an then snatched about fifty feet in the air into a
cloud of machine-made mist—an to tell the truth, it did
look kinda realistic. The visitors could pay ten dollars apiece
to get to do this themsefs.

"Gump," the reverend says, "I have got a brand-new
attraction that I want you to be a part of. It is called 'The
Battle of David and Goliath'!"

It didn't take a whole lot of smarts for me to figger out what part I was sposed to play.

I thought the deal playin in "David and Goliath" was gonna be easy, but of course it wadn't.

First off, they dressed me up in a big ole leopardskin tunic, an give me a shield an a spear an pasted a big black beard on me. What I am sposed to do is growl an roar an generally act like a asshole. An just when I am lookin my fiercest, the David character, he comes out wearin a set of diapers an starts thowin rocks at me with a slingshot.

David is played by that nut Hinckley, who has got hissef into the program by claimin he is really crazy an don't belong in jail anymore. When he is not throwin rocks at me with the slingshot, he spends all his times writin letters to Jodie Foster, who he describes as a "pen pal."

Problem is, they is real rocks he is thowin an ever so often one of em hits me—an let me say this: It hurts! We be doin our act five or six times a day, an by closin time, I probly been hit two dozen times by rocks. Hinckley, he seems to enjoy it, but after about a week or two, I done complained to Reverend Bakker that this don't seem fair, me havin all these bruises an lumps an gettin two of my teeth chipped out by this little bastid, when I don't never get to do anythin back to him.

But the reverend says it is okay, account of in the Bible story, that was the way it was, an you can't change the Bible. Damn if I wouldn't, if I could, but of course I didn't say so, account of the reverend, he say if I don't like it, I can go on back to jail. I am sure missin little Forrest, an Jenny, too, an somehow, I feel that I am seriously forsaken.

Anyhow, the time come when I had had enough. It was a big day at Holy Land, an the theme park was filled with visitors. When the crowd gets to my attraction, I begun roarin an lookin fierce an threatenin David with my spear. He begun thowin his rocks with the slingshot, an damn if one of them don't hit me on the hand an I dropped my shield. I bent over to pick it up, an the little bastid done thowed another rock that hit me in the ass. This is totally uncalled for! A man can put up with just so much.

Well, I lurched over to David, who is just standin there with a stupid smirk on his face, an I grapped him by the seat of his diapers an spun him around a few times, an then let go. He sailed all the way over the trees an landed right in the middle of the lake where Jesus was doin his loafs an fishes thing.

David's arrival must of set somethin off wrong with the main switchboard, cause all of a sudden the pumps begun operatin an the Red Sea begun to part. Without no warnin, the gas jet at the Burnin Bush went off, an Moses, who was standin too close to it, was set on fire. About this time, the mechanical whale took off right out of the lake an came up on shore, chompin an bitin like mad. Now the crowd begun to riot; women was hollerin an children was cryin an men was runnin for they lives. All this got the lion over at Daniel's Den upset, an he busted loose an started to run amok. At that point, I appeared on the scene, which sort of added to the confusion. The guy what was playin Jesus ascendin into heaven was standin there drinkin a soda pop, waitin for his act to start, when all of a sudden the bungee cord snatched him up an flung him into the sky. He wadn't strapped in or nothin, so it just let him go, an he landed in the middle of the fish-fry pavilion, right in a big pot of warm grease.

Somebody had called the police, who showed up an immediately begun beatin people on the heads with nightsticks. Meantime, the lion had got loose in the bulrushes, where he surprised the Reverend Bakker an Jessica Hahn, who was havin some kind of relationship minus their clothes. They come tearin out right in the middle of things, with the lion in hot pursuit. When the police got an eyeful of this, first thing they do is arrest the reverend for "indecent exposure," an cart him off to jail. Last thing he says before they tossed him in the paddy wagon is "Gump, you idiot, I'll have your head for this!"

Chapter Eight

$\mathbb{A}$fter that, it was all over for
he Reverend Bakker. One thing led to another, an in the
end he gone on to jail hissef—where he can now help
rehabilitate the prisoners full-time, not to mention his own
pious ass.

Me, however, it looks like, will be returnin to jail also,
but that was not to be.

The national media had got wind that there was a riot at
Holy Land, an somehow my picture got into the papers an
on TV. I am actually waitin for the bus to take us back to
prison, when a feller shows up with a document in his hand,
says it is my "release."

He is dressed all nattily in a suit with suspenders an has
big flashy teeth an spit-shined shoes, look kinda like a
stockbroker. "Gump," he says, "I am gonna be your 'Angel
of Mercy.'"

Ivan Bozosky is his name.

Ivan Bozosky says he has been tryin to find me ever
since the Capitol Hill hearins with Colonel North.

"Have you seen the newspapers today, Gump?" Ivar Bozosky ast.

"No, sir, I haven't."

"Well, then," he says, "perhaps you'd like to," ar hands me a copy of *The Wall Street Journal*. Headline reads STOOGE SHUTS DOWN IMPORTANT ECONOMIC THEM PARK.

THE WALL STREET JOURNAL.

A recent releasee from a Washington hospital for the criminally insane ran amok yesterday in a small Carolina town, ruining economic opportunities for thousands of hardworking American citizens by setting off a chain of events that caused the downfall of one of Carolina's most revered citizens.

According to sources, the culprit's name is Forrest Gump, a man of low IQ who has been identified in similar disturbances in Atlanta, West Virginia, and elsewhere.

Gump, who was serving time for expressing contempt for the U.S. Congress, was on a work-release project at a Bible-oriented enterprise under the tutelage of the Reverend Jim Bakker, a devout entrepreneur of our American way of life.

In his role as the giant Goliath, Gump, who is said to be a large-figured man, apparently began to disport himself yesterday in a manner described by authorities as "inappropriate," at one point hurling his fellow Bible character David over several stands of trees and into a lake inhabited by a mechanical whale, which, in the words of Holy Land authorities, "became distressed by the intrusion," and began to seethe and set upon the guests and visitors.

Somewhere in the confusion, Reverend Bakker and his secretary, one Jessica Hahn, became embroiled in the exhibit's biblical bulrushes, which tore off their clothing, and they were swept up in a police dragnet, which the spokesman described as "unfortunate."

An shit like that. Anyway, ole Ivan Bozosky, he took back the newspaper an turns to me.

"I like your style, Gump," he says, "because way back before all this, you had every chance there was to rat on Colonel North an the President, but you didn't. You covered it all up an took the blame yourself! Now, that's what I call real corporate spirit! My outfit can use a man like you."

"What outfit is that?" I ast.

"Well, we buy an sell shit—stuff on paper, actually. Bonds, stocks, bidnesses—whatever. We don't buy an sell anything really, but when we get through talkin on the phones an shufflin all the papers, we wind up with a shit-pot of money in our pockets."

"How you do that?"

"Easy," Ivan Bozosky says. "Meanness, dirty tricks an stuff, peekin over people's shoulders, goin behind their backs, pickin their pockets. It's a jungle out there, Gump, an right now, I am the big tiger."

"So what you want me to do?"

Ivan puts his hand on my shoulder. "Gump, I am starting a new division in my company in New York, called the Division of Insider Trading, an I want you to be its president."

"Me? Why?"

"Because of your integrity. It took a lot of integrity to stand up there and lie to the Congress and take the rap for that fool North. Gump, you are just the kind of feller I've been looking for."

"What's it pay?"

"Sky's the limit, Gump! Why, do you need money?"

"Everbody needs money," I says.

"No, I mean *real* money! The kind with half-a-dozen zeros behind it."

"Well, I gotta earn somethin to keep little Forrest in school, an pay for his college someday, an stuff like that."

"Who's little Forrest—your son?"

"Well, sort of. I mean, I'm in charge of takin care of him."

"Good godamighty, Gump," Ivan Bozosky says, "with what you're gonna make, you can send him to Choate, Andover, St. Paul's, and Episcopal High School all at once, and when you're done, he'll be so rich he can send his shirts off to Paris to be laundered."

So that's how I begun my corporate career.

I had never been to New York City, an let me tell you: It was a sight!

I didn't know there was so many people in the whole world. They was millin in the streets an sidewalks an up in the skyscrapers an in the stores. The racket they made was unreal—horns blowin, jackhammers jackin, sirens wailin, an I don't know what-all else. I had the immediate impression that I was in a anthill, where all the ants was half crazy.

Ivan. Bozosky first took me to his company's offices. They was in a big ole skyscraper down near Wall Street. They was hundrits of people workin there at computers, all was wearing shirts an ties an suspenders, an most of em had little round horn-rimmed glasses, an their hair was slicked back. To a man, they was talkin on their telephones, an smokin cigars so much at first I thought the room was on fire.

"This is the deal, Gump," Ivan says. "What we do herein is, we make friends with the folks that run big companies, an when we learn they are gonna issue a big dividend or earnings statement, or sell their company, or start a new division—or do anything else that will make the price of their stock go up—why, we start buying their stock ourselves before the news officially gets in the papers an lets every sonofabitch on Wall Street have a fair chance to get in on the profits."

"How you make friends with them people?" I ast.

"Simple. Just hang around the Harvard or Yale clubs or the Racquet Club or any number of places where these morons do their thing. Buy em a bunch of drinks, play dumb—take em to dinner, get em a girl, kiss their asses—whatever it takes. Sometimes we fly em out to Aspen to ski or to Palm Beach or something. But don't you worry about that, Gump. Our fellers know how to run that scam—All I want you to do is be the president, and the only person you'll report to is me—about, oh, say, once every six months or so."

"What I'm gonna report?"

"We'll figure that out when the time comes. Now, let me show you your office."

Ivan took me down a hall to a big ole corner office that has a mahogany desk an leather chairs an couches, an a Persian rug on the floor. All the windows look out over the city an the rivers, where there is all sorts of boats an steamships goin up an down, an in the distance I can see the Statue of Liberty, shinin in the evenin sun.

"Well, Gump, what do you think?"

"Nice view," I says.

"Nice view my ass!" says Ivan. "This shit cost two hundred dollars a square foot to lease! This is prime real estate, my man! Now, your private secretary will be Miss Hudgins. And she is knock-dead gorgeous. And what I want you to do is, just sit at this desk here and when she brings you in some papers to sign, sign your name on them. You don't need to bother to read them—they'll just be a bunch of bullshit and details anyway. I've always thought bidness executives shouldn't know too much about what's going on in their bidness—you know what I mean?"

"Well, I dunno," I says. "You know, I done got into a lot of trouble in my life doin stuff I didn't know what it was."

"Now, don't worry any about that, Gump. All this is on the big-time up and up. It is the chance of a lifetime for you—and your son." Ivan puts his arm around my shoulder an flashes a big ole toothy grin at me. "Want to ask anything else?"

"Yeah," I says. "Where is the bathroom?"

"Bathroom? Your bathroom? Why, it's right here through this door. You wondering if you got a private bathroom? Is that it?"

"Nope. I got to pee."

At this, Ivan jumps back a little. "Ah, well, that is a rather straightforward way of putting it, I must say. But you go right ahead, Mr. Gump—in the privacy of your own bathroom."

An so that's what I did, but I was still wonderin if I was doin the right thing with this Ivan Bozosky. After all, seems I had heard some of his kind of shit before.

Anyway, Ivan, he gone off an left me in my new office. Big brass nameplate on the desk says Forrest Gump, President. I had just set down in the leather chair an put my feet up when the door opens an in walks a beautiful young woman. I figger this to be Miss Hudgins.

"Ah, Mr. Gump," she says. "Welcome to the insider trading division of Bozosky Enterprises."

Miss Hudgins is certainly a looker—enough to make

your teeth chatter. She is tall an brunette with blue eyes an a big toothy smile an skirt so short that I am afraid her underpants might show if she bends over.

"Would you like some coffee or anything?" she ast.

"No. Thank you, though," I says.

"Well, is there anything I can do for you? How about a CokeCola—or perhaps a whisky sour?"

"Thanks, but I really don't want nothin."

"Then perhaps you would like to see your new apartment."

"My what?"

"Apartment. Mr. Bozosky has ordered you an apartment to live in, since you are president of the division."

"I thought I was gonna stay here on the couch," I says. "I mean, since there is a bathroom an all."

"Heavens, no, Mr. Gump. Mr. Bozosky asked me to find you suitable living quarters over on Fifth Avenue. Something where you can entertain."

"Who I'm gonna entertain?"

"Whoever," Miss Hudgins says. "Will you be ready to go in, say, half an hour?"

"I am ready to go right now," I says. "How we gonna get there?"

"Why, in your limousine, of course."

In no time, we is down on the street gettin into a big ole black limousine. It is so big I think it cannot turn a corner, but the driver, whose name is Eddie, is so good that he can even drive right past the taxicabs by goin up on the curb, an in a few minutes we is arriving at my new apartment after scatterin people all over Madison Avenue. Miss Hudgins says we are now "uptown."

The buildin is a big ole thing of white marble with a

canopy an doormen dressed up like in one of them old-time movies. The sign out front say Helmsley Palace. As we is goin in the door, a woman wearin a fur coat come out walkin a poodle. She be eyein me pretty suspicious an lookin me up an down, account of I am still wearin my work clothes from Holy Land.

When we get off at the eighteenth floor, Miss Hudgins opens the door with a key. It is like goin in a mansion or somethin. They is crystal chandeliers an big gold-leaf mirrors an paintins on the walls. I see fireplaces an fancy furniture an tables with pitcher books on em. There is a library all paneled in wood an beautiful carpets on the floors. In the corner is a bar.

"You want to see your bedroom?" Miss Hudgins says.

I was so speechless, all I could do was nod.

We gone on in the bedroom, an let me say this: It was a sight. Big ole king-size bed with a covered top an fireplace an a TV set built into the wall. Miss Hudgins says it gets a hundrit channels. The bathroom is grander than that, marble floors an a glass shower with gold knobs an jets that spray in ever direction. There are even two toilets, although one is kinda funny lookin.

"What is that?" I ast, pointin to it.

"That, is a bidet," she says.

"What's it for? It ain't got no seat on it."

"Er, well, why don't you just use the other one for now," Miss Hudgins says. "We can talk about the bidet later."

Like the sign out front announces, this place *is* a palace, an "Sooner or later," Miss Hudgins says, "I imagaine you're gonna get to meet the nice lady who owns it. She's a friend of Mr. Bozosky. Her name is Leona."

* * *

Anyway, Miss Hudgins says we got to go out an get me some new clothes that is "fittin for the president of one of Mr. Bozosky's divisions." We gone on over to a tailor shop called Mr. Squeegee's, an is greeted at the door by Mr. Squeegee hissef. He is a little short fat guy with a Hitler-lookin mustache an a bald head.

"Ah, Mr. Gump. I have been expecting you," he says.

Mr. Squeegee done showed me dozens of suits an jackets an pants an cloth patterns an materials—ties an even socks an underpants. Ever time I pick out somethin, Miss Hudgins says, "No, no—that won't do," an she picks out somethin else. Finally, Mr. Squeegee stands me in front of a mirror an begun to take my pants measurements.

"My, my, what a fine specimen you are!" he says.

"You got that right," Miss Hudgins chimes in.

"By the way, Mr. Gump, what side do you dress on?"

"Side of what?" I ast.

"Side, Mr. Gump. Do you dress to the left or the right?"

"Huh?" I says. "I guess it don't matter. I just put on my clothes, you know?"

"Well, er, Mr. Gump . . ."

"Just dress him for both sides," Miss Hudgins say. "A man like Mr. Gump looks like he can swing any way he wants."

"Right," says Mr. Squeegee.

Next day, Eddie picked me up in the limousine an I gone on down to the office. I had just got there when Ivan Bozosky came in an says, "In a little while, let's do lunch. I got somebody I want you to meet."

All the rest of the mornin I signed the papers Miss Hudgins brought in. I must of signed twenty or thirty, an even though I sort of glanced at what was in a few, I could not understand a word that was in them. After a hour or two, my stomach begun to growl, an I started thinkin about my mama's srimp creole. Good ole Mama.

Pretty soon, Ivan come in an says it is time for lunch. A limo took us to a restaurant called The Four Seasons, an we is showed to a table where there is a tall skinny guy in a suit with a wolfish look on his face.

"Ah, Mr. Gump," Ivan Bozosky says, "I want you to meet a friend of mine."

The guy stands up an shook my hand.

Mike Mulligan is his name.

Mike Mulligan is apparently a stockbroker who Mr. Bozosky does some bidness with. Mike Mulligan deals in somethin he calls junk bonds, though what anybody would want with a bunch of junk is beyond me. Nevertheless, I get the impression that Mike Mulligan is some kind of big cheese.

After Ivan an Mike had done some chitchat, they get down to bidness with me.

"What will happen, Mr. Gump," says Ivan Bozosky, "is that Mike, here, is going to give you a call from time to time. He will tell you the name of a company, an when he does, I want you to write it down. He will spell the name out very carefully, so you will not make any mistakes. When you have done that, give the name of the company to Miss Hudgins. She will know what to do with it."

"Yeah?" I ast. "An what is that for?"

"The less you know, the better off you are, Gump," says Ivan. "Mr. Mulligan and I occasionally do each other favors. We trade secrets between us, you know what I mean?" At this, he gives me a big ole wink. There is somethin about all this I don't like, an I am about to say so, but then Ivan, he springs me the big news.

"Now, Gump, what I'm thinking is, you need a proper salary. You gotta have enough to keep your son in school and put yourself in the catbird seat financially, and I am thinking about, oh, let's say, two hundred and fifty thousand a year. How does that sound?"

Well, I was sorta dumbstruck. I mean, I have made a bit of money in my day, but that's a lot of bread for an idiot like me. An so I thought about all this for a few seconds, an then just nodded my head.

"Okay," says Ivan Bozosky. "It is a done deal, then." An Mr. Mike Mulligan, he be grinnin like a Cheshire cat.

Over the months, my executive duties went into full swing. I am signin papers like crazy—mergers, acquisitions, buy-outs, sell-outs, puts an calls. One day I come across Ivan Bozosky in the hallway, chucklin to hissef.

"Well, Gump," he says, "this is the kind of day I like. We done bought out five airlines. I changed the names of two of them, and shut the other three down flat. Them sombitchin passengers ain't gonna know what the hell is happenin to em! They get their asses strapped into a city-block-long steel cylinder an shot up in the air at six hundred miles an hour, an when they come down, they ain't even on the same airline as they was when they left!"

"I reckon they will be surprised," I says.

"Not half as much as those turkeys that was flyin on the ones I shut down!" Ivan chuckles. "We sent out orders by radio for the pilots to land immediately, wherever the nearest field is, an let the bastids off, then and there. There's gonna be assholes thinkin they're headed for Paris, gonna be put off cold in Thule, Greenland. Or those who booked in for LA, they gonna wind up in Montana or Wisconsin or someplace!"

"Ain't they gonna be mad?" I ast.

"Screw em," says Ivan, wavin his hands. "That's what it's all about, Gump! Base capitalism! The old fuckeroo! We gotta consolidate, fire people, get folks scared, an then, when they ain't lookin, get our hands in their pockets. That's what the deal is, my boy!"

An so it went, me signin papers an Ivan an Mike Mulligan buyin an sellin. Meantime, I was gettin my taste of the high life in New York City. I gone to Broadway plays an private clubs an charity benefits at Tavern on the Green. Seems like nobody don't cook at home in New York, but go out to restaurants ever night an eat mysterious-lookin food that cost as much as a new suit of clothes. But I guess it don't matter to me, account of I am makin so much money. Miss Hudgins, she is my "escort" at these affairs. She says Ivan Bozosky wants me to keep a "high profile," an indeed this is so. Ever week I am mentioned in the newspaper gossip columns, an many times they run my picture, too. Miss Hudgins says there are three newspapers in New York—the "smart people's paper," the "dumb people's paper," an the "stupid people's paper." But, Miss Hudgins say, everbody who is anybody reads all three, account of they want to see if they are in there.

One night we had got through with a big charity dance an Miss Hudgins was gonna drop me off at the Helmsley Palace before Eddie took her home. But this time, she say she'd like to come up to my suite "for a nightcap." I am wonderin why, but it is not nice to say no to a lady, so we went on up.

Soon as we get inside, Miss Hudgins turns on the hi-fi, goes over to the bar, an makes a drink. Straight scotch. Then she kicks off her shoes an plops down on the sofa in a reclinin pose.

"Why don't you kiss me," she asts.

I gone over an give her a peck on the cheek, but she graps me an hauls me down on top of her.

"Here, Forrest, I want you to sniff this." With one hand, she dumps a little white powder from a vial out on her thumbnail.

"Why?" I ast.

"Cause it'll make you feel good. It'll make you feel powerful."

"Why I need to feel that?"

"Just do it," she says. "Just this one time. If you don't like it, you don't have to do it again."

I didn't much want to, but it seemed harmless enough, you know? Wadn't but a little bit of white powder. An so I done it. Made me sneeze.

"I've waited a long time for this, Forrest," she says. "I want you."

"Ah, well," I says, "I thought we had a sort of workin relationship, you know?"

"Yeah, well, it's time you get to working!" she pants, an begun to undo my tie an grap at me with her hands.

Well, I didn't know what I was sposed to do. I mean, I had always heard it was a mistake to git involved with persons you work with—"Do not foul your own nest" was what Lieutenant Dan used to say—but at this point, I am truly confused. Miss Hudgins was certainly a beautiful woman, an I had not been with a woman, beautiful or otherwise, in a long time . . . an after all, you are not sposed to say no to a lady . . . an so I done made all the excuses I could think of in the time allowed, an the next thing I knowed, Miss Hudgins an I was in bed.

After it was over, she smoked a cigarette an thowed on her clothes an left, an I was there alone. She had lit the fire in the fireplace an the logs was flickerin low an orange, an I was not feelin good, like I reckon I was sposed to, but sort of lonely an scared, an wonderin where my life is headed up in New York City. An as I am lyin there, starin at the fire, lo an behole, there suddenly appeared Jenny's face in the flames.

"Well, bozo, I spose you're proud of yourself," she says.

"Oh, no, I'm not, in fact, I'm sorry. I didn't never want to get into bed with Miss Hudgins in the first place," I tole her.

"That's not what I'm talkin about, Forrest," Jenny says. "I didn't expect you to never sleep with another woman. You're a human. You got needs. That's not it."

"Then what is it?"

"Your life, you big moose. What are you doing here? When was the last time you spent any time with little Forrest?"

"Well, I called him a few weeks ago. I sent him money . . ."

"And you think that's all there is to it, huh? Just send the money and make a few phone calls?"

"No—but what I'm gonna do? Where I'm gonna *get* the money. Who else is gonna give me a job? Ivan's payin me top dollar here."

"Yeah? For what? Do you have any idea what those papers are you're signing every day?"

"I ain't sposed to, Jenny—that's what Mr. Bozosky said."

"Uh huh. Well, I reckon you're just gonna have to find

out the hard way. And I spose you don't have any idea what that crap was you just stuck up your nose, either."

"Not really."

"But you did it anyhow, just like you always do. You know, Forrest, I've always said you might not be the brightest feller in town, but you're not as dumb as you act sometimes. I've known you all my life and the problem is, mostly, you just don't *think*—You know what I mean?"

"Well, I was kinda hopin you'd help me out there a little."

"I told you, it ain't my turn to watch you all the time, Forrest. You gotta start lookin out for yourself—and while you're at it, you might pay a little more attention to little Forrest. Mama's gettin old, she can't do it all. Boy like that, he needs a daddy in his life."

"Where?" I ast. "Here? You want me to move him up to this dump—I might be stupid, but I ain't so dumb I don't see that this ain't no place to raise a boy—everbody either rich or poor, an no in between. These people, they ain't got no values, Jenny. It's all about money an shit, an gettin your ass in the newspaper columns."

"Yeah, an you're right in the middle of it, aren't you? What you're describing is just one side of this town that you're seeing. Maybe there's another one. People are pretty much the same, everyplace."

"I am doing what I am tole," I says.

"What ever happened to doin the right thing?"

To this, I had no answer, an all of a sudden, Jenny's face begun to fade behind the fire.

"Now, wait a minute," I says. "We is just beginnin to get things straight—Don't go now—It ain't been but a couple of minutes . . ."

"See you later, alligator," she says, an then she is gone. I set up in the bed an tears come to my eyes. Ain't nobody understands what is happenin with me—not even Jenny. I wanted to pull the sheets over my head an not get up at all, but after a while, I gone on an got dressed an went into the office. On my desk, Miss Hudgins had left a pile of papers for me to sign.

Well, I know that Jenny is right about one thing. I got to spend some time with little Forrest, an so I arranged for him to come up to New York City for a few days' vacation. He arrived on a Friday, an Eddie picked him up at the airport in my limousine, which I figgered would impress him. It didn't.

He come into my office wearin dungarees an a T-shirt, took a quick look around, an delivered his opinion.

"I'd rather be back at the pig farm."

"How come?" I ast.

"What's so good about all this?" he says. "You gotta nice view. So what?"

"It's where I earn my livin," I says.

"Doin what?"

"Signin papers."

"This what you gonna do the rest of your life?"

"I dunno. I mean, it pays the bills."

He shook his head an gone over to the winder.

"What's that out there?" he ast. "That the Statue of Liberty?"

"Yup," I says. "That's her." I can't get over how much he has growed up. He must be more than five feet tall an is certainly a handsome young man, with Jenny's blond hair an blue eyes.

"You wanna go see her?"

"Who?"

"The Statue of Liberty."

"I guess," he says.

"Well, good, cause I done arranged for us to take a tour of the town these next few days. We is gonna see all the sights."

So that's what we did. We gone down Fifth Avenue to see the shops an out to the Statue of Liberty an the top of the Empire State Buildin, where little Forrest says he wants to thow somethin off to see how long it takes to land on the ground. I did not let him do that, though. We gone up to Grant's Tomb an down to Broadway, where they was a man exposin himself, an in Central Park, but not for long, account of there was muggers present. We took the subway an come out near the Plaza Hotel, where we stopped in for a CokeCola. The bill come an it was twenty-five dollars.

"That's a bunch of shit," says little Forrest.

"I reckon I can afford it," I says, but he just shook his head an walk on out to the car. I can see he ain't havin such a good time, but what I'm gonna do about it? He don't want to see no plays, an the FAO Schwarz store bores him. I took him to the Metropolitan Museum of Art, an for a while, he seems interested in somethin looks like King Tut's tomb, but then he says it's all just a bunch of ole stuff, an we are on the street again.

I let him off at the apartment an gone back to the office. When Miss Hudgins brought me in another batch of papers to sign, I ast her what I oughta do.

"Well, maybe he'd like to see some famous people, you know?"

"Where I'm gonna find em?"

"Only place in town," she says, "Elaine's restaurant."

"What is that?" I ast.

"You gotta see it to believe it" was Miss Hudgins' answer.

*   *   *

So we went to Elaine's restaurant.

We go there at five o'clock sharp, account of that's the time most people have they supper, but Elaine's restaurant was deserted. It was not the sort of place I had expected; to say it is nothin fancy is a understatement. There was some waiters hangin around, an at the end of the bar was this big ole jolly-lookin lady doin paperwork. I figger her to be Elaine.

While little Forrest waited by the door, I gone over an introduced mysef, an tole her why I was there.

"Fine," Elaine says, "but you come a little early. Most folks don't start showin up here for another four or five hours."

"What? They eat someplace else an come in here later?" I ast.

"No, you dummy. They are all at cocktail parties or plays or openings or somethin. This is a late-night place."

"Well, you mind if we set down an have our food?"

"Go right ahead."

"Any idea which famous people will be showin up later?" I ast.

"It'll be the usual suspects, I guess. Barbra Streisand, Woody Allen, Kurt Vonnegut, George Plimpton, Lauren Bacall—who knows, maybe Paul Newman or Jack Nicholson's in town."

"They all come here?"

"Sometimes—but listen, there is one rule, and you can't violate it. There will be no goin over to these famous people's tables and disturbin them. No picture taking, no tape recording, no nothin. Now, you just sit right at that big round table. That's the 'family table,' an if any famous people come in that don't have other arrangements, I will put them there, an you can talk to them."

So that's what we did, little Forrest an me. We ate our supper an dessert an then a second dessert, but ain't but a handful of people have arrived at Elaine's. I could tell little Forrest was bored, but I figger this is my last chance to impress him with New York, an just about the time I see him squirmin to leave, the door opens an who should be comin in but Elizabeth Taylor.

After that, the place begun to fill up very fast. Bruce Willis an Donald Trump an Cher, the movie star. Sure enough, in comes George Plimpton with his friend, a Mister Spinelli, an the writer William Styron. Woody Allen arrives with a whole entourage, as does the writers Kurt Vonnegut an Norman Mailer an Robert Ludlum. They was all sorts of beautiful people, wearin expensive clothes an furs. I had read about some of them in the papers, an was tryin to explain who they was to little Forrest.

Unfortunately, all of them seem to have other plans, an are sittin with each other, an not with us. After a while, Elaine comes over an sets down, I guess so we do not feel too lonely.

"I guess it's a light night for bachelors," she says.

"Yup," I says. "But even if we can't talk to them, maybe you could tell us what they is talkin about with each other—just to give little Forrest an idea of what famous people talk about."

"Talk about?" says Elaine. "Well, the movie stars, they are talkin about themselves, I imagine."

"What about the writers?" I ast.

"Writers?" she says. "Huh. They are talkin about what they always talk about—baseball, money, and pieces of ass."

About this time the door open an a feller come in, an Elaine motions him over to the table to sit down.

"Mr. Gump, I want you to meet Tom Hanks," she says.

"Pleased to meet you," I say, an introduce him to little Forrest.

"I've seen you," little Forrest says, "on television."

"You an actor?" I ast.

"Sure am," Tom Hanks says. "What about you?"

So I tole him a little bit about my checkered career, an after he listened for a while, Tom Hanks says, "Well, Mr. Gump, you are sure a curious feller. Sounds like somebody ought to make a movie of your life's story."

"Nah," I says, "ain't nobody be interested in somethin stupid like that."

"You never know," says Tom Hanks. " 'Life is like a box of chocolates.' By the way, I just happen to have a box of chocolates right here—You wanna buy some?"

"Nah, I don't think so, I ain't big on chocolates—but thanks, anyhow."

Tom Hanks looks at me kinda funny. "Well, 'stupid is as stupid looks,' I always say." An at that, he gets up an goes to another table.

Next mornin, there is a serious disturbance at Ivan Bozosky's offices.

"Oh, my God! Oh, my God!" shouts Miss Hudgins. "They have arrested Mr. Bozosky!"

"Who have?" I ast.

"The police," she hollered. "Who else arrests people! They have taken him to jail!"

"What'd he do?"

"Insider trading!" she yelled. "They have accused him of insider trading!"

"But I am the president of the insider trading division," I says. "How come they didn't arrest me?"

"It ain't too late for that, bigshot." The voice belonged to a big ole ugly-lookin detective who was standin in the doorway. Behind him was two cops in uniforms.

"You just come along peaceful, now, an there won't be any trouble."

I done what he tole me, but his last line was pure bullshit.

So I am thowed in jail again. I might of known all this couldn't last forever, but I didn't expect there would be such a big deal about it all. Not only have they arrested Ivan Bozosky, but they have thowed Mike Mulligan in jail, too, an various other folks in the bidness. Miss Hudgins is also locked up as a "material witness." They give me one phone call to make, so I phoned little Forrest at the Helmsley an tole him I would not be home for supper. I just could not bring mysef to say his daddy was in the jug again.

Anyhow, Ivan, he is in the ajoinin cell to mine, an to my surprise, he is lookin rather chipper.

"Well, Gump, I believe the time has come for you to do your trained bear act," he says.

"Yeah, what is that?"

"Just what you did for Colonel North—lie, cover up, take the blame."

"For who?"

"For me, you stupo! Why in hell do you think I made you president of my insider trading division? Because of your brains and good looks? To take the heat, in case of something like this, is why I hired you."

"Oh," I says. I might of knowed there was a catch.

* * *

Over the next few days, I am interrogated by about a hundrit cops an lawyers an investigators for all sorts of financial agencies. But I don't tell em nothin. I just kep my big mouth shut, which pissed em off royally, but ain't nothin they can do. They is so many of them, I can't tell which is representin me an Mr. Bozosky an Mike Mulligan, an who is against us. Don't matter. I am quiet as a clam.

One day the jail guard come by, say I got a visitor. When I gone into the visitors room, sure enough, it was little Forrest.

"How'd you find out?" I ast.

"How could I not find out? It's been all over the papers and television. Folks are sayin it's the biggest scandal since Teapot Dome."

"Since who?"

"Never mind," he says. "Anyway, I finally got to meet Mrs. Helmsley, who you said was sposed to be so nice."

"Oh, yeah? She takin good care of you?"

"Sure—she thowed me out."

"Did what?"

"Thowed us out, bag and baggage, on the street. Said she don't feature no crook livin in her hotel."

"So how you gettin by?"

"I got a job washin dishes."

"Well, I got some money in the bank. There's a checkbook someplace in my stuff. You can use it to get a place to stay till you gotta go home. Might even be enough to make my bail outta here."

"Yeah, all right," he says. "Looks like you really done it this time, though."

In this, little Forrest seems correct.

* * *

After the bail was paid, I was free to go for the time bein. But not far. Me an little Forrest rented a walk-up flat in a neighborhood filled with criminals an beggars an ladies of the night.

Little Forrest was interested to know what I'm gonna do when the trial is helt an, to tell the truth, I dunno mysef. I mean, I was hired to take the fall, an there is a certain amount of honor in doin what you is sposed to do. On the other hand, it kinda don't seem fair for me to spend the rest of my life in the slammer just so's Ivan Bozosky an Mike Mulligan can go on livin the high life. One day, little Forrest pipes up with a request.

"You know, I wouldn't mind goin out to the Statue of Liberty again," he says. "I sort of enjoyed that trip."

So that's what we did.

We took the excursion boat out to the statue, an it was all pretty an gleamin in the afternoon sunshine. We stopped an read the inscription about the "huddled masses yearning to breathe free," an then we gone on up to the top of the torch, an looked out across the harbor at New York, with all the tall buildins that seemed like they go right on up into the clouds.

"You gonna rat them out, or what?" little Forrest ast.

"Rat who out?"

"Ivan Bozosky an Mike Mulligan."

"I dunno—Why?"

"Cause you better be thinkin about it an make a decision," he says.

"I been thinkin about it—I just don't know what to do."

"Rattin's not very nice," he says. "You didn't rat out Colonel North . . ."

"Yeah, an look where it got me—thowed in the can."

"Well, I took a lot of guff about that at school, but I'd o.
probably taken more if you'd finked on him."

In this, little Forrest is probly correct. I just stood there
on top of the Statue of Liberty, wonderin an thinkin—
which is not my specialty—an worryin, which is—ar
finally I shook my head.

"Sometimes," I says, "a man's got to do the righ
thing."

Anyways, the time for our trial has finally arrived. We is
herded into a big federal courtroom where the prosecutor is
a Mr. Guguglianti, who looks like he oughta be mayor or
somethin. He is all surly an unpleasant an address us like
we is axe murders, or worse.

"Your Honor, ladies and gentlemen of the jury," Mr
Guguglianti says, "these three men is the worst kinds of
criminals there is! They are guilty of stealing your money—
your money—personally . . . !"

An it goes on downhill from there.

He proceeds to call us crooks, thieves, liars, frauds, an
expect he would of called us assholes, too, if we had not
been in a courtroom.

Finally, when Mr. Guguglianti gets finished tar-an-
featherin us, it becomes our turn to defend ourselfs. First
witness to take the stand is Ivan Bozosky.

"Mr. Bozosky," our lawyer asts, "are you guilty o
insider trading?"

We are bein represented, incidentally, by the big old
New York law firm of Dewey, Screwum & Howe.

"I am absolutely, positively, one-hundrit-percent *inno-
cent,*" Mr. Bozosky says.

"Then if you did not do it, who did?" the lawyer asts

"Mr. Gump over there," Ivan says. "I hired him on a

hief of the insider trading division with instructions to put
an end to any insider trading, so as to improve my
company's reputation, an what does he do? He immediately
proceeds to be a crook . . ."

Ivan Bozosky goes on like this for a while, an paints a
pitcher of me, black as a beaver's butt. I am "totally
responsible" for all the deals, he says, an in fact, I have
totally kept them secret from him, so as to enrich mysef. His
line is that he knows nothin about anythin illegal.

"May God have mercy on his guilty soul" is the way
van Bozosky puts it.

Next, Mike Mulligan gets his turn. He testifies I phoned
him up with stock tips, but he has no idea that I am in the
know about insider tradin an so forth. By the time they are
finished, I figger my goose is cooked, an Mr. Guguglianti be
cowlin at me from his table.

At last it is my time to take the stand.

"Mr. Gump," says Mr. Guguglianti, "just what was
your line of work before you became president of the insider
trading division of Mr. Bozosky's company?"

"I was Goliath," I answers.

"You was what?"

"Goliath—you know, the giant man from the Bible."

"You stand reminded, Mr. Gump, that this is a court of
law. Do not fool with the law, Mr. Gump, or the law will fool
with you back—and that is a promise."

"I ain't kiddin," I says. "It was at Holy Land."

"Mr. Gump, are you some kind of a nut?"

At this, our lawyer jumps up. "Objection, Your Honor,
counsel is badgering the witness!"

"Well," says the judge, "he does sound sort of nutty—
claimin to be Goliath an all. I think I am gonna order a
psychiatric examination of Mr. Gump, here."

So that's what they did.

They took me away to a insane asylum or somepla
where the doctors come in an begun bongin me on
knees with little rubber hammers, which, of course, is
experience I have had before. Next they give me so
puzzles to work an ast me a lot of questions an give me a t
an, to end it off, they bonged me on the knees some m
with their hammers. After that, I am taken back to
witness stand.

"Mr. Gump," the judge say, "the psychiatrists' rep
on you was just what I expected. It says here that you ar
'certifiable idiot.' I overrule the objection! Counsel, you m
proceed!"

Anyhow, they gone on to ast me a bunch of questic
about what my role was in the insider tradin scam. Over
our table, Ivan Bozosky an Mike Mulligan are grinnin l
Cheshire cats.

I admitted to signin all the papers an to callin M
Mulligan from time to time, an that when I did, I did not t
him it was an insider tradin deal, but just a tip. Finally, N
Guguglianti says, "Well, Mr. Gump, it appears now that y
are just gonna confess that you, an you alone, are guilty
sin in this matter, an save the court all the trouble of pro
it—ain't that so?"

I just sat there for a minute or two, lookin around
courtroom. Judge is waitin with a expectant look on his fa
Mr. Bozosky an Mr. Mulligan is leanin back with they ar
folded across they chests, smirkin; an our lawyers be nod
they heads for me to go ahead an get it over with. Out in
gallery, I seen little Forrest lookin at me with a kinda pair
expression on his face. I figger he knows what I'm gonna
an that I gotta do it.

An so I sighs, an says, "Yup, I reckon you're right
am guilty. I am guilty of signin papers—but that's all."

"Objection!" shouts our lawyer.

"What grounds?" ast the judge.

"Well, er, we've just established that this man is a certified idiot. So how can he testify to what he was or was not guilty of?"

"Overruled," says the judge. "I want to hear what he's got to say."

An so I tole them.

I tole them the whole story—about how I was Goliath an about the riot at Holy Land, an about Mr. Bozosky gettin me out of havin to go back to jail an all his instructions about signin the papers an not to look at them, an how, after all, I am just a poor ole idiot that didn't know shit about what was goin on.

What it amounted to was, I ratted out on Mr. Bozosky an Mr. Mulligan.

When I done finished, pandemonium broke out in the courtroom. All the lawyers are on they feet hollerin objections. Newspaper reporters rushed out to the telephones. Ivan Bozosky an Mike Mulligan are jumpin up an down shoutin at the top of they lungs that I am a no good, dirty, double-crossin, ingrateful, lyin, squeeler. The judge be bangin his gavel for order, but ain't none to be found. I looked over at little Forrest an knowed right then an there I made the right decision. An I also decided that whatever else happens, I am not gonna take the fall for nobody, noplace, nomore—an that's that.

Like I said, sometimes a man's just gotta do the right thing.

Chapter Nine

For a while, it looked lik
was off the hook, but of course it turned out that was wro.

Not long after my testimony they carted Ivan Bozos
an Mike Mulligan off to prison. The judge, he thowed
book at them—literally—big ole law book, hit Bozos
square in the head. Next day, a knock come at my do
Standin there was two military police in shiny black helm
with billy clubs an armbands.

"You PFC Gump?" one says.

"That's my name."

"Well, you gotta come along with us, account of you
AWOL from the United States Army."

"AWOL," I says. "How can that be? I was in jail!"

"Yeah," he says, "we know all about that. But yo
hitch runs two more years—that's what you signed up
with Colonel North. We been lookin for you everplace ui
we seen you in the newspapers in this Bozosky trial."

The MP hands me a copy of the *New York Post*, wh
reads: **DULLARD RATS OUT ON HIGH-ROLLING FINANC**
MEN.

A man with an IQ described as "in the low 70s" yesterday finked on two of this newspaper's most popular subjects, resulting in their sentencing to lengthy prison terms.

Forrest Gump, who sources close to the Post described as being "dumber than a rock," testified before a federal judge in Manhattan that in his capacity as president of the insider trading division of Bozosky Enterprises, he had absolutely no knowledge of any insider trading at the company.

Gump, who has had an apparently checkered career as an encyclopedia salesman, inventor, animal refuse engineer, and sometime spy for the U.S. government, was not immediately available for comment. He was not convicted in the trial, which lasted several weeks.

"So what you gonna do with me?" I ast.

"They probly gonna put you in the stockade till hey figger out somethin," the MP says. About this ime, little Forrest come up behin me, tryin to see what's oin on.

"Who's this?" the MP ast. "This your boy?"

I didn't say nothin, an neither did little Forrest. He just lared at the MPs.

"You give me a minute with him?" I says. "I ain't gonna un off or nothin."

"Yeah, I reckon that'd be okay. We'll be outside here— ust don't do nothin funny."

Fact was, funny was not on my mind at this moment. I hut the door an set little Forrest down on the sofa.

"Look," I says, "them fellers come to take me back to he army, an I gotta go with em, you know? So's I want you to get a bus back home an be ready to start school whe opens. Okay?"

The little guy was starin at his shoes an not lookir me, but he nodded his head.

"I'm sorry about this," I says, "but that's just the v things go sometimes."

He nodded again.

"Look," I tole him, "I'm gonna try to work somet out. I'll talk to Colonel North. They ain't gonna keep me the stockade forever. I'll get this straightened out, an tl we'll make a plan."

"Yeah, right," he says. "You got a lot of great pla don't you?"

"Well, I made my mistakes. But somethin's gotta w out. I figger I've had my share of bad luck. It's about ti things start to break good."

He gets up an goes back to his room to start packin. the door, he turn aroun an looks at me for the first time

"Okay," he says. "You ever get out of the slammer, y look me up. An don't worry about it, hear? I'll be all rigł

An so I gone on with the MPs, feelin pretty low pretty alone. Little Forrest is a good-lookin, smart you man by now, an I done let him down again.

Well, just like the MPs said, when we got back Washington, they put me in the stockade—thowed in again. But ain't long afore they come an turn me loose.

When I got there, I done sent a note to Colonel Nor say I think I'm gettin a raw deal here. Couple of mon later, he stops by the stockade.

"Sorry about that, Gump, but there ain't much I do," he says. "I am no longer in the Marine Corps, an

retty busy these days watchin out for some of the Ayatolja's
riends who say they want to kill me. Besides, I'm thinkin
bout runnin for the U.S. Senate. I'll show them bastids
vhat contempt really is."

"Well, Colonel," I says, "that is all very nice, but what
bout me?"

"It's what you get for makin fools of Congress," he
ays. "See you aroun the stockade." An then he bust out
aughin. "You know what I mean?"

Anyhow, after a few more months on bread an water, I
m summoned to the post commander's office.

"Gump," he says, "you just stand at attention while I
ook over your files." After about half an hour, he says, "At
ase," an leans back in his chair. "Well, Gump, I see you
ave a very mixed record in this man's army. Win the
Congressional Medal of Honor, and then you go over the
ill. Just what kind of crapola is that?"

"Sir, I didn't go over the hill. I was in jail."

"Yeah, well that's just as bad. If it was up to me, I'd have
ou cashiered today with a bad-conduct discharge. But it
eems some of the brass don't cotton much to havin Medal
f Honor winners booted out of the service. Looks bad, I
uess. So we got to figger out what to do with you. Got any
uggestions?"

"Sir, if you let me out of the stockade, maybe I can go
n KP or somethin," I says.

"Not on your life, Gump. I read all about your KP
scapades right here in these files. Says here that one time
ou blew up a steam boiler tryin to make a stew or
omethin. Wrecked the mess hall. Cost the army an arm and
 leg. Nosiree—you ain't going anywhere near a mess hall
n my post."

Then he scratch his chin for a minute. "I think I got a

solution, Gump. I ain't got use for any troublemak
around here, so what I'm gonna do is, I'm gonna tran:
your big ass as far away as I possibly can, an the sooner
better. That is all."

An so I am transferred. The commander, he was
kiddin about transferrin me to the fartherest place away
could find. Next thing I know, I am assigned to a ar
weather station in Alaska—in January, no less. But at le
they begun payin me again, so's I can send home so
allotment money for little Forrest. Matter of fact, I done s
nearly all my pay home, account of what in hell I'm gor
spend it on up in Alaska? In January.

"I see by your files, Gump, that you have hac
somewhat checkered past in the service," says the lieuten
in charge of the weather station. "Just keep your nose cle
an they won't be any trouble."

In this, of course, he was wrong.

It was so cold in Alaska that if you went outside an s
somethin, your words would freeze themsefs in the air—
if you took a pee, it would wind up as a icicle.

My job was sposed to be readin weather maps an st
but after a few weeks, they figgered out I am a numbnuts,
give me the job of moppin the place clean an spit-shinin
toilets an so on. On my day off I'd go out ice-fishin, an
time I got chased by a polar bear an another time by a
ole walrus that ate up all the fish I'd caught.

We was in a little ole town there by the ocean where
the people spent most of they time gettin drunk—Exkir
included. The Exkimos was very nice people, except wl
they got drunk an had harpoon-thowin contests in
street. Then, it could be dangerous to be out an about.

One time after a couple of months, I went with some of
ιe other fellers into town on a Saturday night. I really
idn't much want to go, but in fact I had not been anyplace
ιuch, an so I gone along, for the ride, so to speak.

We got to a place called the Gold Rush Saloon an went
ιside. They was all sorts of activity there—folks be drinkin
ιn fightin an gamblin, an a striptease artist was doin her
ιing on the bar. Sorta made me think of Wanda's strip
ιint, down in New Orleans, an I figgered I probly should
rop her a postcard sometime. Also got me to thinkin about
ιe Wanda the pig, little Forrest's pet, an how she was doin,
ιn then, of course, I got to thinkin about little Forrest hissef.
ιut since thinkin ain't exactly my strong point, I decided to
ιke action. I gone out into the street to buy little Forrest a
ιesent.

It is about seven P.M. but the sun is shinin bright as can
ιe up here near the North Pole, an all the stores is open.
ιost of em, however, is saloons. There wadn't no depart-
ιent store around, so's I gone on into a novelty shop where
ιey is peddlin everthin from gold nuggets to eagle feathers,
ιut finally I seen what I wanted to get for little Forrest. A
ιenuine Alaska Indian totem pole!

It was not one of them big ole ten-feet-tall totem poles,
ιut it was about three feet, anyway, an was carved with
ιagle's beaks an faces of stern-lookin Indians an bear's paws
ιn all, an painted pretty bright colors. I ast the feller at
ιe counter how much, an he says, "For you army grunts I
ιake a special price—one thousan, two hundrit, and six
ιollars."

"Damn," I says. "What'd it cost before the discount?"

"For me to know an you to find out" was his reply.

Well, anyhow, I stood there figgerin that it is gettin late
ιn I don't know when I'm gonna get back into town an little
ιorrest probly need to hear from me, so I dug down deep

into my pocket for what was left of my paychecks an bo
the totem pole.

"Could you ship it down to Mobile, Alabama?" I

"Sure, for another four hundrit dollars," he says.
who was I to argue? After all, we are within spittin dist
of the top of the world, so's I dug down again an coughe
the money, figgerin wouldn't have nothin much to sper
on up here anyhow.

I ast him if I could send a note with it, an he says, "S
but notes are another fifty bucks."

But I thought, what the hell, this is a genuine anti
Alaska Indian totem pole, an I am already gettin a bar
So's I wrote the note, which said this:

> Dear little Forrest,
>
> I spose you been wonderin what has become of me
> up here in Alaska. Well, I have been workin very hard at
> a very important job with the United States Army an
> have not had much time to write. I am sendin you a
> totem pole to fool with. The Indians here say they is
> very sacred objects, so you should put it someplace
> important to you. I hope you is doin well in school an
> mindin your grandma.
>
> Love . . .

Well, I started to put "Love, Dad," but he ain't n
called me that, so I just put my name. I figgered he just
to figger out the rest.

Anyhow, time I got back to the bar my guys
proceeded to get drunk. I was just settin at the bar nurs
beer when I noticed a feller in a chair all slumped ov
table. I could only see half his face, but somehow he loc
familiar, an I gone on over an walked aroun him a coup

imes, an lo an behole, if it ain't Mister McGivver from the
pig-shit farm!

I raised up his head an sort of shook him awake. At first
he don't recognize me, which is understandable, account of
there is a mostly empty quart of gin on the table. But then a
light sort of come on in his eyes an he jumps up an give me a
big hug. I figger he is gonna be real mad at me for lettin the
pig shit blow up, but in fact, he ain't.

"Don't worry yourself, my boy," Mister McGivver says.
"It was all probably a blessing in disguise anyway. I never
dreamed the pig-shit operation would get that big, but once
it did, I was under such pressure to keep up with things, it
probably was taking years off my life. Maybe you even did
me a favor."

As it turns out, of course, Mister McGivver has lost
everthin. When the pig-shit farm blowed up, the towns-
people an the environmental people shut him down an ran
him out of town. Next, because he had borrowed so much
money to build the pig-shit-fueled ships, the banks fore-
closed on him an thew him out of bidness entirely.

"But that's all right, Forrest," he says. "The sea was my
first love anyway. I didn't have any business being an
executive or a magnate. Why, hell, right now I'm doing
exactly what I want to."

When I ast him what was that, he tole me.

"I am a ship's captain," he says proudly. "Got me a
big ole ship out in the harbor right now. You want to see
it?"

"Well, I gotta get back to the weather station in a while;
is it gonna take long?"

"No time at all, my boy, no time at all."

In this, Mister McGivver was never more wrong in his
life.

*   *   *

We gone on out to his ship in a launch. At first I thou
the launch was the ship, but when we finally got ther
couldn't believe my eyes. The ship is so big that from
distance it looks like a mountain range! It is about half a m
long an twenty stories high.

Exxon-Valdez is the ship's name.

"Climb aboard," Mister McGivver shouts. It is cold a
well digger's ass, but we climbed up the ladder an gone o
the ship's bridge. Mister McGivver pulls out a big bottle
scotch an offers me a drink, but since I gotta get back to
weather station, I turn it down. He proceeds to drink
hissef, no ice, no water, just straight in the glass, an
talked over ole times for a while.

"Ya know, Forrest, there's one thing I'd have given a
of money to see," he says, "that is, if I'd had any."

"What's that?"

"The expressions on those bozos' faces when the
shit blew up."

"Yessir," I says, "it was kinda a sight."

"By the way," Mister McGivver says, "what ever h
pened to that sow I gave little Forrest—what'd you
her?"

"Wanda."

"Yeah, she was a nice pig. Smart pig."

"She's at the National Zoo in Washington."

"Really? Doing what?"

"In a cage. They are showin her off."

"Well, I'll be damned," he says. "A monument to
our folly."

After a little while, it become apparent to me t
Mister McGivver is drunk again. In fact, he is not o
drunk, he is reelin. At one point he reeled over to the s
control panels an begun turnin on switches an pullin lev

an knobs. Suddenly, the *Exxon-Valdez* begun to shudder an tremble. Somehow, Mister McGivver had turned on the engine.

"Wanna go for a little spin?" he ast.

"Well, ah, thanks," I says, "but I gotta get back to the weather station. I'm on duty in a hour or so."

"Nonsense!" says Mister McGivver. "This won't take but a few minutes. We'll just go out in the sound for a little spin."

By now, he is lurchin an stumblin an tryin to put the *Exxon-Valdez* in gear. He grapped hold of the wheel an when it begin to turn he follered with it—right down onto the floor. Then he begun to jabber.

"Hoot, mon!" Mister McGivver shouts. "I think I'm about four sheets to the wind! *Arrr*, me buckoes, we be forty leagues from Portobello! Run out the guns! You've a bit of the animal in you, young Jim—Long John Silver's my name—What's yours . . . ?"

Shit like that. Anyhow, I got ole Mister McGivver up off the floor, an about that time a sailor come onto the bridge, must of heard the commotion.

"I think Mister McGivver's had one too many," I says. "Maybe we oughta take him to his cabin."

"Yeah," say the sailor, "but I seen him a lot drunker."

"It's the Black Spot for you, laddie buck!" shouts Mister McGivver. "Old Blind Pew knows the score. Hoist up the Jolly Roger! You'll all walk the plank!"

Me an the sailor carried Mister McGivver to his bunk an laid him down. "I'll keelhaul the lot of you" is the last thing Mister McGivver says.

"Say," the sailor ast, "you know why Captain McGivver turned on the engines?"

"Nope—I don't know nothin. I'm with the weather station."

"What!" says the sailor. "Hell, I thought you were th
bar pilot!"

"Me, no. I am a private in the army."

"Greatgodamighty!" he says. "We got ten million ga
lons of crude oil on board!" An he runs out the door.

It was apparent I could not do nothin for Mist
McGivver, account of he is asleep—if that's what you wa
to call it. So I gone on back to the bridge. Nobody is there a
the ship seems to be sailin along, buoy markers an things t
passin us at top speed. I didn't know what else to do, so
grapped the ship's wheel an tried to steer us at least in
straight direction. We had not gone too far when sudden
there is a great big bump. I am figgerin this is good, since th
Exxon-Valdez has finally stopped. Turns out, though, it is nc

All of a sudden, it seems like there is about a hundr
people runnin around on the bridge, everbody hollerin a
screamin an givin each other orders, an some of them eve
be givin each other the finger. Not long afterward, son
fellers from the Coast Guard come aboard, complainin v
has just dumped ten million gallons of crude awl into Prin
William Sound. Birds, seals, fish, polar bears, whales, a
Exkimos—all will be destroyed by what we has now don
An there is gonna be hell to pay.

"Who was in charge on this bridge?" says a Coa
Guard officer.

"*He* was!" everbody on the bridge shouted at once,
pointin they fingers right at me.

I knowed right then that I am in the doghouse for su

MANIAC ARMY MAN AT HELM OF DISASTER SHIP, sa
one of the headlines. **CERTIFIED NUT DRIVING OIL SPI
BOAT**, says another. **CATACLYSM CAUSED BY DANGERO
FOOL**; this is typical of the kind of shit I got to endure.

In any case, they sent up a three-star general from Washington to deal with me an my problems. In a way this is sort of lucky, since the army does not wish to get involved in any sense with the blame for the *Exxon-Valdez* mess, an the best thing they can do is get me the hell out of there—quick.

"Gump," the general says, "if it was up to me, I would have you before a firing squad for this, but since it isn't, I am gonna do the next best thing, which is to have your big stupid ass transferred as far away from here as possible, which, in this case, is to Berlin, Germany. Maybe, if we are lucky, nobody is gonna be able to find you there, and so they'll have to put all the blame on old Captain McGivver for this disaster. Do you read me?"

"Yessir," I says, "but how I'm gonna get there?"

"The plane, Gump, is on the runway. Its motors are running. You got five minutes."

Chapter Ten

Goin to Germany was not all it was cracked up to be. This was account of I was escorted there in handcuffs an leg irons by four MPs who kept remindin me that their orders was, if I done anythin funny, they was to immediately crack me over the head with their nightsticks.

Somebody high up in command had apparently given the order that I was to be assigned the dirtiest job in the entire army, an the order was faithfully carried out. I was sent to a tank company, where my duty was to clean all the mud off the tank treads—an let me say this: There is plenty of mud on the tank tracks in Germany in the winter.

Also, word had apparently got out that I am a Jonah or somethin, cause ain't nobody wants to speak to me except the sergeants, an all they do is holler at me. The days are cold an wet, an the nights are miserable, an I ain't never felt so lonely. I wrote some letters to little Forrest, but his answers are kind of short an I get the impression maybe he is sort of forgettin me. Sometimes at night, I tried to dream about Jenny but it ain't no use. Looks like she done forgot about me, too.

One day somebody tole me I am getting a helper to clean the tank treads an I gotta show him the ropes. I gone on out to the motor pool an they is a feller standin there starin down at a tread got about a hundrit pounds of mud on it.

"Say, you the new guy?" I ast.

When he turn around, I almost fainted dead away! It is ole Sergeant Kranz from Vietnam an the army base where me an Mister McGivver collected the garbage for our pigs! Cept I noticed right away, Sergeant Kranz, he ain't a sergeant major no more—he is only a buck private.

"Oh, no" is the first thing out of his mouth when he sees me.

It seems that Sergeant Kranz blames me for the misfortune of being busted from sergeant-major to private, though even a moron like me can see he is stretchin things a bit.

What had happened was this: After me an Mister McGivver got out of the pig bidness, Sergeant Kranz decided that the army could actually *sell* their garbage to pig farmers all over the area, an after a while they had so much money they didn't know what to do with it. So he suggested they use it to build a new officers' club, an the general was so pleased with this he put Sergeant Kranz in charge of buildin the new club.

On the day of the grand openin, they had a big celebration, with bands an free drinks an all, an to cap it off at the end of the evenin, they had hired a striptease dancer all the way from Australia to do her thing on the stage. Said she was not only the best stripper in Australia, she was the best stripper in the *world*.

Anyhow, the officers' club was mobbed so's you could

barely see the stripper, an at some point the general hiss
got up on a table in the back of the room to get a better loc
However, it seems Sergeant Kranz has installed the ceil
fans about a foot lower than normal, an when the gener
stands up on the table, it got him in the head. Scalped hir
just like a Indian might do.

The general was furious, hollerin an yellin about "Hc
am I gonna explain this to my wife?" An, of course, l
blames Sergeant Kranz an has him busted on the spot ₁
sent here, to the dirtiest job in the army.

"I was one of the first black soldiers to make it to the tc
of the enlisted ranks in this man's army," he says, "but
seems like ever time I get around you, Gump, there is son
kind of shit fixin to go on."

I tell him I'm sorry, but that it don't exactly seem fair
blame me for what happened.

"Yeah, probly you're right, Gump. It's just that I put
twenty-eight years of a thirty-year hitch, only to find mys
spendin my final time as a buck private," he says. "Som
body got to be responsible—that's the way it is in the arm
Couldn't of been me, else how do you explain that I worke
my way up to the highest enlisted rank in the army?"

"Maybe you was just lucky," I says. "I mean, at lea
you got to be a sergeant for a long time. Me, I have alwa
been at the bottom of the shit heap."

"Yeah," he says, "maybe so. Anyway, it don't matt
anymore, I guess. An besides, it was almost worth it."

"What was?" I ast.

"Seein the fan give that old bastid a flattop," he say

Anyhow, me an Sergeant Kranz have got our work c
out for us. Seems like the division is always on maneuve
an the mud is two feet deep. We are scrapin an hoein

shovelin an hosin mud from daylight to dark. When we get back to the barracks, we is too dirty to let inside, an they make us hose off in the cold.

Sergeant Kranz, when he talks at all, mostly talks about Vietnam, which, for some reason, he remembers fondly.

"Yeah, Gump, them was the good old days," he says. "A real war—not this police-action crap they got goin for us now. Man, we had tanks and howitzers and bombers could sure bring down a load of pee on the enemy."

"Seems like they brought down a load of pee on us, too, sometimes," I say.

"Yeah, well, that the way it is. In war, people are gonna get killed. That's why it's called a war."

"I never kilt nobody," I says.

"What! How you know that?"

"Well, I don't think I did. I never done fired my weapon but once or twice, an then it was just at bushes or somethin."

"That ain't nothin to be proud of, Gump. In fact, you oughta be ashamed of yoursef."

"Well, what about Bubba?" I ast.

"What about him? Who was that?"

"My friend. He got kilt."

"Oh, yeah, I remember now—the one you went out after. Well, he probably done somethin stupid."

"Yeah," I says, "like joinin the army."

It went on like that day after day. Sergeant Kranz was not the most interestin person to talk to, but at least he was somebody. Anyway, I was beginnin to believe I would never get off the mud detail, when one day somebody come up an say the post commander wants to see me. They hosed me down an I went up to headquarters.

"Gump, I understand you played a little football at one time. That so?" the commander asts.

"Yeah, a little," I says.

"Tell me about it."

An so I did. An when I get finished, the commander says, "Greatgodamighty!"

At least, I ain't got to clean tanks all day no more. Unfortunately, I have now got to clean them all *night*. But durin the day, I play football for the post team, Swagmier Sour Krauts, we is called.

The Sour Krauts is not a very good football team, to say the least. We was 0 for 11 last year, an 0 for 3 so far this season. Kinda remind me of the old Ain'ts, back in New Orleans. Anyhow, the quarterback is a little wiry guy called Pete, played a little ball in high school. He is fast an slippery an thows the ball okay, but he ain't no Snake, that is for sure. The post commander is of course unhappy about our record, an makes sure we get in a lot of practice. Like about twelve hours a day. An after that, I gotta go back an clean tanks till about three A.M., but it's all right by me—at least it keeps my mind off other things. Also, they has made Sergeant Kranz—oops, *Private* Kranz—the team manager.

Our first football game is against the steam heat company of the post in Hamburg. They are a dirty, filthy lot, an bite an scratch an cuss the whole game, but I runned over most of them, an at the end it is 45 to 0, our way. It was like that the next three games, too, an so we are now ahead of ourselfs for the first time in memory. The commander is beside hissef an to everybody's amazement, he give us a Sunday off, so's we can go into town.

It is a nice little ole town, with ole buildins an little cobblestone streets an gargoyles on the winder sills. Everbody in town be speakin German, about which none of us understands nothin. The extent of my German is *"ja."*

Immediately, of course, the guys found a beer hall, an before long is swillin down huge glasses of beer, served by waitresses wearin German smocks. It is so good to be off post an around civilians that I even had a beer mysef—even if I couldn't understand a word anybody around us had to say.

We was in the beer hall a number of hours, an I think we are startin to get rowdy, account of there is a bunch of German guys sort of glarin at us from the other end of the room. They is mutterin stuff at us, such as *affenarschs* an *scheissbolles*, but we do not understand them, an so go on about our bidness. After a while, one of our fellers puts his hand on the ass of one of the waitresses. It is not that she minded it so much, but it seems the German guys did. Couple of em come over to our table an begun to say a bunch of stuff real loud.

"Du kannst mir mal en den Sac fassen!" says one of the German fellers.

"Huh?" says our right tackle, whose name is Mongo.

The German guy repeated hissef, an Mongo, who is about ten feet tall, just set there lookin puzzled. Finally, one of our guys who understood a little German says to Mongo, "Whatever it was, I don't think it was very nice."

Mongo stood up an face the German. "Whatever you want, pal, we ain't buyin it—so why don't you shove off."

German ain't buyin it neither. *"Scheiss,"* he says.

"What's that?" ast Mongo.

"It is somethin to do with shit," our feller says.

Well, that was it. Mongo grapped up the German feller an thowed him through a winder. All the other Germans come racin over, an a big ole brawl commenced. People be pokin an gougin an bitin an shoutin. Waitress be screamin an chairs be flyin. It was just like the good ole times back at Wanda's strip joint in New Orleans.

A feller was about to crack me over the head with a beer bottle when I felt somebody grap my wrist an pull me back. It was one of the waitresses, done decided to hep me get out of there. She pulled me to a back doorway, an nex thing I knowed, we was outside. In the distance, I heard the sirens of a police car, an figgered that this time, at least, I am gonna get away from here so as not to wind up back in jail. The waitress is a nice-lookin German girl an she leads me down a side street, away from the commotion. Gretchen is her name.

Gretchen don't speak much English, but we kind of communicated by hand an arm signals, me smilin an sayin *ja* an her tryin to tell me somethin in German. Anyhow, we walked for a long time, right out of the village an up onto some pretty hills outside of town. Little yellow flowers be bloomin an they is snow-covered mountain peaks in the distance, an down below, the valley is all green an dotted with little houses. In the distance, I think I hear somebody yodelin. Gretchen pointed to me an ast my name, an I tell her.

"*Ja*," she says. "Forrest Gump is nice name."

After a while, we got up to a pretty meadow an set down, takin in the scenery. They is some sheep in the meadow an away across the valley the sun is beginnin to set in the Alps. You can look down an see a river from here that is shinin in the afternoon sun, an it is so peaceful an beautiful it makes you want to stay here forever.

Gretchen an me, we is findin it a little easier to communicate. She gets across that she is from *East* Germany, which has been captured by the Russians who have built a big ole wall to keep the people from leavin. But Gretchen somehow managed to escape an has been workin as a waitress for about five years, hopin that one day she can get her family out of East Germany an over here, where they do not put you inside a wall. I tried to tell Gretchen some of my story, but I am not sure it is gettin across. That don't matter, though, account of we seems to be gettin to be friends anyhow. At one point, she took hold of my hand again an give it a squeeze, an before it was over with, she done put her head on my shoulder while we just set there, watchin the end of the day.

Over the next few months we played a lot of football. We played some fellers from the navy an some from the air force an a lot more from the army. I used to get Gretchen to come to some of the games when we was playin close to home. She didn't seem to understand much about it, an mostly what she said was "*ach!*" but it didn't matter. It was just sort of nice to have her around. In a way, I guess it was a good thing we didn't speak the same language, account of she would of probly found out what a stupo I am, an gone her own way.

One day I gone into the village, an me an Gretchen is walkin down the street an I tole her I wanted to buy some kind of present for little Forrest. She is delighted an says she would like to help. We gone into a bunch of shops, an Gretchen is showin me a bunch of stuff like little tin soldiers an wooden toy tractors, but I had to tell her little Forrest was actually not all that little anymore. Finally, I seen what I thought he'd like.

It was a great big ole German ooompa horn, all shiny brass an everthin, just like the kind they played down to the beer hall on Saturday nights.

"But, Forrest," she says, "that's too expensive. Yo
don't have that kind of money on a private's salary in yo
army. I know this."

"Well," I says, "I guess it don't matter. See, I don't g
to spend much time with little Forrest, an the way I got
figgered, if I can give him some nice presents, he wor
forget me."

"*Ach*, Forrest," Gretchen says, "this is not the way. I
bet if you just wrote him nice long letters two or three tim
a week, he'd appreciate it more—more than a big o
ooompapa horn, anyway."

"Maybe so," I answered. "But, see, letter writin air
my specialty. I mean, I kinda know what I want to say, bu
just can't seem to get it out on paper. I guess you could s
I'm better 'in person,' you know what I mean?"

"*Ja*, Forrest, I think so, but *ach* this ooompapa horn
eight hundred of your dollars."

"It don't matter," I says. "I been savin up."

So I gone an bought the ooompa horn. In a way, I got
bargin with it, account of the shopkeeper din't charge me f
the note I sent with it. Wadn't much of a note anyhow. Ju
about the same thing as before, cept I tole little Forres
kinda missed him, an would be home soon. Turned out, th
last was just more bullshit from me.

Anyhow, by the end of the season the Sour Krauts is
an 3, an we is up for the All Army Championships, down
Berlin. Sergeant Kranz is beside hissef, sayin that we
finally gonna get off the tank-cleanin detail if we can ju
win this one more game. Me, I am not too sure.

Finally, the big day come. Night before, I have got c
for a while to go into the village an see Gretchen. She

waitin tables at the beer hall when I arrive, an after servin a big tray of beer, she takes a break an holds my hand.

"I am so glad you came tonight," she says. "I have been missing you, Forrest."

"Yeah, me, too," I says.

"I am thinking," she says, "that we might go on a picnic tomorrow. I have got the day off."

"Well, I'd like to, but I gotta play football."

"*Ach!*"

"But I was wonderin, could you come to the game? It is in Berlin."

"Berlin? But it is a long way."

"I know," I says, "but they got a bus, you know, to carry down some of the wives an stuff. I think I can get you on it."

"*Ach!*" Gretchen says. "This American football, I do not understand. But if you want me to go, Forrest, then I will go."

An so that's what we did.

It was in a big ole field next to the Berlin Wall where we played the All Army Championship game. Our opponents was the Wiesbaden Wizards from the intelligence section of the Third Armored Division, an let me tell you, they was smart.

We was bigger an faster, but them intelligence fellers was craftier. First, they unloaded a Statue of Liberty play on us. Ain't nobody on our side ever seen a Statue of Liberty play, an they scored a touchdown.

Next, they roll out a Tackle Eligible play, an pretty soon the score is fourteen to zip, their way. Everbody, includin Sergeant Kranz, is lookin glum.

In the second half, the Wiesbaden Wizards don
thowed a combination stunt-blitz on defense an get u
backed up to our own two yard line on fourth down. What i
worse, our punter got his knee wrenched, an so is out of th
game. In the huddle, somebody say, "Who is gonna kick th
ball?"

"Don't look at me," I says, but everbody be lookin a
me anyway.

"But I ain't never kicked the ball before," I says.

"Don't matter, Gump," somebody say. "We is getti
the hell beat out of us, an if they is gonna be a scapegoat,
might as well be you. You is on everbody's shit list already
anyhow."

An so that's what happened. I done backed up into ou
end zone, an all of a sudden the center, he centers me th
ball. But somehow, the Wiesbaden Wizards done sut
marined under all our whole defensive line an appear in m
backfield, almost like ghosts. I was fixin to kick, but I de
cided it was better to try to get some more room, so
begun to run around. I run back an forth in the end zone
don't know how many times an probably gained a hundr
yards cept, of course, it was goin the wrong way. Finally,
found a little spare room before the Wiesbaden Wizard
caught up with me, an gave the ball the biggest kick I coul
I stood there an watched the ball sail into the air. So di
everbody else. It sailed so high, it went right out of sigh
They said later they had never seen a kick like that.

Unfortunately, though, it sailed off the playin field rigl
over the Berlin Wall an disappeared to the other side. Nov
we got a problem. Everbody be lookin at me in disgust a
pointin they fingers an hollerin an cussin at me.

"All right, Gump," somebody say, "now you gotta g
get our ball back."

"What? You mean climb over the wall?" I ast.

"How else you gonna get it back, you dummy?"

So that's what I did.

Couple of fellers give me a boost, an over the wall I went. I landed on the other side an looked up where they was a bunch of East German soldiers up in towers, all mannin machine guns. I runned right past them, an ain't none of them done a thing, I guess account of they ain't never seen nobody tryin to get *in* to they country—they was there to shoot the people tryin to get *out*.

Suddenly, I become aware of a huge ruckus, sound like from about a hundrit thousan people, which was comin from where I figgered the ball had landed. Turns out, I had caused some serious trouble.

What was goin on on this side of the Berlin Wall from where our football game was, was the World Cup Finals of the game of soccer. In fact, it was the last two minutes of the game between East Germany an Russia, an they was people from all over the world done come to see it.

These people, the Europeans especially, take their soccer very seriously.

When I got into the soccer stadium, I could not immediately figger out what was goin on, but it did not look good. What had happened, though, was this: East Germany was about to score a goal an take the lead from the Russians, when I kicked my football. The German player had dribbled his soccer ball downfield an was right at the Russian goalpost when my football bounced in front of him. Since he did not expect this, he became sort of confused an kicked my football right into the Russian goal, instead of his soccer ball. At first, all the Germans went crazy, account of they had scored a goal an won the game.

But then word come from the referee that it was not the right ball that was kicked in the goal an the score was no good, an then the whistle blowed an the Russians done tied the game. They was a lot of bewilderment by the Germans, followed by disorder, an when I come on the field an ast for my ball back, it seemed like the whole place erupted into pandemonium. They spilled out of the stands onto the field, shoutin stuff at me like, *"Du schwanzgesicht scheissbolle Susse!"* an a bunch of other stuff like that, which was apparently not very nice.

Now, I don't know what you'd do if you saw a hundri thousan pissed-off German soccer fans runnin at you, but I turned around an hauled ass. I run right past the tower guards again, an this time they took a few potshots at me, I expect just to keep me honest. Finally, I begun to scramble over the wall just as the mob got to me. With all them thousans of people there, I reckon the tower guards didn' know exactly what to do, so they didn't do nothin—jus stood there lookin puzzled. I was almost over the wall when somebody grapped the football pants I was wearin an begun to haul me down, but account of I was almost over, they only pulled off my pants.

I dropped on the other side, but a bunch of angry Germans done climbed over after me, an begun chasin me aroun our football field. Then more Germans begun climbin over the wall, an a bunch of the others, I reckon in a effort to get at me, begun tearin chunks out of the wall. Pretty soon it was apparent they was gonna tear down the whole Berlin Wall, just in order to catch me.

All our people was just standin there, kinda astonished lookin, when I run past the post commander, wearin nothin but a jockstrap.

"Gump, you idiot!" he shouts. "They warned me about you! What is the meaning of this? You have caused some kind of international incident!"

In this, he was correct, but I didn't have no time to think about that now! Sergeant Kranz, he was poundin hissef o

he knee with his fist an was all gray in the face an hollerin
somethin about us bein put on "permanent tank-tread
duty," when I caught sight of Gretchen, up in the stands.

She waved for me to come up there, an then she took
me by the hand an dragged me into the street.

"I don't know what you have done, Forrest, but I will
tell you this—they are tearing down the Berlin Wall, and for
the first time in thirty years our country will not be divided.
Perhaps I can even see again my own family, *ja?*"

Well, Gretchen an me, we hid in a alley for a while, an
then she took me to a house of some of her friends, which
was kinda embarrassin, considerin my dress. But they was
all excited, account of the television was showin the East
Germans tearin down the big ole Berlin Wall an dancin in
the streets an everthin. They seemed to have forgot about
me costin em the World Cup soccer match, an everbody was
happy an kissin an huggin each other.

Anyhow, Gretchen an me, we spent the night with each
other for the first time, an for some reason, I didn't feel
guilty afterwards. I kinda half expected Jenny to show up
again, an when I was walkin down the hall to the bathroom,
I sort of felt like she was watchin me, but she never did show
hersef.

Chapter Eleven

Wellsir, Gretchen an n
caught a train back to Oogamooga or whatever it is that v
lived, an when I got to the post, a surprise was in store f
me. The post commander done took me off tank trea
cleanin duty an put me on permanent latrine duty, right o
of *No Time for Sergeants*.

He is furious because, as he say, what I have done
probably put him out of a job.

"Gump, you moron," shouts the post commander, "c
you realize what has happened because of your screw-up
The Germans have torn down their wall and no
everbody's talkin about the end of communism!

"Just look at what *The New York Times* has to say abo
this!" he hollers, and hands me the paper.

DIMWIT SECURES END OF COLD WAR, says the hea
line.

The New York Times

What was apparently an accidental football punting mistake has led to what some experts believe will be the end of the nearly fifty-year-long breach between the East and West.

Sources told the Times that a U.S. Army private named Forrest Gump allegedly miskicked a football during an interservice playoff game in Germany, yesterday, which sailed across the Berlin Wall and landed in midfield on East German territory during the final seconds of the World Cup soccer match between East Germany and the Soviet Union.

The sources said that Mr. Gump then scaled the wall to retrieve the errant football, which had by that time created a disturbance in the soccer match. Irate soccer fans, estimated at 85,000 to 100,000 strong, then proceeded to chase Mr. Gump, with the apparent intention of doing him bodily harm.

Mr. Gump, who has been described as mentally retarded, fled back to the wall and began to climb over into West German territory. Sources said the soccer fans, in their efforts to apprehend Mr. Gump, pursued him across the wall and in the process began to dismantle the barrier which has stood as a symbol of Communist oppression for several decades.

Subsequently, joyous Berliners of all political persuasions joined hands in tearing down the wall and ultimately held what sources described as "the world's largest free-floating street party and beer bash."

In the confusion, Mr. Gump apparently escaped unharmed.

The final score of the East Berlin–Soviet Union soccer match was a 3 to 3 tie. The score of the American football game at the time of its disruption was not immediately available.

"Gump, you numbnuts," the post commander says, we got no more communism, we got no more reason to be

here! Even the goddamn Russians are talkin about givin
communism! Who in hell are we gonna fight if we ain't g
the communists to fight? You have rendered this whole arr
superfluous! Now they will send our asses home to sor
godforsaken post in Palookaville and we will lose the b
duty we could of dreamed of, which is right here in a quai
village in the German Alps! Gump, you have destroyed
soldier's dream—you must be out of your mind!"

He goes on like that for a while, poundin on his desk
thowin shit around the headquarters, but I get the drift
what his argument is, an it ain't doin much good to arg
with it. Anyway, I gone on down to the latrine an assum
my new duties, which is to constantly scrub ever tile with
toothbrush an some bathroom cleanser. Sergeant Kranz, 1
his association with me, is given the task of wipin up behin
me with Spic and Span, an he is none too happy about th
neither.

"We never had it so good, cleanin them tank treads"
the way he puts it.

Once a week, on Sundays, I get a pass to go into tow
but the post commander have ordered two MPs to escort r
everwhere I go, an to not let me out of their sight. This,
course, makes it somewhat hard for me to have a dece
relationship with Gretchen, but we done the best we cou
It was now generally too cold to go on picnics up in t
mountains, as the Alps become chilly in the winter. Most
the time, we gone into the beer hall an set at a table an j
held hands while the MPs was glarin at us from nearby

Gretchen is really a nice person, an does not wish
spend the rest of her life as a beer maid, but she don't kn
what else to do. She is very beautiful, but say she thin
life's done pretty much passed her by.

"I am too old to be a model," she says, "*und* too you

give up on everything else. Maybe I'll go to university. I
ant to make something of myself."

"Yeah," I says, "that would be good. I went to the
niversity once."

"*Ja*, Forrest? *Und* what did you study?"

"Football," I says.

"*Ach!*"

Good things, as my mama Gump used to say, are not
neant to last forever, an this was no exception.

It wadn't before too long when the post commander
alled us all to the parade ground, an made an announce-
nent.

"Men, there is the good news and the bad news."

At this, they was some low mumblin from the troops.

"The bad news," he says, "is for those of you cowards
rho are just drawin your pay and do not wish to perform
our duties as soldiers."

They was some more mumblin.

"The good news is, for those of you who wish to start
illin an dyin—which, if you din't know, is your bidness—
ou are gonna be afforded ever opportunity—thanks to
ome sombitch called Saddamn Hussein, who is the A-rab
1 charge of Iraq, an who has now started a war with our
wn commander-in-chief, the United States of America
'resident George Herbert Walker Bush."

At this, some of the mumblin turned to cheerin.

"And," the commander says, "we are all gonna go over
) Iraq an whip his heathen ass!"

So that's what we did.

*   *   *

The night before we left I got a pass to go see Gretch
for a last time. She has just saved up enough money to en
the university, an in fact is takin her first classes. I wai
outside the schoolroom for her to come out.

"Oh, Forrest," she says, "it is so wonderful! I a
studying English!"

We helt hands an walked for a while, an then I tole l
what was goin on. She didn't scream or carry on or noth
she just hugged my arm tighter an said she figgered t
kind of thing would happen one day.

"All my life," Gretchen says, "I have learned not
depend on good things happening, but I still always hc
they will. One day you will come back, *ja*?"

"*Ja*," I tole her, but I didn't know if it was the truth
not. After all, things don't seem to work out too good in
life, neither.

"When you come back," Gretchen says, "I will
speaking English as well as you."

"*Ja*," I says.

Anyhow, next mornin we left Germany.

First, we loaded up all our stuff, which was tanks
self-propelled guns an things, an flowed off to Saudi Arat
When we arrived there, our division was eighteen thous
strong. Added to the rest of our army, we is about a milli
against twice as many A-rabs, which our leader, Gene
Norman Scheisskopf, says should make for a fair fight.

Saddamn an his A-rab army are occupyin the li
country of Kuwait, which was known mostly for havir
bunch of awl wells. Matter of fact, they was enough awl
Kuwait to run the entire United States of America for
years—which I spose was why we is here. We is fixin
thow them out, so's we can keep the awl.

The one thing that stood out in my mind about Saudi rabia was sand an dust. They was mountains of sand an ust everwhere we went. Got in your eyes an ears an nose n clothes, an soon as you'd wash it out, more dust an sand ould come along. Somebody says the army have trucked in e dust an sand just so's we would not get to feelin too mfortable before we had to fight Saddamn Hussein.

Since there is no latrine here except a hole in the ound, Sergeant Kranz an me have been returned to our uty cleanin tank treads, although this time it is not mud, ut sand an dust we have to get out. Everday me an the rgeant be whiskin out the treads, which of course are just dirty in five minutes than they ever were.

Anyway, one day we all get some time off an go into wn.

The men are unhappy account of in Saudi Arabia they virtually no whisky or women. In fact, whisky an women against the law—well, whisky is anyway, an women ight as well be, account of they run aroun inside big ole oaks so's you can't see nothin but they eyes. The A-rab en wear them cloaks, too, an most of em have on them ttle shoes with toes that curl up at the ends. Somebody says at is because when they is out in the desert an gotta take a it, they can grap ahold of the ends of the shoes when they end over an it keeps them on balance. Whatever.

Anyhow, I am figgerin that long as I am here in the azaar, I might as well send another present to little Forrest 's he don't think I have dropped off the edge of the earth. I ne into one of the shops an am lookin around at all the it when the shopkeeper come up an ast what I want. I tole im a present for my son, an his eyes lighted up. He isappeared behind a ole curtin to the back of the store an appear with a dusty wood box, which he laid out on the unter. When he open it up, I see inside a big shiny knife.

The shopkeeper very carefully run his fingers over t handle of the knife, which is black wood with a bunch jewels set into it. It is a curved knife, with a fat blade tha inscribed with all sorts of fancy Arab writin.

"This was the dirk that our great liberator, Saladin t Magnificent, wore when he defeated the European crusa ers in the twelfth century!" says the shopkeeper. "It priceless!"

"Yeah?" I says. "So how do I know how much it cos

"For you," he says, "nineteen ninety-five."

So I gone on an bought it, thinkin there must be catch—like maybe the note I wanted to send with it w gonna be a thousan bucks, but it wadn't. In fact, the fel says he will ship it to the U.S. free of charge. I figgered y can't beat that, an wrote little Forrest, tellin him the histo of the knife that the shopkeeper tole me, an I warned hin was so sharp it would cut paper, so not to be rubbin fingers on it. I just knew he was gonna go bananas when got it.

Meantime, me an the guys continued walkin down t streets, everbody sort of grousin since they is really notl to do but buy souvenirs an drink coffee. We gone dowr bunch of dark ole alleys, where folks are sellin evertl from bananas to Band-Aids, when I seen somethin that s of makes me stop. They is a little sunshade laid out w poles in the dirt, an under it is a feller drinkin from a big jar of Kool-Aid, an playin a hurdy-gurdy. I can't see his fa right away, but on the end of a rope he is holdin th is a big ole orangutang that looks pretty familiar. T orangutang is doin dances, an the man has a tin cup on ground in front of him an, basically, he is a beggar.

I walked up closer, an the orangutang kind of looks

e funny for a second an then jumped up into my arms. It eighs so much, it knocked me flat on the ground, an when looked up, I am starin into the face of ole Sue, from the ood ole days when I was a spaceman back in New Guinea. ie be clackin his teeth an givin me big ole slobbery kisses a chatterin an whimperin.

"Take your hands off that ape," a voice says, an guess hat? I looked over under the little sunshade an who do I e settin there but good ole Lieutenant Dan! I was so urprised, I like to of fainted.

"Great God!" says Lieutenant Dan. "Is that you, ump?"

"Yessir," I says. "I reckon it is."

"What in hell are you doing here?" he says.

"I reckon I could ast you that same question" was my ply.

Lieutenant Dan, he is lookin a good deal healthier than ie last time I seen him. That was even after Colonel North ot him put in the Walter Reed Army Hospital. They has omehow got rid of his cough an he has put on weight an iere is a luster to his eyes that was not there before.

"Well, Gump," he says, "I read in the newspapers you n't wasted no time stayin in the doghouse. You done icked the Ayatolja, got thowed in jail for contemptin the ongress, caused a riot down at some religious theme park, ot arrested an put on trial for swindling millions of people, as responsible for the greatest single maritime environ-.ental disaster of the world, an somehow managed to put a end to communism in Europe. All in all, I'd say you've ad a fair few years."

"Yup," I says, "that's about the size of it."

All the while, Lieutenant Dan has been tryin to im-

prove hissef. At first he done almost give up when he go
Walter Reed, but the doctors finally persuaded him he ha
few more good years left. He got his army pension bidn
straightened out, an so he don't quite have to live from ha
to mouth anymore. He traveled around for a while, mo
on military aircraft, which the pension entitles him to do,
which is also how he got here to Saudi Arabia.

One time a while back, he says, he was in New Orlea
just to take in the sights from the days when we lived th
an to get him some good oysters on the half shell. He s
that unlike most places, it ain't changed a whole lot. C
day he was settin in Jackson Square, where I used to play
one-man band, when lo an behole, along comes a ape t
he recognized as Sue. Sue had been supportin hissef
kinda taggin along behind the fellers that was singin
dancin for money in the streets, an had learned to do a li
dance hissef. Then, when everbody done thowed enou
money in the tin cups, Sue would grap what he thought v
his share an haul ass.

Anyhow, the two of them teamed up, an Sue wo
push Dan around town in a little grocery cart, account of
artificial legs still bothered him pretty much, although
still carries them around.

"If I need em, I'll put em on," Dan says, "but frankly
easier just sittin on my ass."

"I still don't understand why you is here," I says.

"Cause it's a war goin on, Forrest. My family ai
missed a war in nine generations, an I ain't gonna be the c
to change that record."

Lieutenant Dan says he knows he is technically unfit
military service, but he is sort of hangin around, waitin
his chance to do somethin useful.

When he finds out I'm with a mechanized armo
outfit, he is overjoyed.

"That's just what I need—transportation! Legs or
o legs, I can kill A-rabs good as anybody else" is how he
uts it.

Anyway, we gone over to the Casbah, or whatever they
ll it, an got Sue a banana, an me an Lieutenant Dan ate
oup that had toad larva or somethin in it. "Y'know," he
ays, "I sure wish these A-rabs had some oysters, but I bet
here ain't one within a thousand miles of here."

"What?" I ast. "A-rabs?"

"No, you stupo, oysters," says Dan.

In any case, by the end of the afternoon Dan had talked
e into takin him back to my tank company. Before I took
im in the compound, I gone to the quartermaster an drawn
vo more sets of fatigue uniforms, one for Dan an one for
ue. I am figgerin it might take some explainin about ole
ue, but that we would give it a try, anyhow.

As it turned out, nobody much give a shit that Lieuten-
nt Dan has joined us. In fact, some fellers are glad to have
im around, since besides Sergeant Kranz an me, he is the
nly other person in our outfit to have had any real combat
xperience. Whenever he is in public, Dan now wears the
rtificial legs, just suckin it up when they hurt him. Says it
in't military to go crawlin around or ridin in a cart. Also,
nost of the fellers taken a shine to Sue, who has turned into
uite a scrounger. Whatever we need to have to steal from
omebody else, Sue is the man for the job.

Ever night we set out in front of our tent an watch the
cud missiles that Saddamn Hussein is shooting at us. Most
f the time, they is blowed up in the air by our own missiles,
n it is all like a big fireworks show, with occasional
ccidents.

One day the battalion commander come around an ca[]
us all together.

"Arright, men," he says. "Tomorrow we gonna saddl[]
up. At dawn, all our jet planes an missiles an artillery a[]
everthin else in our grab bag gonna open up on the A-rab[]
Then our asses is gonna hit em so hard in our tanks they wi[]
think ole Allah himself has come back to do them in. So g[]
some rest. You gonna be needin it for the next few days.'[]

That night I walked out away from camp a little bi[]
right to the edge of the desert. I have never seen a sky s[]
clear as over the desert—seemed like every star in th[]
heaven was shinin brighter than ever before. I begun to say[]
little prayer that nothin would happen to me in the battl[]
cause for the first time in my life, I got a responsibility t[]
take care of.

That day, I had got a letter from Mrs. Curran, sayin sh[]
was gettin too ole an sick to take care of little Forrest. Sh[]
says she is gonna have to go in the rest home pretty soon, a[]
she is puttin her house up for sale, account of the rest hon[]
won't take her unless she's dead broke. Little Forrest, sh[]
says, "is gonna have to go live with the state or somethi[]
until I can figger out what else to do." He is just startin to b[]
a teenager, she says, an is a fine-lookin boy, but is kind []
wild sometimes. She say he makes some extra money []
weekends by thumbin over to the casinos in Mississippi a[]
countin cards at the blackjack tables, but that most of th[]
casinos done kicked him out, account of he is so smart h[]
can beat them at their own game.

"I really feel sorry about this," Mrs. Curran writes, "b[]
there's nothing else I can do. I'm sure you'll come hon[]
soon, Forrest, and everything will be okay."

Well, I feel pretty sorry for Mrs. Curran, too. She dor[]
all she could. But my heart don't feel good that I can []

ything to help, even if I do get home in one piece. I mean,
ook at my record so far. Anyway, I am thinkin about all this
hen all of a sudden from out of the desert, a kind of
hirlwind comes blowin up toward me. It whirled an blew
nder the clear desert stars, an then, before I knowed it,
ere was Jenny, shimmerin in the sand an wind. I am so
ad to see her after all this time, I am about to bust.

"Well," she says, "looks like you've done it again,
uh?"

"Done what?"

"Got your ass in a sling. Aren't you gonna go out an
ght the A-rabs tomorrow?"

"Yup, that's what the orders are."

"What if something happens to you?"

"What happens, happens," I said.

"And little Forrest?"

"I been thinkin about that."

"Yeah, I know. But you don't have any plan, do you?"

"Not yet. I gotta get outta this mess, first."

"I know that, too. And I can't tell you what's gonna
ppen, cause it's against the rules. But I will tell you one
ing, though. Stick with Lieutenant Dan. And listen to him.
sten real carefully."

"Oh, I will," I says. "He is the best combat leader there
"

"Well, just pay attention to him, okay?"

I nodded, an then Jenny sort of begun to disappear in
e whirlwind. I wanted to call her back, but her face begun
fade, an she says somethin else that was very faint, but I
ard it.

"That German girl—I like her." Jenny's voice is almost
one. "She's got spirit, and a good heart . . ."

I tried to say somethin, but my words caught up in my

throat, an then the whirlwind gone on its way, an I am
alone under the desert sky.

I ain't never seen nothin like what I saw next dawn,
hope I don't ever see it again.

Far as the eye could see out in the desert, from hori
to horizon, our tanks an personnel carriers an mechani
guns is lined up in all directions. All the motors is run
so's the sound from half a million men an machines is
one big constant growl from a giant tiger. A mad giant ti

At daybreak the order is given to move forward an I
Saddamn Hussein's A-rabs' asses out of Kuwait. An th
what we done.

Me an Sergeant Kranz, who has now been promote
corporal, an Lieutenant Dan are in command of one of
tanks. Also, we has brought ole Sue along for good l
Now, these tanks is not at all like the tanks we hac
Vietnam, which were as simple to run as a tractor. But
was twenty-five years ago. Nosiree, these tanks look like
inside of a spaceship, with all sorts of computers
calculators an electrical stuff flashin an beepin. They e
got air-conditionin.

We is in the first wave of attack, an afore long, we
spotted Saddamn Hussein's army in front of us, cept t
are goin backwards. Sergeant Kranz done fired a few rou
from our big gun an Lieutenant Dan done pushed
throttle forward to maximum speed. Seems like w
actually skimmin over the desert, an all around us ever t
has opened fire an pretty soon the whole land is alive v
big explosions. The noise is frightful, an ole Sue's got
fingers stuck in his ears.

"*Wahoooo!*" shouts Lieutenant Dan. "Lookit them
tards run!"

It was true. Seems like we is out in front of the whole ack. Ole Saddamn's army is flyin off like a huge covey of uail, leavin everthin behind, vehicles, clothes, stolen cars furniture from Kuwait. At one point we done crossed a g long bridge an just afore we got to the end of it, one of r own jet planes dives down an blows it in half. We got to e other end in the nick of time, afore the whole thing llapsed down into a gorge!

When I look back through the mirror, I can see we is ell ahead of everbody an was about to get on the radio to t for instructions, when a big ole sandstorm blowed up in e desert in front, an in no time, we was engulfed inside it. en the radio went dead.

"You reckon we oughta stop an wait for somebody to ll us what to do?" I ast.

"Hell, no," says Dan. "We got them bastids on the n—Let's keep em there!"

So that's what we did. We was in the sandstorm all day most of the night. Couldn't see two feet in any direction, tell if it was night or day, but we kep on goin. Couple of mes we passed stalled-out tanks of Saddamn Hussein's my an refilled our fuel tanks from em.

"You know," says Lieutenant Dan, "way I figger it, e've come nearly three hundred miles."

Sergeant Kranz done looked at the map.

"If that is the case," he says, "why, we oughta be damn ear to Baghdad by now."

Sure enough, just then the sandstorm let up an we me out to a bright sunshine. A sign on the road says aghdad—10 kilometers.

We stopped for a minute an popped open the tank atch an looked out. Sure enough, we can see Bagh-ad up ahead—a big ole white-lookin city with gold spires on the tops of buildins. But we don't see nothin else around.

"We must of outrunned our own line," says Sergeant Kranz.

"I suppose we ought wait for them," Dan says.

All of a sudden, ole Sue, whose natural eyesight is like binoculars, begun to chatter an wave his hands an point behind us.

"What's that?" Sergeant Kranz ast.

Over the horizon, we could barely make out a bunch of vehicles in a line comin up behind us.

"It's our tanks, finally," says Lieutenant Dan.

"Hell it is!" hollers Sergeant Kranz. He has got out the field glasses an is starin at the line of vehicles.

"That's the whole goddamn A-rab army!" he shouts. "We ain't only outrunned our own army—we've outrunned theirs, too!"

"Well," says Dan, "this is a fine kettle of fish. Look like we is caught between the proverbial rock an the hard place."

That is the understatement of the year, far as I'm concerned. Here is the entire A-rab army bearin down on us in one direction, an up ahead is where Saddamn Hussein hissef lives!

"Well, we gotta get some more gas anyhow," Dan says. "I reckon we might as well go into town an find a filling station."

"What! Are you nuts?" shouts Sergeant Kranz.

"Well, what do you suggest?" Dan says. "We run out of gas, we walk. You rather walk, or ride in a tank?"

I reckon Dan's got a point here. I mean, it probably ain't gonna make no difference one way or the other how we are kilt, so we might as well get kilt ridin in our tank.

"What about you, Gump," Sergeant Kranz asts, "you
t a opinion?"

"I don't give a shit," I says. An that was the truth.

"Arright," say Dan, "then let's go to Baghdad an take in
e sights."

So that's what we did.

Chapter Twelve

Let me say this: Us bein ₁
the city of Baghdad was about as welcome as a tankful
bastids at a family reunion.

People done seen us an run off screamin an hollerin, ₐ
some of them begun thowin rocks at us. We drove down
bunch of streets, lookin for some kind of fuel depot, an
one point Dan says we better stop an try to figger out son
way to disguise ourselfs, or we will be in real trouble. We g
out of the tank an looked around. The tank was so covere
with dust it was barely recognizable, except for the Amer
can flag painted on the side, which showed through a littl
Sergeant Kranz observes that it is too bad we ain't got ar
mud on our tank treads now, cause we could use it to hi₍
over the flag. Dan says that ain't a bad idea, an sends n
over to a ditch in the street to get some water for to make o₁
own mud. Turns out, it ain't water in the ditch, but sewag
which makes my job somewhat less than pleasant.

When I come back with the bucket, everbody be hold
they nose an fannin the air, but we gone ahead an mixed ι
some dirt with the sewage an slapped it over our America

188

bag. Dan remarks that if we are caught, we will now probly be shot for spies. Anyhow, we all got back in the tank an Sergeant Kranz give Sue the slop bucket, with some fresh slop, in case the mud wears off an we have to do it again.

So, off we go. We drove around some more, an our disguise seems to be workin. People might look up when we go by, but other than that, they don't take much notice. Finally we come to a fillin station, looks like ain't nobody home. Dan says for me an Sergeant Kranz to go see if they got any diesel fuel. We get out but ain't got three steps when all sorts of commotion begins. Jeeps an armored vehicles suddenly begun roarin down the streets from all directions an slam to a stop right across from us. Me an Sergeant Kranz crouched down behind a garbage bin to wait an see what's goin on.

Presently, from one of the armored vehicles a man come out, got a big bushy mustache an is wearin a green fatigue uniform an a little red beret. Everbody be sort of kowtowin to him.

"Sombitch!" whispers Sergeant Kranz. "That's Saddamn Hussein hissef!"

I squinted over, an sure enough, it look like all the pitchers I seen of him.

At first, he don't seem to take no notice of us, an begun walkin into a buildin, when all of a sudden, he stops an spins around an does sort of a double take at our tank. Suddenly, all the A-rabs around Saddamn Hussein begun wavin automatic weapons an come rushin over an surround the tank. One of em gets up on top an knocks on the hatch. I guess Dan an Sue done thought it was us, cause they opened the hatch an found themsefs starin at about two-dozen gun barrels.

The A-rabs drag them down from the tank an stand them up against a wall with their hands in the air. Actually, since Dan has took off his artificial legs he, of course, has to sit.

Saddamn Hussein stands in front of them with his hands on his hips, an begun laughin to his guards an flunkies.

"See," he says, "I tole you you ain't got nothin to fear from these American soldiers! Look what we got here drivin one of their best tanks—one's a cripple an the other guy's so fuckin ugly he almost looks like a ape!"

At this, Sue get a pained look on his face.

"Well," Saddamn say, "since they ain't no identification on your tank, you must be spies—Give em a cigarette, boys, an see if they got any last words to say."

Seems that things are lookin pretty bleak, an Sergeant Kranz an me, we can't figger out what to do next. Ain't no sense in us tryin to rush the guards, account of they is so many of them we would just be shot down. Can't get back in the tank, neither, cause they are guardin it as well. Can't even run away, cause it'd be cowardly, an besides, where'd we run away to?

By now, Dan is smokin his last cigarette an Sue begun to take his apart an eat it. I guess he is figgerin it for a last meal. Anyhow, all of a sudden ole Saddamn turns around an goes up to our tank an climbs in. Few minutes later, he come out again an hollers for the guards to bring Dan an Sue over to him. Next thing you know, all three of em are inside the tank.

Turns out, ole Saddamn ain't never been in a modern tank before, an don't understand how it works, an so he has decided to give Dan an Sue a reprieve, at least until they can show him how to run the tank.

They is down inside it for a little bit, an then the tank suddenly starts up. Slowly, the turret begun to turn around an the barrel of the big ole cannon begun to depress till i was sort of lookin right in the faces of the guards. The guards got kind of funny expressions on an begun chatterin to theyselfs, when Saddamn's voice come over the tank's loudspeaker, tellin the guards to lay down they automatic weapons an put they hands up. They done as they was tole, an as soon as they did, ole Sue pop up out of the hatch an motion for me an Sergeant Kranz to hurry over an get in the tank. Soon as we had, ole Sue lifted up the slop bucket an thowed the whole load of shit right in the guards' faces, an we took off at top speed. In the dust behind us, we could see the guards all gaggin an flailin aroun an holdin they noses.

Inside the tank, Dan is drivin with one hand an holdin a pistol to Saddamn Hussein's head with the other.

"Forrest," he says, handin me the pistol, "take over an keep this sombitch covered. An if he makes any false moves, blow his ass away."

Saddamn Hussein is one unhappy bastid, an he is cussin an cryin an callin up to his Allah.

"We got to get us some damn gas or this whole scheme is gonna be foiled," Dan says.

"What scheme?" I ast.

"To deliver this goddamn sand wog back to General Scheisskopf so's he can thow him under the jail—or even better, line his ass up against the wall like he did to us."

By this time Saddamn Hussein is got his hands folded together an is tryin to get down on the floor of the tank an is prayin an beggin us for mercy an all that kind of shit.

"Make him be quiet," Dan says. "He is disturbin my concentration. Besides," he says, "the bastid is stingy. When I asked him if I could have a last meal of some fried oysters, he claimed he didn't have any. Whoever heard of a man that runs a whole country couldn't get himself some oysters if he wanted to?"

Just about then, Dan slams on the brakes of the tank.

"Here's a damn BP station," he says, an starts backin the tank around to one of the pumps. A A-rab guy comes out to see what's goin on, an Sergeant Kranz pops out of the hatch an motions for him to fill up our tank. The A-rab guy is shakin his head an chatterin away an trying to wave us off when I snatched up Saddamn Hussein an lifted his head out of the hatch, too, with the pistol still pointed at it.

At this, the A-rab guy shut up an got a kind of astonished look on his face. Saddamn Hussein is now sort of grinnin an pleadin, an this time when Sergeant Kranz motions for the A-rab to fill up the tank, he does what he is tole.

Meantime, Dan says we got to get a better disguise for the tank, account of we is gonna have to drive back through the whole damn A-rab army, which is headed this way. He suggests we go find a Iraqi flag an tie it on our radio antenna, which is not hard to do, since there is about one billion Iraqi flags draped all over Baghdad.

So that's what we done. With me, Lieutenant Dan, Sue, Sergeant Kranz, an Saddamn Hussein tucked away inside the tank, we headed off to find our way home, so to speak.

One good thing about the desert is that it is flat. It is also hot, an with five people inside the tank it is even hotter. Everbody was sort of complainin about this when all of a sudden we got somethin else to complain about, namely the whole damn A-rab army appeared on the horizon, headed right for us.

"What we gonna do now?" Sergeant Kranz ast.

"Fake it," Dan says.

"How you gonna do that?" I ast.

"Just watch me an marvel," says Lieutenant Dan.

He keeps headin the tank toward the whole damn

A-rab army until I think he means to smash into it an get us kilt. But that is not Dan's plan. Just about the time we are fixin to collide with the A-rab tanks, Dan slams on the brakes an wheels our tank around like we was joinin the A-rabs. I reckon they are so scared from whatever it was General Scheisskopf had done to them, they ain't worrin none about us. Anyhow, soon as we got in line with the A-rab tanks, Dan pulls on the throttle an slows us down, so that the A-rabs go on past an we are finally left settin in the desert all alone.

"Now," Dan says, pointin at Saddamn Hussein, "let's get this Kuwait-invadin bastid to higher headquarters."

From there on, it seemed like smooth sailin, at least till we got near our own lines. Then Dan say it is time to "reveal ourselfs." He stopped the tank an tole me an Sergeant Kranz to go out an get rid of the Iraqi flag an scrape the mud off the American flag on the side of the tank—so that's what we done. And let me say this: It was the first time in all the mud scrapin I had done that I actually felt like I was accomplishin somethin. Turns out, it was the last time, too.

Well, with our American flag all shiny an bright on the side of the tank, we got through the American lines all right. On the way we done drove through big ole clouds of smoke from where Saddamn Hussein had ordered his men to blow up all the awl wells in Kuwait. It struck us all as a very sour grapes thing to do. Inside our lines, we ast some MPs for directions to General Scheisskopf's headquarters. We found it okay after about five hours of drivin around in circles, after which Sergeant Kranz remarked that givin directions is not the MPs' strong suit, but arrestin people is—to which Dan responded that "Gump is livin proof" of that.

Me an Sergeant Kranz gone on into the general's

headquarters to tell him what we has got out in our tank
Inside, General Scheisskopf is givin a big press briefin o
the day's activities, an all the cameras are whirlin a
flashbulbs are goin off. He is showin the reporters som
footage from a camera inside the nose of one of our je
fighters as it dived down on a bridge an dropped a bomb t
blow it up. Just ahead of where the bomb went off was
tank hightailin it across the bridge, which barely escaped t
the other side when the bridge collapsed.

"An you see here," says General Scheisskopf, pointin a
the tank with his ruler, "looking through his rearviev
mirror, is the luckiest man in the whole damn A-rab army!
At this, everbody in the room got a big chuckle, cept fc
mysef an Sergeant Kranz, who were horrified, account c
that picture was of *us* when we crossed over that bridge!

Anyhow, we did not tell this to anybody, because
would spoil General Scheisskopf's story, so we waited till h
was finished an then Sergeant Kranz gone up to him a
whispered in his ear. The general, who is a big ole jolly
lookin feller, got a sort of weird look on his face, an th
sergeant whispered in his ear again, an the general's eye
done bugged out an he grapped Sergeant Kranz by the arr
an had him lead him outside. Me, I follered along.

When we got to the tank, General Scheisskopf climbe
up an stuck his head down the hatch. Few moments later h
jerked back up again. "Jesus God!" he said, an jumpe
down on the ground.

Meantime, Dan hoisted hissef out of the hatch an se
down on the deck of the tank, an Sue, he done come ou
too. While we was in the headquarters Dan an Sue had tie
up Saddamn Hussein hand an foot an to keep him fror
blabberin so much had stuck a gag in his mouth.

"I don't know what in hell happened here," says th
general, "but you boys have screwed up royally."

"Huh?" says Sergeant Kranz, forgettin his manners for a moment.

"Don't you understand it is against my orders to capture Saddamn Hussein?"

"What you mean, sir?" ast Dan. "He's the head enemy. He is why we is fightin over here, ain't he?"

"Well, er, yes. But my orders come directly from the President of the United States—George Herbert Walker Bush."

"But, sir . . ." starts Sergeant Kranz.

"My orders," says the general, kinda lookin around to make sure nobody is watchin, "were specifically *not* to capture that butthole you got in that tank. And now what have you done? You're gonna get my ass in a sling with the President himself!"

"Well, General," Dan says, "we're sorry about that. We didn't know. But, I mean, we got him now, don't we? I mean, what are we gonna do with him?"

"Take him back," says the general.

"TAKE HIM BACK!" we all shout.

General Scheisskopf wave his hands for us not to be so loud.

"But, sir," say Sergeant Kranz, "you gotta understand that we was within a inch of our lifes tryin to bring him here. It ain't easy bein the only American tank in Baghdad in the middle of a war."

"Yeah," says Dan. "An what's worse, the whole damn A-rab army is now back in Baghdad, just waitin for us."

"Well, boys," the general says, "I know how you feel, but orders is orders, an I'm orderin you to take him back."

"But, sir," I says, "maybe can't we just leave him out in the desert an let him find his own way back?"

"Much as I'd like to, that would be inhumane," General Scheisskopf says piously. "Tell you what though, just get him within four or five miles of Baghdad—so's he can see it himself, an then turn his ass loose."

"FOUR OR FIVE MILES!" we all shouted. But like the man said, orders was orders.

Anyway, we gassed up an got somethin to eat at the chow tent an saddled up the tank for our return trip. By this time it was gettin night, but we figgered at least it might not be so hot. Sergeant Kranz brought Saddamn Hussein a big ole plate of greasy pork chops, but he say he don't care for any, so hungry or not, off we went.

It was quite a spectacle out in the desert, which was lit up like a stadium from all the awl fires burnin. We made pretty good time though, considerin havin to dodge all the junk left over from the whole damn A-rab army. Seems that while they was occupying Kuwait, they had also occupied some of the Kuwait people's things—like their furniture an their Mercedes-Benzes an such, but when they left in such a hurry, they didn't bother to take them with them.

The ride back to Baghdad was actually kind of borin, an to pass the time I took the gag out of ole Saddamn's mouth to see what he had to say. When I tole him we was takin him home, he begun to cry an shout an pray again cause he figgered we was lyin an was gonna kill him. But finally we settled him down an he begun to believe us, though he could not understand why we was doin this. Lieutenant Dan tole him it was a "gesture of goodwill."

I piped up an tole Saddamn I was friends with the Ayatolja Koumani, an in fact had once transacted some bidness with him.

"That ole fart," Saddamn says, "he has caused me a lot of trouble. I hope he roasts in hell an has to eat tripe an pickled pigs' feet for the rest of eternity."

"I can see you are a man of great Christian charity," says Lieutenant Dan.

To this, Saddamn has no response.

Pretty soon, we could see the lights of Baghdad in the distance. Dan slowed down the tank to hide the noise.

"Well, that's about five miles, as I make it," says Dan.

"It is not," says Saddamn. "It's more like seven or eight."

"That's your tough luck, buster. We got other shit to do, so this is as far as you go."

With that, Sergeant Kranz an me hoisted Saddamn out of the tank. Then Sergeant Kranz, he made Saddamn take off all his clothes, except for his boots an his little beret. Then he pointed him at Baghdad.

"On your way, you degenerate turd," says Sergeant Kranz, an he give ole Saddamn a big kick in the ass. Last we seen of him, he was joggin across the desert, tryin to cover hissef in front an behind.

Now we are headed back to Kuwait, an everthin seems to be goin smoothly, more or less. Though I am missin little Forrest, at least me an Lieutenant Dan an Sue is back together again, an besides, I figger my army hitch is almost up.

It is almost pitch black dark inside the tank an ain't no sounds cept the noise of the engine, an the instrument panels is glowin faint red in the dark.

"Well, Forrest, I reckon we have seen our last war," says Dan.

"I hope so," I says.

"War is not a pretty thing," he goes on, "but when the time comes to fight it, it is us who have to go. We are the professional army. The shit-shovelers in peacetime, but it's

'Tommy get yer rifle, when the drums begin to beat . . .
Saviors of your country an all that crap."

"Well, maybe that's true of you an Sergeant Kranz,"
says, "but me an Sue, here, we are peace-lovin folks."

"Yeah, but when the balloon goes up, you're ther
every time," says Dan. "And don't you think I don'
appreciate it."

"I'll sure be glad when we're home," I says.

"Uh oh," Dan says.

"What?"

"I said, 'Uh oh.'" He is staring into the instrumen
screen.

"Whassamatter?" ast Sergeant Kranz.

"We locked on to."

"What? Who?"

"Somebody's got us locked on. Aircraft. I imagine i
must be one of ours."

"One of ours?"

"Yeah, they ain't got any Iraqi air force left."

"But why?" I ast.

"Uh oh!" Dan says again.

"What?"

"They have fired!"

"At us?"

"Who else," Dan says. He had begun to spin the tan!
aroun when there is a huge explosion that literally blew th
tank apart. All of us is thowed ever which way, an the cabi
is filled with smoke an fire.

"Out! Out!" Dan screams, an I pulled mysef out th
hatch an reached back for Sergeant Kranz right behind me
He come out an I reached for ole Sue, but he was lyin i
back of the cabin, hurt an pinned down by somethin. So
leaned in to grap Dan, but he can't reach my hand. For

instant we looked in each other's eyes, an he says, "Damn, Forrest, we almost made it . . ."

"C'mon, Dan!" I shout. The flames is all over the cabin by now an the smoke thicker an thicker. I kep reachin way down to get him, but it wadn't no use. He kinda smiled an looked up at me. "Well, Forrest, we have had ourselfs a hell of a war, haven't we?"

"Hurry, Dan, grap holt of my hand," I screamed.

"See you around, pal" is all he says, an then the tank blowed up.

It blowed me in the air an singed me up a little, otherwise I was not much hurt. I couldn't believe it, though. I got up an just stood there, watchin the tank burn up. I wanted to go back an try to get em out, but I knew it wadn't no good. Me an the sergeant, we waited a while, until the tank had burned itself out, an then he says, "Well, c'mon, Gump. We got a long walk home."

All the way back across the desert that night I felt so terrible I couldn't even bring mysef to cry. Two of the best friends a man ever had—an now they are gone, too. It is a loneliness almost too sad to believe.

They had a little service for Lieutenant Dan an Sue at the air base where our fighter planes was. I couldn't help but think that one of them pilots was responsible for all this, but I guess he must of felt pretty bad about it hissef. After all, we wadn't sposed to of been out there, cept we had to return Saddamn to Baghdad.

They had a pair of flag-covered caskets lined up on the tarmac, an they shimmered in the heat of the mornin. Wadn't anythin in em, though. Fact was, they wadn't enough left of Dan an Sue to fill a can of beans.

Sergeant Kranz an me was in the little group, an one time he turned to me an says, "Ya know, Gump, them was good soldiers, them two. Even the ape. It never showed no fear."

"Probly too dumb to understand it," I says.

"Yeah, probly. Kinda like you, huh?"

"I spose."

"Well, I'm gonna miss em," Sergeant Kranz says. "We had ourselfs a helluva ride."

"Yup," I says, "I reckon."

After a chaplain said a little somethin, they had a band that played taps an a rifle squad that fired a twelve-gun salute. An then it was over.

Afterward, General Scheisskopf come up an put his arm aroun my shoulder. I guess he could see I was finally beginnin to get little bitty tears in my eyes.

"I'm sorry about this, Private Gump," he says.

"So's everbody else," I tole him.

"Look, these fellers was friends of yours, I understand. We couldn't find any military records on them."

"They was volunteers," I said.

"Well," says the general, "maybe you'd want to take these." One of his aides come up with two little cans, got tiny plastic American flags pasted on the tops.

"Our graves registration people thought it would be appropriate," General Scheisskopf says.

I took the cans an thanked the general, though I don't know what for, an then I gone on off to find my outfit. Time I got back, the company clerk was lookin for me.

"Where you been, Gump? I got important news."

"It's a long story," I says.

"Well, guess what? You ain't in the army no more."

"That so?"

"Sure is. Somebody done figgered out you got a

riminal record—hell, you wadn't sposed to of ever been let
1 this man's army in the first place!"

"So what I'm sposed to do now?" I ast.

"Pack up your shit an get the hell out of here" was his
nswer.

So that's what I done. I found out I was due to leave on
 plane that night for the States. Didn't even have time to
hange my clothes. I put the little cans with Sue's and Dan's
shes in my pack an signed out for the last time. When I got
n the plane, it was only half full. I got me a seat in the back,
y mysef, cause my clothes, well, they had the stink of death
n em, an I was embarrassed of the way I smelled. We was
yin high over the desert, an the moon was full an the
louds was silver all over the horizon. It was dark inside the
·lane an I begun to feel terribly alone an downcasted, when
ll of a sudden I look over at the seat across the aisle, an
here is Jenny, just settin there, lookin at me! She is got a
ind of sad expression on her face, too, an this time, she
on't say nothin, but just looks at me an smiles.

I couldn't hep it. I reached out for her, but she waved
ne off. But also, she stayed there in the seat across the aisle, I
eckon to keep me company, all the way home.

Chapter Thirteen

It was a cloudy an gray da when I got back to Mobile. I gone to Mrs. Curran's house, a she was settin inside in a rockin chair, knittin a doily c somethin. She was glad to finally see me.

"I don't know how much longer I could of lasted," sh said. "Things have been pretty hard around here."

"Yeah," I says, "I can imagine."

"Forrest," she says, "like I told you in my letter, I gott sell the house so's I can get into the Little Sisters of the Poc old folks home. But once I do, they'll take care of me fc good, so I will turn over the money from the house to you t help raise little Forrest."

"Aw, no, Mrs. Curran," I says, "that's your money— can't accept that."

"You got to, Forrest. I can't even *get* into the Littl Sisters of the Poor home unless I'm dead broke. And littl Forrest is my grandson and the only family I have lef Besides, you gonna need all the money you can get. Yo ain't even got a job."

"Well, you are right about that, I guess."

About that time the front door opened an a big ole young man come bustin in, says, "Gramma, I'm home."

I didn't recognize him at all at first. Last time I seen him was nearly three years ago. Now he has growed up to be almost a man, fine an straight an tall. Only thing is, he is wearin a earrin in his ear, which leads me to wonder what sort of underwear he has got on.

"So, you're back, huh?" he says.

"Looks that way."

"Yeah, for how long this time?"

"Well," I says, "way I got it figgered, for good."

"What you gonna do?" he ast.

"That one I ain't figgered out yet."

"I wouldn't of thought so," he says, an gone on back to his room.

Ain't nothin like a warm welcome home, is it?

Anyhow, next mornin I begun lookin for work. Unfortunately, it ain't as though I have got a lot of high-end skills, an so my choices are limited. Like becomin a ditchdigger or somethin. But even that was a hard card to play. Seems they weren't no big market for ditchdiggin at the moment, an besides, one of the bosses tole me I was too old for such work.

"We need up-an-comin young fellers who are lookin to make a career of this—not some old fart who is just wantin enough work to buy a quart of jug wine" was the way he put it.

After three or four days I got pretty discouraged, an after three or four weeks it become downright humiliatin. Finally I took to lyin about it to Mrs. Curran an little Forrest. I tole em I done found work so's I could support em, but the truth was, I begun usin up my separation pay from the army to pay the bills an spent my days at a soda fountain drinkin CokeCola an eatin Fritos, at least when I wadn't out poundin the pavement for a job.

One day I figgered I'd go on down to Bayou La Batre an see if they was anythin for me there. After all, one time I'd owned the biggest bidness in that town.

What I found in Bayou La Batre was pretty depressin. The ole Gump Srimp Company was in a sorry state— buildins an wharfs all dilapidated an fallin in, winders busted out, an the parkin lot's growed up in weeds. It was clear that part of my life was over.

I gone down to the docks, an they is a few srimp boats tied up, but ain't nobody hirin.

"Srimpin's finished down here, Gump," say one captain. "They done fished out all the srimp years ago. Now you gotta have a boat big enough to go all the way down to Mexico afore you can make a profit."

I was about to catch the bus back up to Mobile when it occurred to me I ought to visit poor ole Bubba's daddy. After all, I ain't seen him in nearly ten years. I gone out to where he lived, an sure enough, the ole house was still there, an Bubba's daddy was settin on the porch, drinkin a glass of iced tea.

"Well, I swear," he said when I come walkin up. "I'd heard you was in jail."

"I might of been," I said. "I guess it depends on when you heard it."

I ast him about the srimpin bidness an his picture was bleak as everbody else's.

"Nobody's catchin em, nobody's raisin em. Too few to catch an too cold to grow. Your operation was the heyday down here, Forrest. Ever since then, we been on hard times."

"Well, I'm sorry to hear that," I says. I set down, an Bubba's daddy fixed me a glass of tea.

"You ever catch up with them fellers that looted your company?" he ast.

"Which fellers?"

"That Lieutenant Dan, an ole Mr. Tribble—an that ape, too—what was its name?"

"Sue," I says.

"Yeah, them was the ones."

"Well, I don't think Dan an Sue was to blame. Besides, I guess it don't matter now, anyhow. They are dead."

"Yeah? How'd that happen?"

"It is a long story," I said, an Bubba's daddy, he didn't pursue it no further, for which I was grateful.

"So," he asts finally, "what you gonna do now?"

"I dunno," I says, "but I gotta do somethin."

"Well," say Bubba's daddy, "there is always oysters."

"Oysters?"

"Yeah. Ain't as profitable as srimp used to be, but there some oyster beds still left out there. Problem is, people scared of eatin em raw these days—too much pollution or somethin. They can make you bad sick."

"Can a man make a livin catchin oysters?" I ast.

"Sometimes. Depends on a lot of things. Pollution gets bad, they close down the beds. Then there is storms an hurricanes an, of course, your competition."

"Competition? Who is that?"

"All them other fellers out there tryin to catch oysters," he says. "They don't take kindly to somebody new comin in here. An they is a very rough bunch, which I suppose you know."

"Yeah, I kinda remember em that way," I says. It was too true. Them oystermen was not people to fool around with, at least back in the ole days.

"So how do I get started?" I ast.

"Ain't too hard," say Bubba's daddy. "Just get you a ol skiff an some oyster tongs. Don't even have to buy outboard motor if you don't want to—you can get som oars an row, like they did when I was young."

"That's all?"

"Pretty much, I reckon. I can show you where most the oyster beds are. Course, you'll have to get a license from the state. That's probly the most expensive part."

"You know where I can buy me a skiff?"

"Matter of fact," says Bubba's daddy, "I got one myse you can use. It's tied up behind the house. All you'll have t do is find some oars. Mine done broke ten or fifteen year ago."

So that's what I done.

Well, it seemed to me pretty ironic, me bein in th oyster bidness, after ole Lieutenant Dan was all the tim talkin about gettin some good oysters to eat. Man, I wish h could be here today. He'd be in hog's heaven!

I started out bright an early next mornin. The da before, I'd used the last of my army pay to buy the oars a get a oysterin license. I also bought a pair of coveralls a some baskets to put the oysters in. The sun was just comi up over the Mississippi Sound when I begun to row towar where Bubba's daddy tole me some oyster beds was. Wha he tole me was to row out to where I could see Buoy No. line it up with a water tower on shore an with the tip of Pet Bois Island to the south. When I had done this, I was to wor my way toward the Lake Aux Herbes, an that's where th oysters would be.

It took me about a hour to find Buoy No. 6, but wadn't no time from then that I got on the oyster beds. B unch I had tonged up four bushel baskets of oysters, which was my limit, an so I rowed back into shore.

They was a oyster processin plant in Bayou La Batre, an carried my oysters there to be counted an sold. Time they ally everthin up, I done made forty-two dollars an sixteen ents, which struck me as a little low for upwards of four undrit oysters they would turn around an sell in restau-ants for a dollar apiece. Unfortunately, though, I wadn't in no position to argue.

I was walkin down the street to catch the bus back to Mobile, the forty-two dollars an sixteen cents still warm in my pocket, when half-a-dozen fellers come aroun the corner n block my way on the sidewalk.

"Kinda new around here, ain't you?" one big feller ast.

"Sort of," I said. "What's it to you?"

"We hear you out there tongin up our oysters," another guy says.

"Since when is they *your* oysters? I thought they was verbody's oysters in the water."

"Oh, yeah? Well, they *is* everybody's oysters—if you appen to be from here. We don't take kindly of people who y to barge in on our bidness."

"Well," I says, "my name is Forrest Gump. Used to own he Gump Srimp Company. So I'm kinda from here mysef."

"Oh, yeah? Well, my name's Miller. Smitty Miller. I member your bidness. Fished us all out of srimp an put verybody out of work to boot."

"Look, Mister Miller," I says, "I don't want no trouble. I ot a family to look after, an I just want to tong up a few ysters an be on my way."

"Issat so? Well, you look here, Gump. We gonna be eepin a eye on you. We hear you was hangin aroun with at ole coon thats son got kilt over in Vietnam."

"His name was Bubba. He was my friend."

"Yeah? Well, we don't mix with them people dow∎ here, Gump. You gonna hang aroun in this town, you bette∎ learn the rules."

"Who makes the rules?" I says.

"We do."

Well, that's how it went. Smitty ain't outright tole me t∎ stop oysterin, but I got a feelin that trouble lay aheac∎ Anyhow, I gone on back home an tole Mrs. Curran an littl∎ Forrest that I done got a real job, an they seemed pleased. ∎ might even be I can earn enough to keep Mrs. Curran fron∎ sellin her place an goin to the po house. It wadn't much, b∎ it was a start.

Anyhow, the oysterin bidness was, for now, my salv∎ tion. Ever mornin I'd ride the bus down to Bayou La Batre a∎ tong up enough oysters to get us by another day, but wh∎ happens when the season is over or the beds is closed b∎ pollution, I do not know. It is very worrisome.

Second day I was there, I gone to the dock where m∎ skiff is, an it ain't there. I look down in the water, an it ∎ settin on the bottom. Took me a hour to pull it on shore, a∎ when I did, I find somebody has knocked a hole in th∎ bottom. Took me three hours to fix the hole, an I only g∎ enough oysters to make twenty dollars that day. I a∎ figgerin this is some kind of message from Smitty an h∎ friends, but I got no proof for sure.

Another time, my oars is missin, an I got to buy ne∎ ones. Few days later, somebody done smashed up my bush∎ baskets, but I am tryin to take it in stride.

Meantime, I am havin some problems with little F∎ rest. Seems he is engagin hissef in some typical teena∎ activities, such as stayin in trouble all the time. First, ∎ come home drunk one night. I noticed this, since he f∎

own twice tryin to get up the steps. I didn't say nothin bout it next mornin, though—the truth was, I wadn't eally sure of what my position with him was sposed to be. When I ast Mrs. Curran, she shakes her head an say she on't know, either. She says he ain't a bad boy, but he is ery hard to discipline.

Next, I caught him smokin a cigarette in his bathroom. I et him down an tole him how bad it was. He listened, but as kinda sullen, an when I was finished, he don't promise • stop, he just walked out of the room.

An then there was his gamblin. Account of his bril-ance, he could beat just about anybody at cards an stuff, an roceeded to do so. This got him a stern note from the :hool principal sayin that little Forrest was fleecin all the ther kids at school with his gamblin activities.

Finally, he didn't come home one night. Mrs. Curran ayed up till midnight, but finally went to bed. I was up till awn, when he finally tried to sneak in the bedroom rinder. I decided the time had come to set him down an ave a serious talk.

"Look," I says, "this shit has got to stop. Now, I know oung fellers like you gotta sow some wile oats ever so ften, but you is carryin it to the extreme."

"Yeah?" he says. "Like what?"

"Like sneakin in past midnight—an smokin cigarettes your bathroom."

"Whatsittoyou?" he says. "You been spyin on me, uh?"

"I ain't spyin. I'm noticin."

"Well, it ain't nice to notice. Besides, it's the same as byin."

"Listen," I says, "that ain't the point. I got some esponsibility here. I'm sposed to look after you."

"I can look after myself," he says.

"Yeah, I can see that. Like you lookin after yoursef b hidin a six-pack of beer in your toilet tank, huh?"

"So you *have* been spyin on me, haven't you?"

"I have not. The toilet started runnin, an when I went look I saw one of your beer cans have fallen over an plugge up the flusher hole. How could I not notice that?"

"You could of kept it to yourself."

"The hell I will! If you can't behave yoursef, it is m duty to make you—an that's what I'm gonna do."

"You can't even speak English right—or keep a dece job. What gives you the idea you got some authority ov me? I mean, who are you to tell me what to do? Is it becau you sent me those cheap presents from everyplace? goddamn fake Alaska totem pole? An that ridiculo ooompa horn that I'd look like a fool playin? Or that gre antique knife from Saudi Arabia—when it got here, th little pieces of glass you said were jewels had all fallen ou and besides, the thing's so dull it can't cut butter, let alor paper! I threw em all away! If you've got some authority ov me and what I do in life, I'd like to know what it is!"

Well, that did it—an so I showed him. I snatched hir up an thowed him across my knees an afore I raised m hand I said the only thing that come to my mind.

"This is gonna hurt me more than it's gonna hurt you

An I give him a big ole spankin. I ain't sure if what I ju said was true, but ever time I swatted him, it was like I w swattin mysef. But I didn't know what else to do. He was s smart I couldn't reason with him, cause that ain't m specialty. But somebody gotta exercise some control arour here, an see if we can get back on track. Whole time, litt Forrest ain't sayin nothin, ain't hollerin or cryin or anythi an when I am through, he got up, face beet red, an gone his room. He didn't come out the whole day, an when h

ome to the supper table that night, he ain't sayin much,
ept things like "Pass the gravy, please."

But also, over the next days an weeks, I noticed a
narked improvement in his behavior. An I hope he noticed
hat I noticed that.

A lot of days when I am out oysterin or doin my other
tuff, I am thinkin about Gretchen. But what I'm gonna do
bout it, anyway? I mean, after all, here I am livin barely
and to mouth, while she is gonna be a college graduate one
ay. A lot of times I thought about writin her, but can't
gger out what to say. It would probly just make it worse, is
hat I am thinkin. So's I just kept the memories an went on
bout my bidness.

One time after he got home from school, little Forrest
ome into the kitchen, where I am tryin to clean up an wash
y hands after a long day on the oyster beds. I have cut my
nger on a oyster shell, an though it don't hurt much, it
led pretty good, an that is the first thing he noticed.

"What happened?" he ast.

I tole him, an he says, "Want me to get you a Band-
id?"

He gone in an got the Band-Aid, but before he put it on
y finger he washed out the cut with some peroxide or
methin that stang like hell.

"You gotta be careful with oyster-shell cuts," he say.
They can give you a pretty serious infection, ya know?"

"Yeah, how come?"

"Cause the best kind of place for oysters to grow is
here there is the dirtiest nastiest kind of pollution there is.
in't you know that?"

"Nope. How'd you find out?"

"Cause I studied up on it. If you could ask a oyste where it wanted to live, it'd probly say, in a cesspool."

"How come you studin up on oysters?"

"Cause I'm figgerin I need to start pullin my weigh around here," he says. "I mean, you goin out there ever day an tongin up oysters, an all I'm doin is goin to school.

"Well, that's what you sposed to do. You gotta lear somethin so's you don't wind up like me."

"Yeah, well, I already learned enough. I mean, to te you the truth, I don't do nothin in school. I'm so far ahead everybody in the class that the teachers just let me go sit i the library an read whatever books I want."

"That so?"

"Yeah, that's so. And I am figgerin that maybe I coul just not go to school every day anymore, but maybe com down to Bayou La Batre sometimes an help you out with th oyster-tongin bidness."

"Uh, well, I appreciate that, but uh . . ."

"That is, if you want me to. Maybe you don't want m around."

"No, no, it ain't that. It just that about the school. mean, your mama would of wanted . . ."

"Well, she ain't here to have a say-so. And I think yc might could use some help. I mean, tongin oysters is ha work, and maybe I could be of some use."

"Well, yeah, sure you could. But . . ."

"Okay then, that's it," he says. "How about I sta tomorrow mornin?"

An so, right or wrong, that's what we done.

Next mornin before dawn I got up an fixed us son breakfast an then I peeked in little Forrest's room to see

's awake. He ain't, so's I tippy-toed in an stood there
okin at him, sound asleep in Jenny's bed. In a way, he
oks so much like her I kinda got choked up for a moment,
it I caught mysef, account of no matter what, we got work
 do. I leaned over to shake him awake, when my foot
uched somethin under the bed. I looked down, an damn if
ain't the head of the big ole totem pole from Alaska I had
nt him. I bent over an peered under the bed, an sure
iough, there is the other stuff, too, the ooompa horn an the
iife, still in its case. He ain't thowed them away after all,
it is keepin em right there. Maybe he don't play with em
uch, but at least he has em close, an all of a sudden I am
eginnin to understand somethin about children. For just a
cond I felt like reachin over an kissin him on the cheek,
it I didn't. But I sure felt like it.

Anyhow, after breakfast me an little Forrest set out for
ayou La Batre. I have been able finally to make a down
iyment on a ole truck so's I don't have to ride the bus no
ore, but it is a real question ever day whether or not the
uck will make it there an back. I have named the truck
'anda, in honor of, well, all the Wandas I have known.

"What you spose happened to her?" little Forrest ast.

"Who?" I said. We was drivin on a ole two-lane road in
ie dark, past broke-down houses an farm fields, toward the
ater. The lights on the dashboard of the ole truck, a 1954
hevy, was glowin green an I could see little Forrest's face
 the reflection.

"Wanda," he says.

"Your pig? Well, I reckon she's still up at the zoo."

"You really think so?"

"I guess. I mean, why wouldn't she be?"

"I dunno. It's been a long time. Maybe she died. Or
iey sold her."

"You want me to find out?"

"Maybe both of us should," he says.

"Yeah. Maybe so."

"Hey," he says, "I wanted to tell you I was sorry abo[ut] what happened to Sue an Lieutenant Dan, ya know?"

"Well, I appreciate that."

"They was real good friends, huh?"

"Yup, they was."

"So what'd they die for?"

"Oh, I dunno. Cause they was doin what they was to[ld] to, I guess. Ole Bubba's daddy ast me the same question[s] long time ago. They was just in the wrong place in t[he] wrong time, maybe."

"Yeah, I know that, but what was the war about?"

"Well, they tole us it was account of Saddamn Husse[in] done attacked the people in Kuwait."

"That so?"

"It's what they said."

"So what do you really think?"

"A lot of people said it was about awl."

"Oil—yeah, I read that, too."

"I reckon they died for awl" was what I had to s[ay] about that.

Well, we got on down to Bayou La Batre an put t[he] baskets in the boat, an I rowed us out to the oyster beds. T[he] sun was comin up off the Gulf of Mexico an they was pi[nk] fluffy clouds in the mornin sky. The water was clear an fl[at] as a tabletop, an the oars was the only sounds. We got out [to] the beds, an I showed little Forrest how to stick one oar [in] the mud to hold the boat still while I raked over the beds a[n] then used the tongs to pull up big globs of oysters. It was [a] pretty good mornin, an after a while little Forrest said h[e] wanted to do some tongin, too. He seemed happy as [he] could be, almost like he was tongin pearls instead of oysters, which in fact there were some—but they wadn't worth nothin, at least not for money to amount to anythin. Wadn't them kind of oysters.

Anyhow, after we had got all our limit, I begun to row us back to the oyster processin plant, but I ain't got halfway there before little Forrest ast if he can try his hand at rowin the boat. I moved over an he begun to pull on the oars, an after about half a hour of weavin us this way an that, he got the hang of it.

"How come you don't get a motor for the boat?" he ast.

"I dunno," I says. "Sometimes I kinda like rowin. It's pretty quiet an peaceful. An it gives me time to think."

"Yeah, about what?"

"I dunno," I says. "Nothin much. After all, thinkin ain't my specialty."

"A motor would save time," he says, "and efficiency."

"Yeah, I spose."

Well, we got on into the dock where the oyster packin plant was an unloaded our bushels of oysters. Price was a little higher today, account of, the man says, they has closed a bunch of oyster beds because of pollution, an so our oysters were rarer than yesterday, which was arright by me. I tole little Forrest to go on over to the truck an get us our lunch buckets so's we could have our sambwiches down here on the dock, kinda like a waterfront picnic.

I had just settled up with the paymaster when little Forrest come up, lookin unhappy.

"You know a guy called Smitty?" he ast.

"Yup, I know him. Why?"

"Well, somebody's punched a hole in both our front tires on Wanda. An this guy was standin across the street laughin, an when I asked if he knew who did it, he just said, 'Nope, but tell your friend that Smitty says hello.' "

"Umph" was all I could manage.

"So who is this guy?"

"Just a feller," I says.

"But he looked like he was enjoyin it."

"Probly. He an his friends don't like me oysterin do[w]
here."

"He had a oyster knife in his hand. You spose he w[as]
the one who did it?"

"Maybe. Problem is, I got no proof."

"So why don't you go find out? Ask him?"

"I think it's best to let them people alone," I says. [They]
ain't nothin but trouble to fool with them."

"You ain't scared, are you?"

"Not exactly. I mean, they all live here. They're m[ad]
cause I'm tongin their oysters."

"Their oysters! Oysters in the water are anybod[y's]
oysters."

"Yeah, I know that, but they don't see it that way."

"So you gonna let them push us around?"

"I'm gonna go on about my bidness an let them be," [I]
says.

Little Forrest, he turn around an went on back to t[he]
truck an begun fixin the flat tire. I could see him from dow[n]
the street, talkin an cussin to hissef. I knowed how he fe[lt]
but I just can't afford no screw-ups now. I have got a fam[ily]
to look after.

Chapter Fourteen

Then one day it happened. They shut us down.

Me an little Forrest got down to the dock one mornin an they is big ole signs posted everwhere, say Due to Pollution in the Water There Will Be No More Oysterin Under Penalty of Law Till Further Notice.

Well, this come as bad news, indeed. After all, we is hangin on by just about a thread, but they wadn't nothin to do cept go on back home. It was a pretty dreary night all round, an in the mornin I am feelin glum, settin at the breakfast table, drinkin coffee, when little Forrest come in the kitchen.

"I got a idea," he says.

"Yeah, what?"

"I think I have figgered out a way to start harvestin oysters again."

"How is that?" I ast.

"Well, I been studyin up on it," little Forrest says. "Spose we can convince the state fish n wildlife people that any oysters we harvest is gonna be free of any pollution?"

"How is we gonna do that?"

"Move em," he says.

"Move what?"

"The oysters. See, a oyster thrives in pollution, but y
can't eat em, cause it'll make you sick. We all know that. B
accordin to the research I done, a oyster purges its
completely every twenty-four hours."

"So what?"

"Well, spose we tong up the oysters in the pollut
water, an then move them out to the Gulf, where it is cle
an clean an salty? All we have to do is sink the oysters in
few feet of water for a day or so, an they'll be clean an pu
an fresh as a whistle."

"We can do that?" I ast.

"Yeah. I'm pretty sure. I mean, all we need to do is g
another ole skiff an tow it out to one of them islands whe
the water is clear, put the oysters we tonged up here in it,
sink it for a day. Those oysters will have purged themsel
entirely of anything bad and I bet they'll taste better, to
cause they'll pick up the salt from the Gulf water."

"Hey," I says, "that sounds like it really might work

"Yeah. I mean, it'll be a little more to do, account of v
gotta move the oysters and then pick em up again, but i
better than nothin."

So that's what we did.

Somehow we managed to convince the state Fish
Wildlife Service that our oysters wasn't gonna be no thre
to nobody. We started out movin em from the bay beds
the Gulf in the skiff, but pretty soon we was so busy we ha
to buy us a barge. An also, the price we got for our oyste
went sky high, account of we was the only big-time game
town.

As the weeks an months went by, we added to our peration by gettin more an more barges, an we had to hire 1ore people to help us in the oysterin bidness.

Little Forrest also done come up with another idea, an 1 fact, it was what made us rich.

"Listen," he says one day after we brought in a big load f oysters, "I been thinkin—Where is the best place to grow oyster?"

"In shit," I answered.

"Exactly," he says. "An where is there the most shit in 1e whole bay?"

"Probly by the sewage treatment plant," I says.

"Exactly! So here's what we do, we go out there an lant oysters! Thousands of em—millions. We can use lanks or somethin to mature the spat—which is the baby ysters. Set the whole thing up on a regular basis with boats ngin up the new oysters an movin em to our barges out in 1e Gulf. I've even got a idea for a submersible barge, so's e just take it out an sink it with the polluted oysters, then . a day or so pump it out, an presto, we got a bargeload of 1re, fresh oysters!"

So that is also what we done.

In a year, we are harvestin more oysters by the sewage eatment plant than the law ought to allow an we have panded our operation to include a oyster processin plant 1 shippin section, an we have also got a marketin division, o.

GUMP & COMPANY is what I have named ourselfs, an e is sellin premium-grade oysters all over the United States America!

All this has cheered up Jenny's mama so, that she come our receptionist. She says she feels "totally rejuve- ited" an don't want to go to the po house no more. She has en bought herself a new Cadillac convertible that she

drives around with the top down, wearin a sleeveles
sundress an a bonnet.

As the months go by, we have got so big I went on
hirin spree. I located Mr. Ivan Bozosky an Mike Mulligan, ar
put them in charge of the accountin department, figgerir
they have learned a lesson durin their terms in jail.

Ole Slim, from my encyclopedia days, I put in charge c
sales, an he has increased our volume by five-hundr
percent! Curtis an Snake, whose football playin days wit
the Giants an Saints is over, I put in charge of "security."

Now, ole Alfred Hopewell, from the new CokeCol
bidness, I put him in the position of research an develop
ment. His wife, Mrs. Hopewell, whose circumstances hav
been considerably reduced since the riot in Atlanta, she i
now our government liaison director, an let me say this: W
ain't had no problems with the state Fish an Wildlife Servic
since she got on the job. Ever time she have a meetin wit
them fellers in her office, I hear her Chinese gong sound, a
know that all is well.

Mister McGivver, from the pig-farmin enterprise, wa
havin trouble findin a job after the *Exxon-Valdez* disaster, a
so I put him in charge of our oyster barge operations. He ha
quit drinkin, an none of our barges have had so much as
bump on the bottom, now that he is in control. However, h
still enjoys talkin like a pirate, which I figger might hel
keep his crews in line.

Ole Colonel North is also havin a bit of trouble of h
own, an I give him a job runnin our covert operatior
department, which is basically makin sure that our oyste
come up fresh an pure, an have no taint or stain to em.

"One day, Gump," he says, "I am gonna run for tl
U.S. Senate, an show them bastids what common decency
all about."

"Right, Colonel," I tell him, "but meantime, just ke

ır oysters' noses clean down here—You know what I
ean?"

I was gonna try to hire the Ayatolja to run our moral an
iritual relations department, but he gone an died, an so I
)t the Reverend Jim Bakker for the job. He is doin pretty
)od, blessin all our boats an barges an everthin, but his
ife, Tammy Faye, don't get along so good with Mrs.
opewell an her Chinese gong, an so I am gonna have to do
•methin about that.

As crew for our harvestin an processin operations, I
ıve got the entire staff from Reverend Bakker's Holy Land:
[oses from the "Burnin Bush," Jonah from the whale scene,
cob an his "Coat of Many Colors," an all of Pharaoh's
rmy are now our oyster shuckers. Also, I have got the feller
at played Jesus in the "Ascendin into Heaven" act an
aniel with his lion from the "Lion's Den" attraction,
owin out oyster spat in our maritime farmin bidness. The
)n, who has gotten kinda ole an moldy, he just sets outside
ıe door to my office, an lets out a roar sometimes. He has
st most of his teeth by now, but has developed a taste for
ysters on the half shell, which I spose is all to the good.

Miss Hudgins, from my Ivan Bozosky days, is now our
ıief shippin dispatcher, an Elaine, from Elaine's restaurant
. New York City, is one of our main customers for Gump &
ompany farm fresh oysters. The venerable old New York
w firm of Dewey, Screwum & Howe represent us in our
gal matters, an the prosecutor, Mr. Guguglianti, who has
)und hissef another job, is a sometimes "adviser" on
riminal matters—assumin we have any.

I have also found jobs for all members of the army
)otball teams in Germany, the Swagmien Sour Krauts an
'iesbaden Wizards, who do various things around the
lant. An Eddie, the limo driver from my New York tycoon
ays, I put in charge of transportation. Furthermore, I have

offered jobs to ole Saddamn Hussein an Gener
Scheisskopf, but they both wrote back nice letters sayin th
had "other weenies to roast." Saddamn, however, says he
keepin his "options open," an may be back in touch late

Finally, I hired good ole Sergeant Kranz to be my pla
manager, an it is good to see the ole sergeant again, an g
his ration of shit.

But actually, I am savin the best for last. After v
become successful, I got up the courage to write
Gretchen. Lo an behole, after a week I got a really beautif
letter back from her, tellin me all about hersef an how she
comin in the university, an the letter is in such good Engli
I can hardly read it.

"Dearest Forrest," she writes, "I have missed you eve
day since you left for the war and was terrified somethi
had happened to you. I even checked through the America
Embassy here, and after some research, they told me yo
were now out of the army and were well. That was all th
mattered . . ."

Gretchen gone on to say that aside from English, she
workin on a bidness degree an hopes one day to open
restaurant, but that she would sure like to see me. She g
her wish. In two weeks she was settin right down in o
plant in Bayou La Batre, headin up our international oper
tions division. At night, we'd take long walks along t
beach an hole hands like we did in the ole days, an I w
finally beginnin to feel sort of happy again. Kinda like I ha
a purpose in life, but I am takin it slow.

Meantime, Bubba's daddy was kinda lookin for a jo
so I made him processin supervisor, and let me say this: F
rides them oyster shuckers hard.

An so, here we all are, growin, tongin, bargin, shucki
processin, cannin, an shippin oysters. An makin mon
hand over foot! Above my desk I have a quotation that litt

orrest has had done up for me. It is solid gold on a face of
black velvet an is from the ole writer Jonathan Swift, an
says: "He Was a Bold Man That First Ate a Oyster," which is,
of course, too true.

Only problem is, ole Smitty an his crew are not likin
our bidness one bit. I even offered em jobs, but Smitty say
his people don't work in no "integrated" positions, an so we
re havin sort of a Mexican standoff. Ever so often, somebody will cut our boat lines at night, or put sugar in our gas
tanks, or other chickenshit stuff, but I am tryin to take it in
tride. After all, we is doin so good, I do not want to blow it
by gettin in a personal feud.

So far, the months is goin by fairly peaceful, when little
orrest one night ast the question, what about ole Wanda?

"Well," I says, "I reckon they probly treatin her pretty
ood up at the zoo in Washington," but he ain't satisfied.

"Well," I says, "let us write them a letter an see if they
will send her back."

So that's what we did.

Few months later, there come the reply.

"The National Zoo does not return animals that right-
ully belong to it" was pretty much the gist of it.

"Well," little Forrest says, "that don't seem fair. I mean,
fter all, we raised her from a piglet, didn't we?"

"Yup, I reckon," I says. "We just lent her to the zoo
while I was away with the Ayatolja."

Anyway, we went to see Colonel North, who was
peratin out of a guardhouse he had built on our grounds,
n tole him the situation.

"Them bastids," he began, employin his usual tact an
iplomacy. "Then we will just have to organize a clandestin
peration to get Wanda back."

An we did that, too.

Colonel North spent months preparin for th
clandestin operation. He has bought all sorts of camouflag
clothes, an greasepaint for our faces, an scalin wire a
hacksaws an knives an compasses an stuff. When I ast hi
what the plan is, he says we will figger it out when we g
there.

The day finally come when we get to Washington, a
we went out near the zoo an hid out in a park till nighttim
By midnight, all we can hear from the zoo is the bears a
lions an tigers growlin an an occasional bellow from th
elephant.

"Arright, it's time to saddle up," says Colonel Nortl
an the three of us begin to sneak into the zoo. We have ju
gone over the wall when all of a sudden seemed like eve
light in the place come on, an sirens go off an bells clang, a
in no time, we is surrounded by about fifty police.

"I thought you was sposed to be a expert at this sort o
thing," I says to the colonel.

"Yeah, I thought I was, too," he says. "Maybe I'm just
little rusty."

Anyhow, the colonel, he tries to get us out of it by telli
the police we is spies practicin for a top secret clandesti
operation in the Iraqi zoo in Baghdad, so's as to captur
some of Saddamn Hussein's animals an hole them hostag
an a bunch of other shit like that. The head policeman a
everbody else begun laughin so hard that it give little Forres
time to slip away in the confusion. Finally, they was loadi
us up in the paddy wagon, when a shout broke out in th
night, follered by a oink.

It was little Forrest an Wanda, who he had hacksawe
out of her cage. They run by us so fast that the policema
drop everthin an go chasin after, which also gives me an th

lonel a chance to escape. The police, I guess, do not know
at one of the few things little Forrest inherited from me is
y speed, an he gone sailin into the night like a bat out of
ell. Colonel an me take off in the opposite direction, an
ally we meet up at our secret hideout in the park, as we
ave agreed to do. Little Forrest an Wanda is already there.

"Goddamn, Gump!" shouts the colonel, "we done
lled it off! That was a brilliant clandestin operation on my
art, huh?"

"Yeah, Colonel," I says, "you was slicker than owl
it."

Anyway, we sneaked out of the park an down by the
ilroad tracks just about sunup, an lo an behole, they is a
oxcar there on a sidin filled with pigs.

"This is great," says the colonel. "What could be a
etter disguise than to hide in there?"

"For Wanda, maybe," I says. "I ain't sure about us."

"Well, Gump, it's the only game in town. Climb
oard," he says.

So that's what we did, an let me say this: It was a long
n uncomfortable ride home—especially since the boxcar
as headed out to Oregon, but somehow we made it, an the
olonel, he is pattin hissef on the back the whole way.

Anyhow, we got on home with Wanda, an little Forrest
eems happy as he can be, now he has his pet back. Ever
ay, ole Wanda sets outside my office door, across from the
on, which, fortunately for Wanda I guess, ain't got no
eth. But he looks at her all the time in a kinda longin
anner, sorta as if he wanted to marry her, or somethin.

One day, little Forrest comes up an wants to talk. We
one out to the dock, an he says what's on his mind.

"Listen," he says, "we been workin pretty hard he lately, haven't we?"

"Yup."

"So I was thinkin, maybe it's time for a vacation."

"What you got in mind?"

"Well, maybe we can get away from this bay, ya know Maybe go up to the mountains. Maybe go river raftin, somethin, huh?"

"Yeah, okay," I says. "You got some particular pla you want to go?"

"I been studin up," he says, "an they is a place Arkansas that looks pretty good."

"Yeah, what is it?"

"It's called the Whitewash River," he says.

So that's what we did.

Before we left, I took ole Sergeant Kranz aside an ga him his instructions as plant manager.

"Just keep things movin," I says, "an try not to get in any shit with Smitty or any of his people. We got a bidne to run, okay?"

"Sure, Gump," he says. "An I meant to tell you, I su appreciate the opportunity here, ya know? I mean, r retirement from this man's army after thirty years wadi somethin I was lookin forward to. An now you give me r first real job. I just want to say thanks."

"It's okay, Sergeant," I tole him. "You doin a fine jc It's good havin you around. After all, we been together mc or less since them days in Vietnam, with Bubba an them, that's been more than half my life ago."

"Yeah, well, that's so, I guess. War or peace, I gues can't get rid of you, can I, Gump?"

"Let's just hope they ain't no more wars to figl

ergeant," I says. But in fact, they was one more, though I
lidn't know it at the time.

In any case, little Forrest an me, we got packed up to go
o Arkansas an the Whitewash River. Ever since we got in
he oyster processin bidness, little Forrest an me have had a
ort of uneasy truce. I mean, he is on his best behavior, an
as saved me from mysef an my own stupidity more than
nce. He is vice-president an chief executive officer of
Gump & Company, but in truth, he really runs the bidness,
ause I certainly ain't got the brains to.

Well, it is a cool spring day when me an little Forrest get
p to the Whitewash River. We hired ourselfs a canoe an
acked it with pork n beans an Vienna sausages an cheeses
n bologna an bread for sambwiches, an off we went.

The Whitewash River is very beautiful, an all the way
lown it, little Forrest is explainin to me the geologic history
f the area, which you can see cut into the riverbanks from
ime to time. Like he says, it is to be seen in fossils—like me,
guess. We are close to the beginnin of the famous
Smackover Formation, he says, which is where all the awl in
he whole southeastern United States comes from.

At night we'd camp out on the banks of the river an
uild a little fire from driftwood an set around an cook our
ork n beans an eat our supper, an I am thinkin that this is
he first vacation I have ever had. Little Forrest is pretty
heery, an I am hopin me an him can get along better as the
lays go by. I sure am proud of the way he has growed up an
aken charge of so much stuff at the Gump & Company
yster plant, but I am also worried that he is growin up too
ast. I mean, I wonder if he has ever had a real boyhood, an
ot to play football an stuff like I did. I ast him about it, but
e says it don't matter.

One night he give me a big surprise. He reaches in h
knapsack an pulls out a ole harmonica, which in fact is th
one I have kep all these years when I played it over i
Vietnam an later with Jenny's band, The Cracked Eggs. T
my amazement, he done begun to play some of the ol
tunes, an he played em sweeter an prettier than I ever coul
of. I ast him how he learned to play the thing, an he ju
says, "Natural instinct, I guess."

We is almost finished with our trip down the river whe
I seen a feller on the banks hollerin an wavin at us a
motionin to come over. So that's what we did. We pulled i
at the bank, an he come on down an grap our bow line.

"Hi," he says. "You fellers new in these parts?"

We tole him we was from Mobile, Alabama, an that w
was just passin through, but he says we gotta come up a
look at some property he is tryin to sell on the river. He say
it is the best property in the whole state of Arkansas, an wi
give it to us real cheap.

Now, I tole him we was not in the property buyi
bidness just yet, but he is so persistent that I figgered
wouldn't hurt to foller him to his property, so as not to hu
his feelins. Well, when we got there, I gotta admit, I wa
somewhat disappointed. I mean, it was nice land an all, bt
they was a lot of sort of shabby buildins aroun, an peopl
with car gardens an rubber tires in they yards, painte
white. It kinda looked like a place I might of lived i
mysef—at least till a year or so ago.

Anyhow, he says to just call him Bill, an not to worr
about how the "outstructures" looked, account of in a wee
or so they would all be torn down an replaced by millio
dollar houses, an so if we signed up now, we would be th
first to get in on this good deal.

"Let me tell you fellers somethin," Bill says, "I am

olitician in these parts, but politickin don't pay enough, an
o I have made the investment of my lifetime in the
Vhitewash River enterprise, an I guarantee it can't bring
one of us nothin but satisfaction and success. You know
vhat I mean?"

Well, ole Bill looked like sort of a nice guy. I mean, he
eemed pretty genuine an had a husky down-to-earth voice,
vhite woolly hair, a big ole reddish nose look like Santa
Claus's, an a nice laugh—an he even introduced us to his
vife, Hillary, who come out of a trailer wearin a granny
ress an a hairdo look like a Beatle wig an brung us some
ool-Aid.

"Listen," Bill says in almost a whisper, "I ain't sposed
ɔ say anythin to anybody about this, but the truth is, this
Vhitewash River property is right over the Smackover Awl
ormation, an even if you don't build you a house here, if
ou buy it now, afore anybody else finds out, you will be
nillionaires a hundrit times over, account of the awl."

Just about then, a ole feller shows up on the scene, an
vhen I seen him, I like to of fainted dead away.

"Fellers," Bill says, "I want you to meet my partner."

It was Mister Tribble, my ole chess championship
nentor, who everbody says was the one that stole all the
noney from me in the srimp bidness way back when.

When he seen me, Mister Tribble jumped back an
ɔoked sort of like he's gonna run off, but then he got hissef
ɔgether an come up an shakes my hand.

"Well, it's good to see you again, Forrest," he says.

"Yeah," I says. "What you doin here?"

"It is a long story," he says. "But after your srimp
•idness went bust, I needed a job. So I heard the governor,
ere, needed an adviser, an he took me on."

"Governor?" I ast.

"Why, yes, Bill is the governor of this state."

"Then how come you out sellin real estate?" I ast hir

"Cause it's the steal of a lifetime," Bill says. "Why, a
you gotta do is sign here an the deal is done. An ole M
Tribble here, he will make his commission an profits, an v
will all get rich."

"We is already rich," somebody says. It was litt
Forrest done piped up at last an said that.

"Well, then, you can get even richer," Bill says. "Why,
is rich people makes the world go around. I love rich peopl
Rich people are my friends."

Kinda sounded to me like he was runnin for presiden
but then, I am just a poor ole idiot. What in the world do
know?

"Now, I guess, Forrest," says Mister Tribble, "you ai
wonderin what happened to all your money from the srim
bidness?"

"Well, it crosses my mind, from time to time,"
answered.

"Frankly, I took it," Mister Tribble says. "I mean, yo
were away assin around in New Orleans, an when the srim
begun to run out, I figgered I'd better put it in safekeepin fc
you."

"Yeah? How'd you do that?" I ast.

"Why, I purchased this lovely tract here on the White
wash River. It is the investment of a lifetime," Mister Tribb!
says.

"That's bullshit," says little Forrest. "This land ain
worth a peehole in the snow."

"Ah, now, who are you, son?" Mister Tribble ast.

"Name's Forrest—An I ain't your son."

"Oh, I see. Well . . ."

"An what you're sayin is, we own this dump?"

"Ah, well, not exactly. You see, I used the srimp company money just for a down payment. I mean, a man has to live on somethin. So with the exception of the one-point-seven-million-dollar loan I had to take out, you own every square inch of this place."

"Yeah," Bill says, "but don't worry about the debt or anythin. After all, you know how federal savins and loan bidnesses are. They don't care if you pay it back or not."

"Issat so?" I ast.

"Never will, if I ever get to be president," Bill says.

Well, after that, we took our leaves from Bill an Mister Tribble, an little Forrest is hoppin mad.

"You oughta sue them bastids," he says.

"For what?"

"For stealin your money an puttin it in that hole of dirt, damnit! Can't you see that place is one of them scam real state deals? Who the hell would want to live there?"

"I thought you liked this river. You could go campin out on it ever night."

"Not anymore, I don't," he says. An so we paddled down the Whitewash River the rest of the day, an little Forrest, he ain't sayin much. It look like I am in the doghouse again.

Well, like it will happen, spring turned to summer an the summer to autumn, an the Gump & Company bidness is still goin great guns. It almost seems like we can do no wrong, an sometimes I just can't believe it, you know? But me an Gretchen is doin fine together, an little Forrest seems to be happy as a clam—or a oyster. One day I ast Gretchen

an little Forrest if they wanted to go see a football game
Actually, I first thought about astin just little Forres
account I remember all Gretchen used to say about footba
was "*ach!*" But this time, she didn't say no such thing.

"I have been reading about your football now, Forres
and I'm looking forward to the game" was how she put i

Well, it wasn't exactly a game I took them to, it wa
more like a *event*. This was the Sugar Bowl down in Nev
Orleans where the University of Alabama was to play th
University of Miami for the national championship on Nev
Year's Day.

The University of Miami players was runnin all ove
town before the game braggin about how they was gonn
whup the Crimson Tide an make us ashamed to show ou
faces anyplace. Kind of sounded like them cornshucke
jackoffs from the University of Nebraska that we had to pla
in the Orange Bowl when I was on the team. But that was
long, long time ago, an gettin longer.

Anyhow, we gone on to the game, an let me say this: I
was a sight! They play the game these days inside a big ol
dome on fake grass an all, but they ain't nothin fake abou
the game. In fact, it was a war. I had me a private box a
invited some of the rinky dinks I had assed around wit
over the years, includin good ole Wanda from the strip joir
down in the quarter. She an Gretchen got on just fine
especially when Gretchen tole her she'd been a barmai
back in Germany.

"They all just want one thing, honey—but it ain't a ba
deal" was how Wanda handled the situation.

Well, not to get to describin things too far, let me ju
say that the Crimson Tide of Alabama whupped ther
Hurricanes from the University of Miami so bad they le
town with they tails between they legs, an so I finally got t

ee my ole alma mater win a national championship—an so
id Gretchen.

Little Forrest was beside hissef—especially when they
nnounced my name at halftime as bein one of the ole
:llers present—but Gretchen, now, she like to of gone
:azy!

"Defense! Defense! Defense!" was all she could shout,
n lo an behole, our defense got so good it would literally
natch the ball out of the hands of them Hurricanes.

When it was over, we all hugged each other, an I could
:e that whatever else happened, we was all three gonna be
:iends forever. Which is good, account of I am always fond
: havin friends.

One day it is sort of misty on the bay, an I been thinkin
hat now is the time for me to do my thing with ole
:ieutenant Dan an Sue. Poor ole Sue.

So I got out the little ashes cans General Scheisskopf
ive me back in Kuwait that day, an I gone an got me my ole
kiff an untied it from the dock an started to row out of the
:ayou. I had tole Gretchen an little Forrest what I was fixin
) do an they both ast to come with me, but I says, no, this is
:omethin I gotta do by mysef.

"Hey, Mr. Gump," somebody shouts out from shore.
Why don't you take one of these new boats with the
:otors on em? You don't have to row no boat anymore."

"Aw, sometimes I kinda like to," I called back to him,
just for ole times' sake."

So that's what I done.

All through the channel an out into the back bay I could
:ear the foghorns of boats an bells from the buoys an things,
n the sun is settin like a big ole red biscuit through

the mist. I rowed on out to our new oyster beds by tl sewage treatment plant. Everbody else done gone home l this time, so I got the place to mysef—an man, it sho smells ripe!

I drifted downwind a little an then pointed the bow the skiff up a bit so's to have some room, an where I figgere the biggest an fattest oysters would be growin I open tl little cans an I begun to say a prayer that Dan an Sue w gonna be okay, an then I thowed em overboard, into tl dark waters, an while I ought to of been sad, I wadn somehow. They done come to the end of their journey, w the way I looked at it. Actually, I would of preferred to hav a jungle to leave Sue in, but since there ain't any aroun here, I figgered the oyster beds was the next best thing. Aft all, he'd be down there with Dan, who was his pal. watched the tin cans sort of flutter to the bottom, an for ju a moment, they kind of shined back up at me like stars, then they was gone.

I turned the skiff around an was fixin to row back whe I heard a gong from one a them big ole bell buoys, an whei look up, there is Jenny settin on top of it, slowly rockin ba an forth, an lookin as beautiful as ever. Good ole Jenny. Sl always seems to be there when I need her.

"Well, Forrest," she says, "I guess you finally listened me, huh?"

"What about?"

"Way back when. About payin attention to Dan."

"Oh," I says. "Yeah, I spose I did. Pretty good, huh?

"Yes, I'd say it was. You just needed somebody to kee repeating 'oysters' to you, and finally you'd get the picture

"Well, I hope I don't screw it up this time," I says.

"I don't think you will. Not this time."

"You look kinda sad," I said. "Somethin wrong?"

"Nope. It's just this time might be our last, you know"

.ean, I think you're really all right now. An I got other fish
• fry—or oysters to shuck—if you get my meaning."

"But what about little Forrest? I thought it was all about
im?"

"Nope, not really. It was always about you. Little
orrest is a fine young man. He can take care of himself. But
ou, you needed a little lookin after."

"I ain't sure he likes me," I said.

"I think he does," Jenny says. "It's just kids. I mean,
:member how we were at his age?"

"It's been a long time ago."

"Now, what about Gretchen?" Jenny ast. "How's that
omin along? You know I told you I liked her a while ago.
he's, well—she's real people."

"I dunno," I says. "It's kinda embarrassin, you astin
uff like that."

"It ought not to be. After all, we had our run."

"Yeah, well, not all the way. I mean, it kinda got cut
iort."

"That'll happen. Memories are what counts in life,
orrest; when there's nothing else left, it'll be the memories
1at mean everything."

"But, is what you're sayin is, I won't get to . . . ?"

"Probly, but look, you got the rest of your life in front of
ou. An I think you're okay now. I don't know how you're
onna do it, but would you say good-bye for me to my
iama an little Forrest—just in your own special way?"

"Well, sure, but . . ."

"I just want you to know that I loved you, and also,
orrest, you are very fine."

"Hey," I says, but when I looked up, they was just the
ig ole bell buoy rockin back an forth in the mist. Nothin
lse. An so I rowed on back to shore.

* * *

So I gone back into the processin plant that afternoo
Most everbody else has went home now, an I sort
wandered around by mysef, feelin a little bit alone. In a fe
offices I could see lights on, people workin late, so's v
could have a successful bidness.

They was one little room in the plant that I liked. It w
where we kept the pearls. It wadn't no bigger than a clos
but inside, with some tools an other stuff, we kept a buck
Actually, it was the workers that kept the bucket, an in tl
bucket was the pearls.

They weren't much as pearls go. Japanese oysters g
all the nice pearls, but ever so often our shuckers will find
ole pearl or so, usually kinda funny-shaped or ugly-colore
but by the end of the year, they would usually be enou₃
pearls that was usable for us to sell em an get enough ca:
for a beer bust for the shuckin an floor crews, so that's wh
we did.

But when I gone by the pearl closet, I heard a o
sound comin from it, an when I opened the door, there w.
Sergeant Kranz, settin on a stool, an when I looked at hir
settin under a twenty-watt bulb, I could see his eyes w.
red.

"Why, Sergeant, what's wrong?" I ast.

"Nothin" was what he said.

"Sergeant Kranz. I have known you for many years.
ain't never seen you cryin before."

"Yeah, well, you won't again, neither. Besides, I air
cryin."

"Uh-huh. Well, I am the head of this here operation, ;
it is my bidness to know what's wrong with my people."

"Since when have I become 'your people,' Gump?" I
says.

"Since the day I met you, Sergeant." An we kind

ared at each other for a moment, an then I seen big ole
ars begun to roll down his cheeks.

"Well, damn, Gump," he says, "I just guess I'm too ole
r this shit."

"What you mean, Sergeant Kranz?"

"It was that Smitty, an his crew," he says.

"What happened?"

"I gone down to check on our boats, an he come after
e with his gang. An when I was checkin the lines on our
iffs, he begun to pee in one of my boats, an when I said
methin, he an the others grapped me an begun beatin me
ith dead mullets . . ."

"They done what!"

"An Smitty, he called me a nigger. First time anybody
er done that to my face."

"Issat so?" I ast.

"You heard what I said, Gump. Wadn't nothin I could
o—Hell, I'm fifty-nine years old. How I'm gonna defend
ysef against eight or ten big ole white boys, ain't half my
;e?"

"Well, Sergeant . . ."

"Well, my ass. I never thought I'd see the day I wouldn't
f fought them. But it wouldn't of done no good. I'd of just
ot beat up—an that wouldn't of mattered, either, cause of
hat he called me—except you tole me not to get into any
it with Smitty an his bunch. I would of tried, but it
ouldn't of done no good."

"You look here, Sergeant Kranz. That don't matter now.
ou just stay here till I get back, you hear. An that's a order."

"I don't take orders from privates, Gump."

"Well, you'll take this one," I says.

An so I gone on down to see about this Smitty bidness.
ll my life I have tried to do the right thing, the only way I

saw it. An my mama always tole me the right thing is not
start pickin fights with folks, especially account of I am $
big an dumb. But sometimes, you cannot let the right thir
stand in your way.

It was a long walk down the street in Bayou La Batre
where the docks is, an so I spose Smitty an his people see
me comin, cause when I got there, they is all lined up, a
Smitty is standin in front of the bunch.

Also, I din't notice it, but a lot of the folks from ov
Gump & Company oyster plant has follered me down ther
an the ones that can, are lookin unhappy, like they mea
bidness, too.

I gone up to Smitty an ast him what happened wit
Sergeant Kranz.

"Ain't nothin to you, Gump," he says. "We was ju
havin some fun."

"You call a gang of you beatin a fifty-nine-year-ole ma
with dead mullets fun?"

"Hell, Gump, he ain't nothin but a ole nigge
Whatsittoyou?"

An so I showed him.

First I grapped him by the jacket an lifted him off th
ground. Then I thowed him into a pile of seagull shit th
had been collectin on the dock. An wiped his nose in it.

Then I turned him around an kicked his big ass over th
dock into one of his own oyster boats. An when he landed i
it on his back, I unzipped my pants an peed on him from th
wharf above.

"You ever fool with one of my people again," I tole hir
"you will wish you had been brought up as a vegetable o
somethin." It was probly not the wittiest thing I could
thought of to say, but at the moment I was not feelin witt

Just about then somethin hit me in the arm. One of
nitty's men has got a board with nails in it, an let me say
is: It hurt. But I was not in no mood to be screwed with. So
grapped him, too, an they happened to be a big ole ice
achine nearby, an I stuffed him into it, headfirst. Another
y come at me with a tire tool, but I seized him by the hair
. begun swingin him around an around until I let him go,
e a discus or somethin, an last time I looked, he was
adin for Cuba or maybe Jamaica. All them other goons,
:er seein this, they backed off.

All I says was "Remember what you seen here. You
n't want it to happen to you." An that was it.

It was gettin dark by now, an all the folks from Gump &
mpany was cheerin, an also booin Smitty an his collec-
n of turds. In the dimness I got a glance of Sergeant Kranz
ndin there, noddin his head. I give him a wink an he give
e the thumbs-up sign. We has been friends for a long time,
e an Sergeant Kranz, an I think we understand one
other.

About this time, I feel a tuggin at my sleeve. It is little
rrest, who is lookin at the blood on my arm from where
e goon hit me with the board full of nails.

"You arright, Dad?" he ast.

"Huh?"

"I said you arright, Dad; you are bleedin."

"What you call me?"

"I love you, Dad" was what he said. An that was
ough for me. Yessir.

Yessir.

An so that's how it ends, more or less. After the crowd
ifted away I walked on down to the bayou where they is a
int that looks out over the bay an the Mississippi Sound

an then on out into the Gulf beyond it, an if you could, y
could see clear down to Mexico, or South America. Bu
was still a little misty that evenin, an so I went an set do
on a ole park bench, an little Forrest come an set beside
We didn't say nothin, cause I think it had been about
said, but it got me to thinkin what a lucky feller I am. I
me a job, a son proud an tall, an I had me some friends
my day, too. I couldn't help but remember em all. (
Bubba, an Jenny, an my mama, an Dan, an Sue, is gone nc
but probly not too far, cause ever time I hear a big
foghorn on the water, or a bell from a bell buoy, I think
them; they is out there someplace. An there is little Forr
an Jenny's mama, an Sergeant Kranz, an all the rest, s
here. An I ain't forgot what Jenny said about Gretch
neither. An so, in a way, I am the luckiest feller in the wor

They is just one more thing to tell, an that is when th
decided to make a movie of my life's story. That is unusu
even for me. Somebody got wind of the fact that I am a id
who has made good, an in these days it is what they cal
"man bites dog" sort of story.

So one day these Hollywood producers come an info
me I am gonna be in the motion pitchers. Well, a lot of y
know the rest. They done made the show, an everbody
over the world went to see it. Mr. Tom Hanks that I met
New York that night, he played my part in the movie—
was pretty good, too.

Well, finally it become the night to go to the Acade
Awards show in California, an I took everbody that was
friends there, an we set in the audience—I even got to
with Bubba's folks. An damn if the pitcher didn't win m
of the Academy Awards, an at the end, after they

rough thankin everbody else, they decided to thank me, o.

They was a Mister Letterman, as the host, a nice feller ith big picket teeth an a trick dog an shit, an as the last em on the menu, so to speak, he announces they is a ecial award for ole Forrest Gump, for bein "The Most vable Certified Idiot in America," an I am called to the age.

An after they give me the award, Mister Letterman ast if ey is anythin I would like to say to the TV cameras. An in ct, they is, an I been savin it up. An so I look out there on l them fancy dresses an expensive jewelry an pretty omen an handsome men, an says the first thing that comes mind, which is, of course,

"I got to pee."

Well, at first, ain't nobody clappin or commentin or thin. I think they is all embarrassed, account of we is on tional television an all. An after a moment or two, the dience begun a kind of deep mumblin an whisperin to eyselfs.

An Mister Letterman, who feels like he must be in arge, I think he ain't sure what to do, so he motions hind the curtains for the hands to get a big ole stage hook, haul my fat ass off the stage. An the stage hook has just apped me behind the collar when all of a sudden, out of e audience, a missile sails across the footlights. Little rrest, it seems, has got so excited he has chewed up his tire Academy Award program, account of they don't serve popcorn at the Oscars, an so he is armed with what ight be the world's largest spitball. An when they are tryin pull me off the stage, little Forrest thows the spitball an ts Mister Letterman square between the eyes!

Gretchen is horrified, of course, an cries out, "Oh, my

goodness!" But let me say this: It was a sight! All of
sudden, all hell bust loose. People begun jumpin up
hollerin an pointin an shoutin, an the nice Mister Letterm
is flounderin around behind the speaker's platform, tryin
pick the spitball off his face.

But then from out in the audience, I hear one sho
above all the rest, an it is this: "That's my dad! That's
dad!" An I gotta tell you, that was enough for sure. S
reckon you can say we been there, an then the curtain con
down on all of us.

You know what I mean?